The Agent

Lynn Erickson

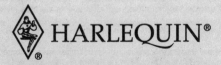

HARLEQUIN®

TORONTO • NEW YORK • LONDON
AMSTERDAM • PARIS • SYDNEY • HAMBURG
STOCKHOLM • ATHENS • TOKYO • MILAN • MADRID
PRAGUE • WARSAW • BUDAPEST • AUCKLAND

ISBN 0-373-71054-2

THE AGENT

Visit us at www.eHarlequin.com

Printed in U.S.A.

"I can sugarcoat everything or I can be blunt. Your choice."

My God, he's direct, Meg thought. She almost said, *sugarcoat everything. I can't take the cold truth.* "Please be as blunt as necessary" came out of her mouth, and she prayed she wouldn't regret her words.

"Okay." He stood comfortably in Meg's living room, and his eyes held hers. "Your husband's missing." He paused for a moment, then continued. "There are a lot of people out there who'd give good money for his research. They'd pay for it, and if they couldn't buy it, they might use force to obtain it."

"Force?" she repeated weakly.

"Abduction, perhaps. Threats of physical violence."

She knew that Howie's vaccine research was valuable and she also knew the relationship between a vaccine and a biological warfare agent—flip sides of the same coin. But to think anyone would abduct *Howie.*

"Mrs. Afferton—" the agent's voice broke into her thoughts "—I realize this is upsetting, but it's important that you know the whole story. The reason I'm here is to find your husband, negotiate his return if necessary and ensure that you are not used as a pawn. But for now, I think you should get some rest."

Meg turned away. She placed a hand on her stomach and wondered whether a child really grew within her. Hers and Howie's, a tiny new life, deep in her womb.

Get some rest, the agent had said. She wondered if she'd ever rest again.

Dear Reader,

Sometimes we come up with a story that is too close to the truth for comfort. Sometimes we downright scare ourselves. Who would have known, as we wrote *The Agent* only months before the events of September 11, 2001, that our world would change so much? Who would have known bioterrorism would become a real threat?

The Given Institute exists exactly as described, and we conducted a chilling interview with the director, a doctor who listed all the possible biological warfare agents and how they could be spread. We invented the country of Turghistan, but ones like it figure largely in the news these days.

Perhaps Canadian Customs—on high alert—would have detained a man like Howie Afferton when he entered the country, because he appeared suspicious. Perhaps not. Perhaps this story *could* happen, made even more dangerous in today's world.

And it all started with a *what if*?

We hope you enjoy *The Agent*.

Regards,

Carla and Molly (Lynn Erickson)

The Agent

CHAPTER ONE

MEG AFFERTON'S HUSBAND did not come home from his seminar at the Given Institute on that Friday in July. At first she thought he'd gone out with his colleagues for a beer or two at one of Aspen's trendy bars, but by the time seven o'clock rolled around, she began to get worried.

The day was already chalked up in her mind as one of the worst of her life. Howard had woken early and wanted to make love. She'd felt her flesh shrink when his hand slid beneath her nightgown and sought her. She'd closed her legs to him. To her husband.

Was *that* why he hadn't come home yet? Was he brooding, punishing her?

Then, before he'd climbed into the shower—his expression granite because he hadn't gotten his once-a-week sexual *fix*—she'd admitted to him how unhappy she was and that she was considering taking a break—time by herself to think things out.

"And what does *that* mean?" he'd demanded.

What a coward she was. Instead of telling him she was afraid their marriage was failing, she'd said, "I just need to get my head straight, Howie. I told you. I'm not happy…."

But in typical Howard Afferton fashion, he had

sneered at her. "God, Meg, what more do you want from me? Blood?"

Now she thought back on the scene and wished she'd told him the truth. That she craved warmth and affection and respect. A loving partner for life.

Yes, he must be punishing her by being late. She was certain of it, because Howard was a punctual man. Always organized, scrupulous, the absolute antithesis of the absentminded professor, although he was a scientist, a brilliant biochemist. He never stayed out without calling Meg; he liked his meals on time, his sheets ironed, his shirts on hangers, light starch, his shoes shined.

Yet the fact remained: he wasn't home.

She walked to the front window of their condo again, looked out onto Hyman Avenue, peered down the tree-shaded street in the direction from which Howie would be returning from the Given Institute. The shadows of the tall cottonwoods lay in stripes across the street. *Prison bars,* Meg thought for a moment, then chased the errant thought away.

His seminar, titled Emerging Diseases and Global Medicine, should have been over at four. He'd told her he'd be home by five, because people might hang around to ask questions. Two hours ago. No phone call. No Howie. Nothing.

She glanced at the stove, where her special gourmet dinner sat, ruined now. Needing to make up for her coldness in bed, wanting to explain her discontent in a civilized manner, she'd spent all afternoon on that dinner—Howie's favorites—broccoli soufflé, shrimp scampi, new potatoes in butter and dill. And the rhubarb custard pie he loved. Well, the pie would keep, the potatoes she could microwave, but the soufflé had fallen and the shrimp lay cold and limp in congealed butter.

Where was Howie?

They'd been married six years. She'd met him when she went to work as a lab technician for his biotech company in the University of Colorado's new Health Sciences Center.

Married the boss, yes, that's what she'd done. He'd been handsome, older, brilliant. Anglo-Irish, he'd told her. From Boston. Tall and reed-thin, black hair and blue eyes that gleamed with intensity, a masculine, high-bridged nose. He'd gone to Harvard for graduate school. *Harvard.*

She was so flattered, so grateful to Howard for marrying her, she had never, in six years, dared to question anything he did. Until this morning, that was.

Seven-thirty. She paced and worried. "Where are you, Howie?" she asked the empty condo.

On top of everything, Meg's brother was staying with them. Brian was only twenty, twelve years her junior. Meg had invited the surly, spoiled and unhappy boy to visit her in Aspen, figuring their mother, who'd never been able to handle her younger child, needed a break. But Howie, Meg knew, wasn't terribly keen on having her brother around.

Was that another reason Howie hadn't come home? Because Brian was here? Oh, my God... Last week Howie had thrown a fit when Meg had planned an overnight camping trip with her brother. She'd planned the outing hoping she could have a real heart-to-heart talk with him. Just Meg and Brian and the Rocky Mountains. But Howie had told her that he expected her to attend a cocktail party in *his* honor at the institute that evening.

"Did you conveniently forget?" he had asked coldly. "Is your brain turning to mush?"

So the camping trip hadn't materialized. And Brian wasted his time sleeping late, watching TV and hanging out on the picturesque pedestrian malls of Aspen.

She remembered something her mother Lucy had said, hope strong in her voice. "Maybe Brian could find a job for the summer in Aspen. I know they need workers up there."

Well, that was true. Housing—and thus employees—was scarce in the mountain resort. Summer activities—sightseeing, hiking, camping, fishing and biking—kept Aspen as busy as it was in the winter. The rodeos and jeep rides, the town's fine dining and shopping, the Aspen Music Festival with its two months of superb classical concerts in the brand-new tent with its white peaked roof mimicking the surrounding mountains. The Physics Institute, where learned physicists debated black holes, quarks and the Big Bang Theory of the universe. And, of course, the Given Institute, a think tank extension of the University of Colorado School of Medicine, a private enclave in the heart of Aspen dedicated to the sharing of cutting-edge developments in the fields of biotechnology and human health.

But Brian hadn't been interested in working. He'd lost his summer job in Denver, neglected to finish the course work he'd left dangling at the end of his sophomore year at CU in Boulder. In Howie's words, he was a bum. In his mother's, he was troubled. To Meg, he was her baby brother. She'd been more of a mother to him than Lucy, who'd given up any effort to discipline the boy after the death of her husband eleven years ago.

Oh, God, where was Howie?

The worst part of it was that Meg was starving. Too sick with concern to eat, but still, she was hungry. Her body didn't care that Howie wasn't home; her body required sustenance. And she knew why. Meg Afferton was almost positive she was pregnant.

After dinner had been prepared, she'd put on a pair of khaki slacks that were growing tight at the waist, and an emerald-green blouse, which she knew flattered her coloring. All to assure Howie's good mood, because she'd planned on telling him tonight that she'd missed two periods, which made her about three months pregnant. She had to know what the future held.

And her husband wasn't home.

All right, she thought. *How long do I wait before I start calling his friends?* How long? If she panicked too soon, everyone would think she was unhinged. A man is a couple of hours late, and his wife instantly assumes a calamity?

But Howie was never late. Never. Not unless he called.

She moved around the living room, touching things. He had been lecturing at the institute for several years now, but he'd only bought this condo recently. In previous summers they'd stayed at a funky old ski lodge right on Main Street. A noisy affair at best.

"How can we afford it?" Meg had asked when Howie had told her he'd purchased the condo. She knew full well the astronomical prices of real estate in Aspen.

"Don't you worry," he'd said. "We got approval of our last funding request, so Jerry and I gave ourselves raises."

The condo was one in a building of four units, an unpretentious three-bedroom place, at the base of the outcropping called Shadow Mountain on the west side of Aspen Mountain. Only a few blocks from the Given Institute and Aspen's downtown malls.

It had come completely furnished and renovated by the previous owner. Meg would have liked very much to have chosen the furniture herself, to have picked out carpet and paint and cabinets, but Howie was pleased with the earth-toned utilitarian decor.

"Perfect," he'd said. "Easy to keep and easy to rent out when we're not here." And that was that.

She moved into the kitchen, picked one shrimp from the pan and ate it, standing over the stove, chewing slowly, feeling the garlicky flavor burst on her tongue. Feeling utterly disloyal. A traitor.

Thank God Brian was out. He loved the nightlife in Aspen. Even though he was still a few months under legal drinking age, he hung around downtown, slipping into bars if he could get away with it, Meg supposed, or using a phony ID. Right now she didn't care; she was only grateful that he was not home making sarcastic remarks.

She could just hear him. "Wow, sis, it's like two whole hours since the big man was supposed to be home. Maybe he got lost. Want me to send out the bloodhounds?"

She looked out the front window for the umpteenth time and pushed Brian from her thoughts. Howie might walk in any second. He wouldn't pull a stunt like this over her behavior this morning. There was some other explanation for his lateness. There had to be. Something logical, important.

Still, wouldn't he have phoned?

Another woman? No, she thought. Ridiculous. Howie loved her. He'd never been interested in other women. He liked his home life, his routine. He liked being able to discuss technical problems in his research with Meg. Except for his once-a-week sexual needs, he was not particularly romantic; he was not the least bit spontaneous. No, it couldn't be another woman.

But even if he did come home, if he walked in the front door right now, the mood was ruined. She couldn't talk about her hopes and doubts tonight, much less a possible pregnancy. And that made Meg nervous. She'd been steeling herself to confess to Howie for a month now. She wasn't at all sure how he'd take the news, either. Although he'd never actually said he didn't want children, Meg knew he had no fondness for kids, their noise, their mess, their need for attention. He didn't much like his partner Jerry Riggs's two children, and they were old enough to be reasonably behaved. Whenever Meg had brought up the subject of children, Howie had invariably said, "Later. Plenty of time. Later." End of subject.

No, Howie wouldn't be thrilled at all, but she hoped he'd warm to the idea. A baby. *Don't worry,* she'd assure him, *I'll take care of it. You won't have to do a thing, Howie, honestly. This could be the miracle cure for our marriage.*

She could almost hear him. "You're on the pill. How in the devil did you get pregnant?" Angry, with that hard voice and cold blue stare that frightened her. That almost always made her want to take back whatever she'd said or done to prompt his disapproval.

She would never tell him that she'd been unable to keep down the pill for several days when she'd had the flu a few months ago—that was her secret. Hers and the baby's.

The phone rang. Her heart seized, then loosened. Relief washed away her fears. *Howie, it was Howie.*

But it was not her husband; it was one of his friends from the institute, wanting to set up a tennis game the next day.

"I'm sorry, Tom, but Howie isn't home," she heard herself say, the polite wife, not the near-hysterical woman who screamed inside. "Can I take your number? I'm sure he'll be home soon."

She carefully wrote down Tom's number on the notepad by the phone, where Howie always checked for messages. "Um, Tom, you haven't seen Howie this evening?" Her voice trailed off weakly.

No, Tom hadn't. Was there anything wrong?

"Oh no, nothing. Howie's, um, he's a little late. I was just wondering…"

Stupid, she thought when she hung up. Asking Tom. Of course he hadn't seen Howie. The words had come out of her mouth without thought. Just as Howie pointed out so often: "You don't *think,* Meg. You're a chump. Everything that goes on in your brain just comes out your mouth."

Not true. If only he knew how many times in the last month one thought had been on the tip of her tongue. How many times she had *thought*…and not let the words come out?

Were other women afraid of their husbands?

She never objected to anything Howie said or planned for them. His reaction would be too… uncomfortable. He would never hit her, God forbid. He'd never laid a hand on her. He was not a *physical* person. He was an intellectual. And a shrewd businessman. But he did intimidate Meg. He had from the beginning.

As soon as they were married—in a simple civil ceremony in Denver's city hall—he'd asked her to stop working. When she'd demurred, he explained that he wanted to cherish her and take care of her. Not work her to the bone like his father had done to Howie's mother.

"But I like working. What would I do all day?" she'd protested.

"Whatever pampered women do," he'd replied, and when she'd refused his request, he'd sulked and turned his disapproving gaze on her until she had given in and quit her job at the lab.

Six years. She'd taken to reading and long walks and music appreciation courses. Once she'd suggested she get a dog for companionship, but Howie was allergic. Cats, too. Even birds. He'd finally—just last year—agreed she could work as a volunteer at Presbyterian-St. Luke's Hospital one day a week. She often put in two or three days a week, though, because her fellow volunteers knew they could count on her to fill in for them. Howie complained, and she always promised she'd get her schedule down to one day—which somehow she never did.

The minutes dragged, slow and ponderous, full of unnamed fears. Still no Howie. Her heart beat the seconds off in a heavy cadence. She walked onto the back deck that looked out at the bulk of Shadow Mountain. It was growing dark, the sun far down on the horizon, the sky a deep, pure sapphire, the air smelling of cut grass and flowers and pine trees, dust motes dancing in a bright sliver of light that reached through the trees to gild the redwood decking. Somewhere a backyard chef was grilling meat on a barbecue, and the scent floated on the cooling air. From a tree nearby the contented cluck-cluck of a robin readying itself for bed.

She loved Aspen. It was a beautiful, exciting place. Sometimes Howie took her to a restaurant or to a concert or an art film at the stately, century-old Wheeler Opera House. Of course, she and Howie attended many institute social affairs—her husband's colleagues were fascinating people. But mostly Howie liked a settled, routine life. Home and hearth, as he liked to put it. Peace and quiet and dinner on the table at precisely six-thirty. His desire for routine, he'd told her, was due to an insecure and unsettled family life as a child. His father drank, his mother worked like a dog. He'd gotten out as soon as he could and never looked back.

And that was all he'd say about his family. She'd offered many times to call them in Boston, to visit with them, but Howie refused. Rapprochement was not contemplated. His family probably didn't know Meg existed. And now, whether or not they stayed married, there was to be a grandchild, and Howie would never tell them that, either.

Not that her own family was a model of homespun values. Howie wasn't really interested in Meg's mother or Brian, either. He was, she guessed, protective of her.

Then why, *why* hadn't he called? Where was he?

She shivered—the evenings grew cold quickly at eight thousand feet in the mountains—and went inside. The aromas of her ruined dinner lay heavily on the air, and her stomach constricted.

Where was he? Sex was not important enough to him to keep him away. And he'd barely considered her announcement that she needed a break. Something had happened to him; she knew it. He was an excessively orderly person. He never left loose ends. Even if…even if he was with…another woman, he would have called with a lie, an excuse. Meg knew her husband—he wasn't a complicated man—and she *knew* he wouldn't leave without a word.

She glanced once again at the clock on the wall of the kitchen. Almost nine o'clock. Four hours late, five hours since his lecture was over. He wouldn't still be at the institute answering questions, would he? Good God, no.

She couldn't bear it another second. She had to do something. She strode to the phone and punched in the familiar number of the Given Institute. The phone rang and rang, then the answering machine clicked on: "You have reached the Given Institute in Aspen, Colorado. Our hours are 9:00 a.m. to 5:00 p.m. In case of an emergency, please call 555-2213."

She scribbled the emergency number down, not trusting her memory, then punched it in. A click, then someone picked up the phone. "Hello, Givens Institute," said a man.

"Oh, oh, hello. Excuse me—" her voice rushed, breathless "—this is Meg Afferton, Dr. Howard Afferton's wife? I'm trying to locate him. Is he there?"

"Well, I'm the security guard, ma'am, and I can tell you this place is closed up tight, not a single soul here."

"Oh…oh, I see."

"The last person left here over two hours ago, and that was Janet Fusaro. You know Janet?"

"Yes, of course." Janet was the director of the institute.

"Do you want her number, Mrs. Afferton?"

"Uh, no, that's all right. I, ah, I have it." She took a deep breath. "Thank you."

"Okay, ma'am, glad to help."

She clicked the off button and laid the cordless phone down. She stood there, pressing her hands against the neutral-colored kitchen counter, head hanging, heart pounding out a terrible rhythm.

He was dead. There'd been an accident. A car crossing Main Street had hit him. He'd fallen in the river. He'd had a heart attack and was in the hospital, unable to speak. No, no. Someone would have notified her. Howie had his wallet with him. His name, address, everything was on his driver's license and his business cards.

So he must have been mugged. His wallet stolen, no ID, he was lying somewhere bleeding....

No, not in Aspen, for God's sake.

He'd met another brilliant biologist, a gorgeous sexy woman, and he'd been swept off his feet, gone with her to her hotel room and they were, right now they were...

No. Not Howie. No.

But did she really know her husband? Did you ever really *know* another person?

She was suddenly weary. Exhausted. It seemed as if she were always tired these days. She wanted to collapse onto the couch, turn the television on to the news, or some light sitcom. To relax. But her mind refused to let her rest; it whirled sickeningly, testing out hypotheses, discarding them, taunting her with possibilities, dreadful scenarios.

She heard someone at the door just after ten o'clock. She stood bolt upright, her heart lurching. The door opened. What would she say? Would she be angry, yell at him? Sob and fall into his arms?

It was her brother.

"Hey," he said brightly, "you're still up?"

"Yes—" she tried to say, and then had to clear her throat and try again. "Yes."

"What's the matter? You look…awful."

Humiliation swept her. "It's…it's Howie."

"Huh…?"

"He's not home."

"Where is he?"

She looked down. "I don't know."

"He didn't call you?"

She shook her head.

"Oh, geez. Howie, the perfect husband," he said sarcastically.

"Brian, please."

"Sorry." But he didn't sound sorry.

"I'm afraid something's happened to him. I'm worried."

"Did you guys have a fight or something?" But he answered his own question. "Of course not. You don't fight. He just tells you what to do."

She turned away.

"Look, he probably just got hung up with someone. Maybe a rich investor."

She bit her lip and shook her head.

"When did you expect him home?"

"Five," she whispered.

"Well, hey, that's only a few hours. It's not like he…"

"Like he what?" she said, turning to face her brother.

"Um, well, like he drinks or hangs out with girls or stuff like that."

"*That's* why I'm worried," she said, more sharply than she'd intended.

Brian shrugged. *No big deal*, his gesture said. And

she really didn't want to make such a big deal of it, because Brian would tell their mother, and Lucy had enough problems of her own.

Brian was a young twenty. He hadn't filled out yet, and even though he was nearly six feet tall, he was thin. He'd be handsome, though, when he matured— dark, longish hair, dark eyes like Meg's. Fair skin, but while hers was pale, his held more color. His beard was still patchy. He hated to shave, so he had scraggly whiskers. He had a great smile when he was in the mood, but he tended to look dissatisfied. He favored sarcasm that he mistook for wit.

He wandered to the TV set, found the remote, then dropped onto the couch, his legs stretched out before him, and started clicking through shows. Channels flashed across the screen, sound bites grabbed out of the ether—news, movies, sports, sci-fi.

"I'm going to make some phone calls," Meg said, trying to sound calm. "Upstairs."

"Okay." *Star Trek Voyager, David Letterman*, the Weather Channel, *Friends*.

Upstairs, Meg sat on the edge of the bed, opened Howie's night table drawer, took out his list of phone numbers. He'd be mad if he knew she had it; he was strangely secretive about some things. But this was an emergency. Maybe other men could be five hours late without upsetting their wives, but not him.

She ran her finger down the list. Yes, David Barach, there it was. An Israeli who taught at MIT, an old friend of Howie's. She quailed at the thought of phoning so late—it was after ten—but she had to. What would she say?

She punched in the number. The phone rang once, twice, three times. Maybe David and his wife were out, maybe asleep, maybe...

"Hello?"

"David, this is Meg Afferton. I'm sorry to call so late, but..."

"What is it, Meg?"

"Howie hasn't come home, and I'm worried, so I thought you might have seen him, or..."

"I went to his lecture this afternoon, but I haven't seen him since...around four, I'd say."

"Oh."

"You think something has happened to him, Meg?"

"Oh, I'm just trying to figure out..."

"He's probably charming some wealthy biotech investor. You know him."

I thought I knew Howie. "Yes," she said, falsely cheerful, "that's probably it. Sorry to have bothered you, David."

"No problem. *Shalom.*"

She hung up, then quickly dialed a Denver number from memory. Jerry Riggs, Howie's partner.

"Hello?" came a bleary voice.

"Oh, Jerry, sorry to call you at this hour, but have you heard from Howie?"

"What? Oh, Meg. Aren't you still in Aspen?"

"Yes, I'm calling from there. I was just wondering if Howie got in touch with you tonight. About, well..."

"No, I haven't heard from him. Wasn't he supposed to give his seminar today? How'd it go?"

"Yes, today. It went well, yes, just fine. Thanks, Jerry."

Her face flushed with humiliation as she hung up. Calling at this hour, begging for information. It was awful. Chasing down an errant husband. Oh, God, what would people think? And then... What if he walked in right now, or in the next five minutes, or the next half hour, and he found out she'd been pursuing him all over the state, for God's sake. He'd be so angry. She quaked inside.

But she made a few more phone calls, anyway, going down Howie's list. Ben from UCLA, Donald from the University of Chicago, Peter from the biotech firm in San Francisco, all of them here for the conference. No, not one of them had seen her husband since his seminar.

After the last call, she put the phone down and buried her face in her hands. She wanted to cry, to burst into tears. But she didn't. Brian might hear.

She stood and went downstairs to the living room, where her brother was watching a program with a canned laugh track.

"I'm going for a walk," she said. "If Howie comes home while I'm gone, tell him..."

"Yeah?"

"Tell him I got restless, I needed some fresh air."

"Okay."

"Did you hear me, Brian?"

"Ah, sure." Then he went back to his show.

She grabbed a sweater and walked outside. The stars were scattered like diamonds on an endless black velvet sky, a glittering mystery. But Meg barely noticed. She took several deep breaths, trying to fight down panic. What if Howie came in while she was gone? What if Brian gave him a flip answer when he asked where she was? Maybe she should have waited. But she couldn't have stayed in the condo another moment. No, not a second.

She walked quickly toward the lights of downtown. A dogged determination took hold of her. Anger growing from the seed of worry. How dare he do this to her?

She didn't care what people thought. She simply didn't care. She was going to find her husband—whether he wished to be found or not.

She ducked into the Mother Lode bar, the first place she came across. Warm and dim, the scent of cigarette smoke and Italian food in the air. She walked around the bar, peered into the restaurant. No Howie. She tried Bentley's a block down at the Wheeler, the J-Bar two blocks away at the Hotel Jerome, then back up Mill Street to the Cooper Street Mall. The Red Onion, the bar of Syzygy's and the Little Nell Hotel, and finally, L'Hosteria, where people sat relaxed in deep armchairs sipping from glasses of red wine that caught the light like sparkling rubies. No Howie.

The hours became a whirling nightmare of jazz and the smells of fine cuisine. And strange faces—disparaging faces—staring at her. What must she look like? A crazy woman, wan, uncombed hair, a frozen expression on her face. Walking into bars, searching, turning on her heel and leaving.

No Howie.

Finally exhausted, she stood on the rough bricks of the west end of the Cooper Street Mall. People—happy people, celebrating their vacation—partied around her. Friday night in the old mining town. Young, attractive couples, rich older ones. A lady in bicycle shorts, two guys in climbing gear, straight off the mountain. A couple kissing.

Walking home, Meg hugged herself. She was shivering, from the cool dry air, from panic and shame and frustration. It was after eleven; her husband had been missing for six hours. Seven really, because apparently no one had seen him after his talk.

Howie, Howie, where are you?

A seven-hour absence was nothing, she told herself. *But it was. It was.* Something had happened to him.

She tried to calm herself. She didn't want to alarm Brian. He was such a lost soul, poor kid. If only their father had lived… But he had died when Meg was twenty-one and Brian only nine. She recalled him perfectly, fondly, but of course Brian had only hazy memories. She certainly didn't want her brother relating her troubles to her mother, who considered Howie beyond reproach.

Life was hard enough for Lucy—still working as a librarian at the same high school she'd been at for years. A slim, pretty lady, her hair straight and gray, pulled back and clenched in a tortoise-shell clip, her glasses on a gold chain, resting on her chest, unless she was reading, two furrows between her eyebrows. Mrs. Deverall to the students, who—Meg was sure—laughed at her mother behind her back.

Meg arrived back at the condo and stood at her front door. She didn't want to go in. The place seemed like a cage to her now, a prison. But perhaps Howie was home. Could he be? And if he were, he'd be furious that she hadn't been there to greet him. That she'd gone for a *walk*. "At this hour?" She could almost hear his voice.

She forced herself to open the door, felt her heart beating against her ribs like a wild thing.

No Howie. Only Brian, half asleep in front of the TV set, a plate that held the remains of her gourmet dinner on the glass-topped coffee table.

"Howie...?" she began.

"Nope," Brian managed to reply.

She felt herself sag, half in relief, half in dread. "Why don't you go to bed?" she suggested.

"You gonna be okay?"

"Of course I'll be okay."

"You still worried about Howie?"

She waved a hand dismissively. "Oh, he must have made some plans I forgot about. A meeting where they got to talking about how to cure some disease. You know."

"Sure. He's out till—" Brian looked at the wall clock "—twelve-forty, and you're a mess, and he's just arguing about germs with his pals? Right."

"Everything's fine, Brian."

"If you say so. Frankly, I don't think he's much of a loss."

"*Brian!*"

"He doesn't like me, he doesn't like Mom. I'm not sure how much he likes *you*. He uses you, Meg, and he keeps you cooped up like some kind of pet. A show dog.''

"God, Brian, who are you to judge my marriage?''

He stood, tall and lanky, his absurd beard a shadow on his face. "Who am *I*? Nobody. I'm nobody.'' He slashed the air with a hand.

"Oh, Brian...'' She felt near tears again. Howie, Brian... The men in her life, tormenting her. What was there about her that made her so easy to hurt?

"All right, I'm going to bed,'' he said, and he turned toward the stairs.

"You'll see,'' she said to his back, "in the morning Howie will be home, and all this will be just a misunderstanding.''

"Sure, he forgot to tell you he was leaving you.''

But she barely heard, didn't bother replying as her brother went upstairs to his room. She was thinking about the next step, the only possible thing left to do.

She waited until Brian was done in the bathroom and had closed his bedroom door, then she took the cordless phone, retreated into the far corner of the kitchen where he wouldn't hear her and took a deep breath.

Her finger didn't seem to belong to her as she watched it press the numbers: 911.

"Aspen police dispatch. Can I help you?''

"I—'' she had to swallow the lump in her throat "—I wish to report a missing person.''

CHAPTER TWO

MEG PULLED THE TAN SWEATER more tightly around her and hugged herself as she sat on the couch in her living room. Hugging herself was a defensive gesture, but right now she was unaware of her body language or her wrinkled khaki slacks or the collar of her green blouse curled up on one side.

"That's David Barach, Mrs. Afferton?" the young policewoman asked.

"Yes, B-A-R-A-C-H. He's one of my husband's closest friends."

"And he's staying at the Gant Lodge, you said?"

"Ah, yes, but I already spoke to him earlier. He hadn't seen Howie—"

"Howie?" the other officer said, a tall buff blond in his late twenties.

"Oh, sorry. My husband never goes by Howard, his given name."

"All right. So you spoke to Mr. Barach at around nine o'clock this evening?" The female officer sitting across from Meg glanced up from her notepad.

"Nine. I, ah, think it was nine. It could have been later, I guess. In fact, maybe it was. Yes, I remember thinking I'd wake him up. David, that is." She felt a tick of a nerve at the corner of her mouth. "I'm sorry, I'm not much help, am I?"

The male officer replied. "That's okay, Mrs. Afferton. Under the circumstances, you're doing fine."

Meg gave them the names of everyone she remembered contacting that evening. Ben and Donald and David, of course. "Oh, and I also phoned Peter. That's Peter Marrs from GeneUSA in San Francisco. He's here for the conference, too, and he's at the Mountain House with his wife and two boys. But I don't suppose you need to know that. Sorry. I'm just…worried. I'm not thinking straight at all right now."

The policewoman smiled sympathetically and scribbled more notes.

"Do you always respond to these sort of calls so quickly?" Meg asked. "I mean, isn't it usually twenty-four hours or something before a person is officially considered missing? Or maybe that's just on TV."

The male officer, who'd been standing near the kitchen alcove all this time, exchanged a look with his female counterpart.

"What?" Meg said, catching the exchange. "What is it? Is there something…? I mean, do you *know* something?" Her belly coiled sickeningly.

But the policewoman was quick to calm her fears. "No, there's nothing like that, Mrs. Afferton. We have no idea where Dr. Afferton is. To answer your question, though, we respond immediately to these calls because Aspen is so unique. Fourteen-thousand-foot mountains and hiking and biking trails surround us. People kayak and river raft and backpack in the summer. They often go into potentially dangerous wilderness areas. When someone is reported overdue or missing, we pay attention.''

She was grateful for their understanding, but she knew they were thinking of a scenario as yet unvoiced. But any minute now, one of these nice cops would ask if it was possible her husband was having an affair. *She'd* thought of it, and surely they would. It was a logical question.

And what would she reply?

''Was Dr. Afferton wearing clothes suitable for hiking?'' the woman asked. ''Boots?''

''Oh, no, he had on tan pants and a dark blue short-sleeved shirt and loafers. For the lecture. It's pretty informal up here.''

The woman wrote more notes.

Meg spoke into the silence. ''He had no other plans, certainly nothing athletic. He did say that he would stay to chat with his associates after the seminar, but that's what he normally does. And, of course, sometimes scientists lose track of time. For hours.'' Meg laughed humorlessly.

''Yes,'' the policeman said, ''I can imagine.'' He looked at his wristwatch. ''But people don't lose track of the time till one in the morning.''

''Does your husband ever go out for a drink after the lectures?'' the policewoman inquired.

Here it was at last. She spoke carefully. ''Once in a while, yes. But he never stays out for more than a couple hours. He's a social drinker, he never loses control. He's a very controlled man,'' Meg added, and again she laughed nervously. "And that's why I'm so concerned. Howie does everything on schedule. He's never late."

"Never?"

"Never without phoning." She hesitated. "Look, I know what you're thinking, but Howie is not the sort of man to stay out with another woman. Honestly."

"There haven't been any...problems between you and your husband lately?" the woman asked. "Sorry, but I have to ask."

"No, not a thing." *Only my wretched unhappiness and a pregnancy he doesn't know about,* she thought.

The male officer used his radio to contact Dispatch and request a search of the downtown bars and nightclubs despite Meg's assertion that Howie would never pull such a wild stunt. She'd mentioned to the police when they'd first arrived that she'd already walked the downtown malls looking for her husband, but they nevertheless wanted another check.

"We have about six or seven officers on duty downtown, anyway," Meg was told. "You never know when an Old-West-style brawl will break out."

Both officers smiled. Then the male one sobered and said, "Not that we think Howard...Howie, that is, would be downtown drinking or involved in anything like that, but we only want to point out that in this town...*stuff* happens. People sometimes leave their good sense at home."

"Um," Meg said, but she thought: *Not Howie, not in a million years,* and her stomach knotted. He was in trouble. If not mugged then...maybe he'd gone for

a walk on the Rio Grande bike path that snaked along-
side the banks of the Roaring Fork River. A walk to
clear his head after an intense day. Maybe he'd spotted an eddy. Noticed a rainbow trout in the crystal
clear mountain water, made his way to the bank, lost
his footing. Just last spring when she and Howie had
driven up from Denver for a long weekend she'd read
about a couple—a man and wife—who'd both
drowned in the white-water runoff not a quarter mile
from the core of the town.

Could Howie have been swept away by the river?

She was suddenly dizzy with fear. And exhaustion
and hunger. Or was she dizzy because she was going
to have a baby? Was she pregnant? She couldn't think
about that now.

The female officer recontacted everyone in
Howie's address book who was in Aspen for the seminar at the Given Institute. The woman woke everybody up—*again*—and got the same information Meg
had received hours and hours ago. No one had seen
Howard Afferton since his 3:00 p.m. lecture had let
out.

The male officer was on the phone with Howie's
partner Jerry Riggs in Denver when Brian appeared
downstairs, scratching his sleep-tousled head and
yawning. His torso was naked, sweatpants that he'd
slept in riding low on his hips till he saw the cops.
He straightened, pulling the drawstring tight before
tying it.

Meg prepared herself for the wisecrack he'd surely
make upon seeing the police, but fortunately, for once

in his life her little brother held back his sophomoric wit.

"This is Brian," Meg explained when the officers raised questioning brows. "Brian Deverall. He's my brother, visiting from Denver."

"Hi, Brian," the policewoman said.

Brian sat on the arm of the couch next to Meg. "Yeah, I'm the black sheep, you might say."

"I don't suppose you have any input as to your brother-in-law's whereabouts?"

"Not a clue." Brian shrugged.

The female officer wrote something down then looked up. "And you last saw Dr. Afferton...?"

"God, I don't know. Around lunch? I sort of slept in this morning, er, yesterday morning now."

"I see."

"How about the other side of the family, Mrs. Afferton? Your husband's relatives?"

Meg shook her head. "No. No one would have any idea of his whereabouts. Howie was—is—what you'd call estranged from them. And they live in Boston, anyway."

"Still, I'd like a contact there if you have it. A mother, father, sibling?"

Oh, God, Meg thought, cringing inwardly. But now was not the time to withhold anything. "I'm afraid I can't help at all," she admitted, her gaze slipping away. "I've never met them, and I don't have a phone number, not even a name other than Afferton. I realize how that sounds...." She took a breath. "But I met Howie in Denver at his lab, and we were married in a civil ceremony. What I'm saying, I guess, is that

Howie was already estranged from them when we met.''

Meg knew what was going through their heads. Even Brian. They were thinking: *Well, surely you must have tried to mend fences or at least gotten his father or mother's name. Surely you did that much as a dutiful wife.*

And she had tried. But Howie had only gotten furious, and after a year or so she'd let that sleeping, flea-ridden dog lie.

She kept her gaze averted and tiredly whispered, ''They live in the Boston area. That's all I know.''

''Okay, then,'' the policewoman said, and she flipped her notebook closed and stood up. ''We'll keep checking the bars and malls and the hospital, of course, just as a precaution. In the morning at the shift change two more officers will be by. In the meantime, if you think of anything, no matter how insignificant, please let us know immediately. Even if it seems like a small detail to you, it could help us locate your husband.''

Meg, too, rose to her feet. ''I understand. And thank you. I never expected such an immediate response. I really appreciate the help.''

The man replied, ''No trouble, ma'am. We'll be in touch if there are any developments.''

''Thank you,'' Meg said again, and she wondered whether to tell them once more that Howie would never have pulled a stupid trick like this, that he was Mr. Perfection, but she'd already told them that a dozen times.

''Try to get some rest,'' the policewoman sug-

gested at the door to the condo. "I know how trite
that sounds, but try, anyway. And remember, nine out
of ten times these things turn out to be nothing but a
simple miscommunication."

"All right," Meg said, forcing a weak smile. But
her brain knew better. This was no misunderstanding.
There was only one explanation—he was incapable,
for whatever reason, of getting to a phone or a road
or a house. No matter her doubts, he was still her
husband, the father of her baby, and he was in serious
peril.

BY MIDMORNING TWO MORE officers had arrived to
take charge of the case. Meg was so exhausted, so
drained from stress and hunger and morning sickness
that she could barely answer the questions they put
to her; she stuttered and had moments of utter blank-
ness where she fell silent, unable to recall the question
or what she'd been about to reply. She thought if she
said the word *sorry* one more time she'd scream.

Then Howie's associates began to arrive. First David Barach, then Peter Marrs, and on his heels came
Tom and Donald and a scientist named Ralph something or other, whom Meg had met last year at a cocktail reception here in Aspen.

The condo was crowded, sweet rolls and doughnuts
and bagels—Meg had no idea who'd brought them—
sat half eaten on plates next to empty coffee mugs,
and there was nowhere for the visitors to sit. For some
reason, Peter's kids were there, too, running up and
down the stairs to the bedrooms, jumping on the bed
in the small downstairs guest room, jumping on the

new, never-been-used duvet cover. Howie would have
had a fit.

The police questioned everyone who arrived, but
always came back to her, as if she were withholding
information. At one point it raced through her mind
that they probably thought she'd murdered her husband and was covering up—hacked Howie to pieces
or bludgeoned him to death. She knew the cops had
spoken to the neighbors, and she was positive they'd
asked them if they'd heard arguments, screams, even
gunshots, for God's sake. Of course the police suspected foul play—she wasn't stupid, she knew the
spouse of a missing person was the prime suspect
when the police couldn't come up with anyone else.

"And your husband hadn't scheduled an out-of-
town meeting or something similar that you've simply
forgotten?" one of the new officers was asking.

A shout from Peter's kids came from the guest bath
off the downstairs hall, fraying Meg's nerves even
more.

"What? I'm sorry, I can barely hear...." she muttered to the policeman.

She heard Peter scolding the kids, but a few seconds later they were racing upstairs again. The officer
repeated his question. Someone dropped a coffee mug
in the sink, and voices, seemingly dozens of them,
pounded in her head, and she lost it.

"Do you know how many goddamn times I've answered these same questions? And while you're sitting here grilling me as if I'm a criminal my husband
is out there somewhere in trouble!" she cried.

She felt Brian's hand squeeze her arm.

The officer said something completely officious, and Brian replied, ''Just like all cops, a bunch of ass-holes,'' and both policemen reacted strongly, coming to their feet, warning him that he'd be real smart to shut up right now before the situation escalated.

Thank God, David took Brian aside and calmed him down, and the tension drained out of the police-men. Still, the room was suddenly very silent until the phone shrilled, making her jump. One of the cops hurried to pick it up, not even considering that she might like to answer it.

She sat back down with what little dignity she could muster. ''That was a stupid thing I said, I apol-ogize. You've been wonderful, I know that, and I ap-preciate all you're doing. I can't begin to imagine what happened to Howie. And I'm so afraid that he's…but he just wouldn't be…*gone*. I'd know it. Wouldn't I know it if my husband were…dead?'' She put a hand over her mouth to muffle the sobs, and the tears finally came.

Everyone in the room responded. She got hugs and kisses on her cheek and arms around her shoulder and pats on the back. She heard the words ''He's fine. Everything will be okay, Meg.'' But she lost track of who was saying what.

And all the while she responded with gratitude and false confidence. ''I know, I'm sure there's some log-ical explanation for this.''

She even mustered a few stiff smiles as she gra-ciously accepted each and every well-wisher and every hug and platitude. Dutiful, uncomplaining Meg Afferton.

In her heart she knew they were lying. Howie was not fine. There was no logical explanation whatsoever. He'd been missing now for nearly twenty hours, and with each passing minute, the odds of finding him alive were diminishing.

MARK FIELDER CLASPED his hands behind his head, rocked back in his chair and stared at the computer screen. He'd read the police report twice. Now he simply stared, deep in thought.

Dr. Howard Afferton was missing.

When Mark was lost in concentration, contemplating a case and extrapolating facts, he reminded his fellow DARPA agents of an intensely focused hunter. He could appear benign, his features relaxed, his eyes slightly blurred behind the lenses of the small, wire-rimmed glasses he wore. But when he was on the job, his concentration was ferocious.

His hair was thick and dark blond, the kind that never lay flat on his head, but always looked mussed. He had a fashionably casual look. The ever-present stubble on his cheeks gave him a slightly careless air.

He'd worked for DARPA, Defense Advanced Research Projects Agency, a covert branch of the Defense Department, since leaving military service five years before. He would have stayed in the navy—a lifer—except at thirty-five years old he'd been losing his edge physically, and as an officer in the SEALs, his duty had been to be as tough and combat-ready as the young men under his command.

Now he spent a lot of time behind a desk following the activities of thirty-seven American citizens: his

PCs—Personal Charges. A lot of boring hours spent in a Washington, D.C., complex hidden from the public eye. The downtime, as Mark thought of it, was bearable only because of the sporadic incidents that threw his life into an immediate and intense whirlwind of adrenaline-pumping action.

Mark Fielder lived for those few and far-between moments.

And he could feel one coming on as he sat, stretching his arms, gazing at the name Howard Afferton on the screen.

Howard, no, Howie, he mused, *what have you gotten yourself into?*

"Yo, Fielder," he heard over his shoulder, the sound breaking his concentration, "something interesting? You haven't come up for air all morning."

Mark let out a whistling breath and swiveled in his chair. "Maybe," he said mildly. "Maybe."

"One of your biotech nerds being a bad boy?"

Mark smiled thinly at his fellow agent Janie Weathers. "I don't know, Janie, too early to tell."

"Oh, come on, I'm dying of boredom here. Tell me what you've got."

He laughed lightly. "Biotechnology researcher named Afferton."

"He's one of your biggies?"

Mark nodded. "Yep. Out of Denver."

"What'd he do? Overcharge on his credit card?" Janie's big brown eyes danced with curiosity.

"Not exactly."

"Well?"

"He's missing."

"Missing? That's serious. You mean actually po-lice-report missing?"

"Yep."

"Wow. What's his field?"

Again Mark gave Janie one of his taunting half smiles. "Viruses. Viruses and vaccines."

Janie sat back in her own chair as if an invisible hand had shoved her. "That's really interesting, Mark."

"Uh-huh."

"I mean, does this Afferton character have red flags?" Janie asked, using the DARPA in-house term referring to any unusual activity by one of their cases. All scientists receiving government grants were sub-ject to close scrutiny, though few were aware of the existence of DARPA and its intrusive surveillance methods. Those who did know, kept quiet. The money was too good to make waves.

The agency was by and large a secret government watchdog. DARPA had never received recognition for inventing Stealth aircraft or the M16 assault rifle or even the invention of the Internet over thirty years ago. Nevertheless, DARPA's shadowy hand touched many areas—one of its missions being to scour the globe for evidence of bioterrorism.

As an agent for DARPA, Mark was well aware that the production of vaccines was not far removed from the manufacture of biological warfare material. The vaccine that could rid the world of AIDs could easily be reengineered to exterminate mankind. It was vi-tally important for the government to keep close tabs on its scientists, thirty-seven of whom were Mark's charges.

"Afferton's file already has three red flags," Mark told Janie.

"Holy cow. And he's disappeared," Janie reflected. "Well, all I can say is have fun. I'm jealous as hell, Fielder. My guys are all choir boys."

"I used to think mine were, too." Mark pivoted and went back to the computer, refreshing his screen for updates on the Aspen Police Department's file.

He'd found the missing person's report not ten minutes after arriving at the DARPA complex this morning. Found it easily because his computer was automatically programmed to scan and cross-check hundreds of thousands of public and private files with the names of his charges. If someone purchased an airline ticket, Mark knew about it. If a scientist applied for a new credit card or a new grant or patent or FDA approval for a drug, Mark was instantly privy to that information. He kept tabs on divorces, college tuition, child support payments, alimony, home mortgages, auto loans. After the traitor scandals at the FBI and CIA, no government agency could afford to let down its guard. The watchdog business was ugly, but it was also vital to national security.

He read an update from Aspen—no clue yet as to Afferton's whereabouts—and he thought back to the previous week when one of his charges had couriered computer files on hantavirus to a colleague in England. Mark had been on the case in a microsecond. The red flag incident had turned out to be a false alarm, a harmless error in judgment on the part of the

American scientist. His British counterpart had wanted to compare the modern-day hantavirus, caused by field mice, to a mystery scourge that had killed scores of people in England back in the 1500s. Nevertheless, the man should have known better.

Mark skipped lunch and informed his immediate superior about the missing person report on Afferton. "I think I better get a flight out today," Mark said. "This is the fourth red flag in eighteen months. Maybe the guy got lost on a hike or God knows what. And maybe he didn't. Maybe he wants to be lost."

His boss nodded. "Get Laura to run an expense account for you and keep in close contact."

"Will do, sir."

"Aspen," his superior mused, "some guys have all the luck."

"Uh-huh," Mark replied, halfway out the door.

He was sitting on a flight to Denver within two hours. He stared out the window, his glasses dangling from one hand as he massaged the bridge of his nose with the other. *Four red flags,* he thought. The first had been a ten-thousand-dollar diamond-and-sapphire bracelet Afferton had bought his wife. The second had been the purchase of an upscale house in Denver, which had a very small mortgage on it, and the third had come earlier this year when Afferton paid cash for a condo in Aspen, where real estate was notoriously pricey. And now the doctor had disappeared.

"Would you like juice or soda?" a flight attendant asked.

But Mark never heard her. He was thinking, *Not good, not good at all.*

CHAPTER THREE

BY THAT EVENING, more than twenty-four hours since Howie's inexplicable disappearance, Meg was past frantic. She still couldn't hold down food, nor could she sleep. The strain showed. Normally she would have been appalled at her appearance, appalled that she hadn't washed her face or brushed her teeth or put on deodorant in more than a day. Right now those simple daily chores were the furthest things from her thoughts.

The condo still buzzed with activity. She sat in a hard-backed window seat as evening progressed and gazed out the front window. To onlookers it probably looked as if she were willing Howie to walk up the three front steps. In truth, she was too numb to even think, much less concentrate on the possibility of his magical appearance.

Howie's colleagues came and went. The wives who were with their husbands for the seminar had kindly supplied a variety of food all day long, untouched by Meg, but Brian and the ever-present cops and Howie's fellow scientists had their fill. Like an Irish wake for her Irish husband, Meg thought. But no one knew if he was dead.

"Come on, sis," Brian had said so many times she

lost count, "eat something. There's sliced roast beef, all kinds of bread, cookies, cakes, casseroles, cheese and vegetable platters...."

"I can't," she replied every time. "I won't be able to hold anything down."

Of course, she hadn't mentioned to Brian—or anyone else for that matter—that she had been contemplating leaving her husband and that she might be pregnant. That it was highly likely she *was* pregnant.

She'd been saving those issues to discuss with Howie first. Over dinner. The great dinner she'd cooked last night. A lifetime ago.

She found herself on the back deck of the condo. Had she thought about it, she would have realized she always wandered outside at this hour of the evening when the Steller's jays and robins and magpies were active, and barn swallows swooped among the cottonwoods and aspens in the gathering dusk. She was on autopilot, moving here and there for no apparent reason, then sitting, just sitting and staring into the middle distance for long spells. People spoke to her constantly, and she must have replied, but what she said, she had no inkling, nor could she summon the energy to care.

Then two voices coming from just inside the glass sliding doors penetrated her foggy mind.

David Barach and someone else—it was the policewoman's voice, Meg realized, the same officer who had been on duty last night. The two were saying something about the river. Howie and the river.

Meg forced herself to listen. "Oh, God." David's voice.

Then the policewoman: "It's a natural progression of our investigation, Dr. Barach. We have three volunteer teams searching the banks of the Roaring Fork River right now, though it'll be too dark soon for them to continue."

"But how in hell could Howie have fallen into the river? It wasn't as if he was kayaking, for God's sake. The most he could have been doing was taking a walk along the Rio Grande bike path. A thousand people must walk along that trail every day. Women with baby strollers and joggers and bikes and goddamn dogs all over the place!"

"Dr. Barach, I explained that this search is routine. *Something* has happened to Dr. Afferton, I'd say that's quite clear at this juncture. We're only covering all bases."

A thought flew into Meg's frazzled brain—Howie had taken a walk to think over her discontent and their failing marriage. Then an image assailed her: Howie's body, facedown, caught on a rock. Howie's body washing back and forth, bloated. Howie's white shriveled hand moving in the current. All because of her.

She rushed indoors, brushing past Barach and the policewoman, ran up the steps to her bathroom and vomited into the toilet.

After about ten minutes, she washed her face, averting her eyes from the mirror, and brushed her teeth. Slowly she walked downstairs.

David took her arm and led her to a new face in the living room. "Meg, Anita Massy. She's an internist here in town. I asked her to stop by."

Anita extended her hand and took Meg's. "I'm so

sorry, Mrs. Afferton, for what you're having to en-
dure. I know it's no help, but everyone in town is
pulling for you and your husband.''

"Thank you," Meg muttered.

"I hope it's all right that I came by to speak with
you. David was worried.''

"Sure." The word came out lethargically.

"Is there somewhere we could…''

"Let's go to the guest room. Just over here." Automatically, Meg led the doctor to the small guest
room. The comforter on the queen-size bed was still
flattened and mussed from Peter's kids. *God.* And the
bedside lamps were turned sideways, their shades
tilted. Howie would be so irritated. Howie… But he
wasn't here.

"David tells me you haven't eaten or slept in over
a day. I'm sure my being here feels like an intrusion,
but I'd like you to consider something. In the event
of another crisis or if your husband, he goes by the
name Howie, I understand… If Howie were to walk
in right now, you'd want to be here for him. As it is
you're probably ready to collapse.''

Meg sat woodenly on the edge of the bed and
sighed. "Look," she said, "I don't mind that David
called you, really. In fact, I appreciate it. A *house*
call," she added, trying to smile, but there was nothing left inside her. "It's just that I know what you're
going to say, that I should take some medication, a
sleeping pill, tranquilizer, whatever.''

Anita Massy nodded.

"The thing is," Meg continued, "and I haven't
told a soul, not even Howie…" She bit her lip and

stifled sudden tears burning behind her eyes. "I'm pretty sure I'm pregnant."

"Oh," the doctor said, "I see. And you're thinking medication might harm the fetus."

"Exactly."

Anita sat beside her then. "Well, first, Mrs. Afferton, Meg, it sounds as if you haven't seen your physician yet to confirm your pregnancy, am I right?"

"His office is in Denver, where we live most of the year, and I thought I'd wait till after Howie's seminar. I've only missed two periods."

"Um."

"But I'm always regular and last week I started feeling queasy just before breakfast."

"You understand that there are medications I can prescribe that will be harmless to the fetus?"

"I know they're *supposed* to be harmless, yes. Still, I'd rather not take a chance. Please don't press the issue."

"Okay. But I urge you to get something in your stomach, Meg, and at least try to sleep. If not for yourself, then for the baby."

"You're right. Of course you're right, it's just that I'm so worried. I seem to go from numb to frantic at the blink of an eye, and every time the phone rings, I think…I'm sure it's about Howie, that they've found him…and…"

Meg wept then. She sobbed out the tension she'd been keeping in for the past day, and the doctor kept an arm around her shoulder until her tears subsided. "Don't feel embarrassed to cry, Meg, you need to let go," Anita said kindly. "You can cry all you want and everyone will understand. Okay?"

"Okay," she managed to say, "all right. I'm better now. I really am. Thank you."

"No need to thank me. If you change your mind about the medication, don't hesitate to phone or have David call. Will you do that?"

"Yes," Meg said, but she knew she wouldn't, and she suspected the doctor knew it, too.

She forced down a few crackers and cheese, then climbed the steps to her room, hers and Howie's. Downstairs David was still taking charge of the phone and updating Howie's colleagues who continued to drop in. Brian had gone into town earlier for a walk. Normally Meg would have questioned that, aware of her role as older sister, but right now Brian was the last thing on her mind. The police came and went, though there was always one who stayed in case word came about Howie, in case her husband suddenly called or walked in the door.

She showered and brushed her teeth again, her head heavy and her vision blurred from lack of sleep. She put on her sleeveless blue silk nightgown, the one Howie liked best, the one he'd said looked like a skimpy, sexy evening gown, and she fell into bed.

I'll never ever sleep ran through her mind, and she heard voices downstairs near the front door, David calling to someone, probably the policeman on duty, that he'd be back first thing in the morning. Then the condo grew quiet. It was eleven o'clock when she looked at the digital clock. More than thirty hours since Howie had vanished. Thirty of the worst hours imaginable. What if he was injured, unable to seek help, alone in the mountains somewhere, cold, afraid, growing weaker by the moment as she lay in their big luxurious bed?

She reached under the sheet and felt the cool emptiness where he should have been, and her heart beat against her rib cage. And then she fell mercifully asleep.

The voices rising from the living room awakened her at 3:00 a.m. At first she was disoriented, and then the nightmare of reality rushed in and she was suddenly fully alert.

She sat up, dizzy, sleep-drenched, and heard the voices clearly now. Two men were downstairs. Not Brian. Or David. And certainly not Howie. Who then?

Immediately she was on her feet, her blood pumping furiously, positive something had happened, just as positive it was bad news. If Howie had been found safe, surely someone would have awakened her by now.

Meg summoned what little courage she could muster and went down the steps. The voices were coming from just outside the sliding glass doors leading to the deck. She could make out two men standing in the dim light that spilled from the kitchen. One man was an Aspen police officer she recognized from yesterday, but the other was a stranger. She thought she heard the policeman mention Washington. Someone was here from Washington?

Unconsciously hugging her bare arms around her lace-covered breasts, she padded up to them. ''What's happened? Have you found Howie?'' she blurted out.

Both men turned toward her. "Oh, Mrs. Afferton," the policeman said, "we woke you. I'm sorry."

She shook her head to indicate that was of no consequence, and again asked, "Has something happened. Have you…?"

But the other man cut her off. "Nothing has happened, Mrs. Afferton, there aren't any new developments in the case."

She felt as if she'd collapse, sag to the floor with the wildly disparate feelings of relief and dread. She took a ragged breath and lifted her eyes to the stranger. "And who are you? I don't recall seeing you here before. It's the middle of the night. I don't understand."

The man nodded slowly, and she was momentarily struck by the sense that he was absolutely not a local. There was something too intense, too keen about him, too…her mind searched for the words. *Yes,* she thought, too competent and self-assured for a small-town police department. Was he FBI?

But he was speaking, and she had to focus. "My name is Mark Fielder," he was saying, "and I've been sent here by Merrick Pharmaceuticals. I'm sure you're aware that Merrick funds your husband's research."

"Yes…I…ah…sure I know that. Merrick funds him and the government also helps out." A curious light flickered in the man's blue eyes, sharp deep blue eyes behind stylish round wire-rimmed glasses, then disappeared.

"I'm a security expert," he continued. "Merrick sent me to assist the local police and any other agency involved in the investigation of your husband's disappearance. I caught the last flight from Denver, and I wanted to touch base with the police. And you, of course.''

She stared at him and, without thinking, rubbed her arms against the cold night air streaming in from the deck. ''Why do we need a security expert?'' she began, but before she could receive an explanation, he was removing his summer-weight tan sport coat and draping it over her shoulders.

''You're freezing standing here, Mrs. Afferton,'' he said, his hands tugging the warm jacket around her shoulders, and then he was steering her inside, the policeman following.

The stranger, this security man from Merrick, was unlike anyone she'd ever met. In the space of two minutes she was aware of a deliberateness and control she'd never seen before. He was so unlike the scientists who had been a part of her daily experience for years that it took her a moment to adjust to the difference.

She felt the sudden necessity to sharpen her wits. ''Would you answer my question, please?'' she said, standing now, facing him, in the living room.

But he didn't answer immediately. Instead, he switched on a lamp and carefully touched her arm, nodding at the couch. ''Won't you sit down?'' And she sat, not sure if he'd pressed her down or if she'd sat of her own accord.

Mark Fielder remained standing, however. She was a little put off. A stranger, he'd invaded her home without asking, led her into her own living room and sat her down like a little kid. And she still wore his jacket. She'd known Howie for months before he'd given her a sweater of his, or had it been a shirt?

She shook off the memory and gazed up at Fielder. "A security expert," she prompted.

He met her eyes soberly. "I'm sure you have a lot of questions, Mrs. Afferton."

"Meg."

"All right then, *Meg*. I can answer your questions two ways. I can sugarcoat what's going on here or I can be blunt. Your choice."

My God, he was direct, she thought, and she almost said, *Sugarcoat everything. I can't take the cold truth. I'm too frail right now, too tired, too worried....* "Please be as blunt as necessary" came out of her mouth, and she prayed she wouldn't regret her words.

"Okay, blunt it is," he said, and he stood comfortably in her living room in his expensive pale yellow shirt, casual Levi's and tassel loafers. His eyes held hers from behind his glasses. "You may or may not be aware that Merrick Pharmaceuticals keeps substantial insurance policies on its business associates," he began. "Including your husband, Howard, Howie you call him, I believe."

"Yes, Howie. He never goes by Howard," she explained. Yet she had the distinct impression Mark Fielder already knew that and a whole lot more.

He listened patiently.

"But I don't quite understand," Meg said. "What kind of insurance? You mean some sort of life insurance?"

"Exactly. Merrick keeps insurance on your husband because of their investment in his research."

"I see," she said, and goose bumps rose on her

arms despite the jacket. *Life insurance.* If people knew that she'd fought with her husband, caused him to leave, maybe to injure himself—or worse, they'd think she'd done it for the insurance money.

"It's a routine arrangement," he said.

"Of course. I understand."

"I'm not certain you have the entire picture, Mrs....Meg. In part, the insurance covers any kind of foul play."

"Foul play?"

"A crime against your husband. Kidnapping."

"A crime? Kidnapping?" she whispered.

"We can't rule anything out at this point."

He fell silent then, allowing her a moment. She searched his face, noticing the short, dark blond hair that was slightly rumpled, as if he'd slept wrong on one side or run a hand through it, his heavy eyebrows, his cheeks, nicely chiseled planes covered with fashionable stubble. She stared at his mouth for too long before meeting his dark blue eyes behind the glasses, an incongruous touch that diluted the keen vigilance in his expression.

"A crime," she breathed. "I hadn't...the police... we thought, I mean, they've searched the river and..."

"Yes," he allowed. "But I'm not here for those possibilities."

She waited.

He studied her, a frown drawing vertical lines between his brows. "Your husband's work is on the cutting edge of biotechnology, Mrs....sorry, Meg."

"Yes?"

"There are people out there," he gestured with a hand, "*countries* out there, who'd give a lot for his research. They'd pay for it, and if they couldn't buy it, they might use force to obtain it.''

"Force?" she said weakly.

"Abduction, perhaps. Threats of physical violence.''

"But…but, why…?"

"Bioterrorism.''

"No," she whispered.

"It's a definite possibility.''

His words rocked her. From her training as a lab technician, and of course from her years with Howie, she knew the relationship between a vaccine and a biological warfare agent—flip sides of the same coin. But the concept that Howie's vaccine research, done for the betterment of mankind…to think that anyone would actually abduct *Howie*…

She shook her head vehemently. "No. No, that's not possible," she insisted. "Howie would never cooperate with people like that. You can't think… No. That's wrong.''

"Do you happen to know if your husband had his passport with him?''

"Passport?''

"In case he left the country," he explained carefully.

She thought a minute, feeling utterly stupid. "I don't know if Howie had a passport. We never traveled outside the country. I…I never saw one. But…well, if he had one it would be in Denver. I'm sure it would be there. But I don't think…" Her voice trailed off.

"Look," Mark Fielder said, "I should have talked to you in the morning. It was wrong to initiate this conversation at this hour. I think you should—"

"I'm fine," she interrupted. "I'm wide awake, and I want to hear everything. I couldn't possibly sleep right now, anyway. You said you'd be blunt. Okay. If there's more, I want to know."

"I realize this is upsetting, but it's also important that you know the whole story. Maybe your husband wouldn't voluntarily cooperate with his kidnappers, *if* he's been kidnapped. There are ways of making him cooperate, though."

She sat unmoving, trying to digest the new twist. She hadn't considered any of this. Nor had the local police or his colleagues. Had they all been blind, naive? Or was this security man from Merrick completely off base?

"Another way of gaining your husband's cooperation could be through you, Meg," Fielder was saying.

"Through *me?*" She felt as if she'd been dealt a blow to her stomach.

"Correct. You could be used as a foil to force your husband to turn over his research. In part, that's why I'm here."

"I...you mean you're here to protect me from some out-of-control terrorist organization? That's... crazy. It's absurd. I don't believe you, Mr. Fielder."

"Mark will do."

"Look, *Mr.* Fielder," she said with sudden courage, "I may seem like a distraught wife right now, but I assure you I'm not that dumb. You're here to protect Merrick's interests, not Howie's and not mine."

The hint of a smile etched itself on his lips. "That's true, but our interests may coincide." He paused, then continued. "Look, my job is to find your husband, negotiate for his return if necessary and ensure that you are not used as a pawn. Those are the facts."

Meg sighed deeply and closed her eyes for a minute. None of this could be real. Howie was simply a scientist, a man wholly dedicated to his research. No one would have targeted him. Impossible. And that someone would try to use her to gain Howie's co-operation was ludicrous. Lurking in the shadows of her mind was the feeling that she wasn't important enough for that role, and she wondered if Howie even cared enough about her for such a ploy to work.

No, this was all wrong, her mind cried, and yet the fact remained that Howie was missing. Missing with no other feasible explanation.

The police officer who'd been talking to Mark Fielder earlier was still standing near the door to the deck, and she looked to him momentarily for help, as if he'd tell her it was much more probable Howie had fallen in the river, but his expression was neutral. She glanced back at the security expert, and his face, too, was impassive. She shook her head in denial, but it was no good and she was terribly, miserably afraid this man could be right.

So many questions swirled in her head that she could not pin down a single thought for examination. And then there was a noise at the front door, the knob turning. Meg and the two men spun as if they were puppets on strings. The door opened and Brian walked in. It took several moments before he seemed to realize that three expectant faces were staring at him.

"Whoa," he mumbled. Then he grinned sloppily.

Meg had assumed he'd been upstairs asleep. It

hadn't even occurred to her that he was still out. Then
she looked closer and saw that he was drunk. And
the gleam in his eyes was suspicious. Had he done
drugs, too? "Oh, God," she moaned aloud.

"Who in hell…?" Mark was saying.

The cop stared at the twenty-year-old with no
amusement whatsoever, then he nodded in Brian's direction and said to Mark Fielder, "It's just her kid
brother."

Meg rose and went quickly to Brian. She wanted
to throttle him. Of all the times to pull a stunt like
this. "Dammit," she began, a wave of exhaustion
seizing her, "do you realize what time it is? Where
in God's name…?"

"Hey," Brian slurred, "what are you, my
mother?"

She took his arm, hoping, praying she could lead
him upstairs to his bedroom before he got himself into
real trouble. He started to pull away with a jerk, but
then, mercifully, he subsided and slowly, wobbling,
he climbed the steps.

When she heard the bedroom door close and a subsequent thump, she made her way back to the couch
and sat down ponderously. *What next?* she thought.

By then the cop had gone to the front door. "Mrs.
Afferton," he said, "I'll be at the cop shop if you
need anything. Someone will be over again at seven.
Of course, if there are any developments, we'll be in
touch. All right?"

"But…but, what if…?" she began.

"I think you're in good hands, Mrs. Afferton. I
talked at length with Mr. Fielder here before you
came down tonight, and I'm *sure* you're in good
hands."

Meg did not know what to say. She acquiesced, ducking her head, suddenly overcome by weariness. She'd been given too much information, too many shocks: Fielder and Merrick and kidnapping and then the icing on the cake, Brian. She took a heavy breath and then another and realized something else—obviously Mark Fielder planned to camp out right here. The cop had known that, or he wouldn't have left. Fielder had also known it. She could tell him to leave. Order him out of her house. But would that be foolish? Shouldn't she sleep on it? As if she could sleep again tonight…or this morning, or whatever day or time it was.

And Howie was still missing.

She finally glanced up. The security man was silently studying her. "I'm sorry about my brother's behavior," she said.

"Don't worry about it. The kid went overboard. Bad timing. Now, is there somewhere I can set up my laptop? I need to check in at headquarters, see if there have been any developments."

"I had no idea Merrick Pharmaceuticals was so well *secured*," she reflected. But when no reply was forthcoming, she shrugged. "You can use the downstairs guest room, I suppose. And there's a bath to the right of it. The bed's a little messed up, those kids… I'll just straighten it."

"No need. I'll be perfectly all right. I suggest you try to get some sleep, Meg."

A bodyguard. That's what he was. And now he was playing the protective role. How bizarre, she mused, another jolt in her orderly existence. How many more would there be? And no Howie to take charge.

"I'll say good night, then," Mark said.

Stiffly she rose and walked to the guest room, switching on the lights. Then she shrugged his jacket off her shoulders and handed it to him, feeling abruptly exposed in the flimsy nightgown. She was aware of his quick scrutiny before he switched his gaze away.

"Get some rest," he repeated. "We'll talk more in the morning." Then he closed the door.

She stood for a moment staring at the smooth off-white-painted wood, then rubbed her arms and turned away. She wouldn't sleep, she knew that. Not tonight, anyway, and maybe not tomorrow. She placed a hand on her stomach and wondered if a child really grew within her. Hers and Howie's, a tiny little life deep in her womb.

Get some rest, Mark had said.

She wondered if she'd ever rest again.

CHAPTER FOUR

IT WAS NEARLY DAWN when Mark hung up his jacket on a padded hanger and closed the closet door. Despite his own weariness, he surveyed his surroundings, hands on hips. Queen-size bed with an earth-toned, delicately striped comforter and opposing-pattern throw pillows. Too damn many of them. He'd always wondered where you were supposed to put all the pretty little pillows. On the floor? On the closet shelf and then get them down in the morning? It seemed ridiculous to him, silly and feminine, but then what else did Mrs. Afferton, *Meg,* have to do with her time but shop for decorator pillows?

The carved wooden headboard was Southwest desert style, probably from Santa Fe. As were the matching bedside lamps. Light-colored, hand-carved wood lamps with a green Kokopelli design. The shades were of faux antique paper. The floor was blond wood with two multicolored Navajo-design throw rugs strategically scattered for just the right lived-in effect. The walls were generic white.

He studied the room and could picture Meg there, standing on the threshold, one arm folded across her stomach, the other bent at the elbow, her index finger tapping her full lower lip as she decided exactly where to place the throw rugs and hang the earth-tone prints in the pastel frames.

Oh, yes, he could see her as clear as day. Despite her exhaustion and the inordinate amount of stress she was suffering, she'd been ready to drag herself in here and tidy the duvet cover. Had she always been a Martha Stewart-type or had Afferton demanded his wife be picture-pretty in a picture-pretty home?

He unpacked his laptop and set it up to receive a mobile signal, an encrypted signal that his computer automatically decoded. Phone lines were insecure these days, and data bounced off a satellite to his modem was worse. Thus, every time an agent logged onto DARPA's mainframe, the signals, both incoming and outgoing, were subject to encryption.

He sat at a small desk. Logged on, then waited for the DARPA home site to download.

Meg. The Happy Homemaker. Till two days ago, that was.

Uncharacteristically squandering time, Mark went to Afferton's file and downloaded the photo of Meg he'd saved in his hard drive two years ago—he always saved photos of his charges' wives and children. Her picture filled the screen. She'd been thirty then, dressed in a sleeveless black dress and pearls for a reception at the new Health Sciences Center of the University of Colorado in Aurora, where her husband's biotech lab was situated. The picture had been in *Science Now* magazine, and Meg had been standing between her husband and his partner Jerry Riggs. Riggs's wife, Joanna, had not been at the reception.

One of their two kids had been sick and she'd stayed home.

But it was Meg who held Mark's attention. She was fashionably slender, about five feet five inches tall, though she looked taller. Her reddish-brown hair had fallen just below her ears. Now it was shorter, more layered and more curly. Her eyes were dark brown.

She was, all in all, very lovely, her most outstanding feature in his estimation being her flawless, milky-white skin that seemed almost translucent. The effect of the dark reddish hair and sable eyes against the unusually pale skin was stunning. It was no wonder Howard Afferton had married his new lab technician only a few months after moving from Boston to Denver.

But Meg Deverall Afferton wasn't quite as attractive right now. Forty-eight hours of unrelenting pressure had taken its toll. He felt a curious stab of sympathy for her, then forgave himself for the emotion. Any decent person would sympathize with her predicament.

He clicked off her photo and put his full attention onto the subject at hand, Howard Afferton. There were no new cross-check references such as credit card purchases or airline reservations in his name. Then again, Mark hadn't expected any. He was pretty damn certain his boy Howie had been nabbed. And that was enough for Mark.

He clicked into Afferton's personal file. The man came from a poor Boston family. When Afferton was only seven, his father, a railroad worker and big drinker, had been involved in an on-the-job accident and had never really worked again. Afferton's mother had supported the family.

Childhood had been brutal on the kids. But Afferton had managed to shine through the dimness of poverty. He had been born with brains, an IQ of 155. Harvard had snatched him up with a full scholarship. From that point on, Afferton never looked back.

At twenty-five he had his Ph.D. A classic overachiever. At twenty-seven he met Jerry Riggs, another boy wonder, and they had set up their first biotech lab in a rundown South Boston industrial district with a small government grant. They'd been doing cancer research then. And had some success, receiving FDA approval for second-stage development of their smart gene research. Then they'd been bought out by a larger biotech company for a tidy profit. At that point they'd created R and A Biotech and tried their hands at vaccine research, specifically a vaccine for the Ebola virus, and the University of Colorado noted their progress and offered the use of the state-of-the-art lab at their new Health Sciences Center in the old Fitzsimons Army Medical Center in Aurora, a suburb of Denver.

With the federal grant money flowing in steadily and the new facility near Denver, Merrick Pharmaceuticals had also offered R and A further monetary assistance in exchange for a ten-year exclusive license to develop their patented, FDA-approved vaccine. But for a giant drug company like Merrick, the amount invested in R and A Biotech was a pittance. And besides, the grants were write-off expenses when corporate tax time rolled around.

But for Afferton and Riggs the extra money had been pure manna from heaven. The men had come a long way since their first lab in the crummy Boston industrial district.

Not far enough for diamond-and-sapphire bracelets, though, or the trendy Denver home and the even trendier Aspen condo. All red flags. Afferton was living beyond his means.

The light outside the guest-room window morphed from gray to a luminescent mauve. Mark took off his glasses and set them beside the laptop and unconsciously rubbed the bridge of his nose. Just how much did Meg know about her husband's business? She seemed innocent and naive, living in her own fairytale world, but maybe she was a good actress.

"Why do we need a security expert?" she'd asked. Standing there in the living room, in a blue nightgown, dark fingerprints of shadow under her eyes, her hair disordered from sleep. She'd sounded completely innocent, puzzled, anxious, exhausted. Shivering in the cool night air.

His first impulse had been to be fiercely protective; odd how that feeling had rushed through his veins. Then he'd backed off and studied her reactions. She *could* be acting, he supposed. But he doubted it.

A hint of a smile curved his lips. He certainly had a suspicious nature. *He* was the expert when it came to deceit. Hell, look at his cover story, that he was from Merrick Pharmaceuticals. The story contained just enough truth to be convincing, and if anyone checked up on him, Merrick had his file, cover story and all, loaded into its computer under employee records. He'd used similar cover stories before; DARPA had ongoing arrangements with several companies. It was an arrangement that suited everyone. DARPA agents were neatly protected, while the interests of the companies were also safeguarded. Like now. Merrick had full, if shadowy, government backing to find their man and to retrieve all pertinent research data belonging to them.

He put his glasses on and entered notes on his first encounter with Meg into the laptop. Then he saved the information on the hard drive and shut down the computer.

He was tired. It had been a long day and an even longer night. His plane had arrived late in Denver, his commuter flight to Aspen had been canceled due to a mechanical glitch, and he'd had to wait for the last flight. Still, it had been quicker than taking a three-hour drive on unfamiliar, pitch-black roads over twelve-thousand-foot mountain passes.

He'd gotten a taxi straight to the police department and spoken at length to the assistant police chief, who'd called the chief at home and filled him in. Not surprisingly, the chief, at a dead end in his search for Dr. Afferton, had been willing to turn the investigation over to the government. Then one of the on-duty cops had given Mark a ride to the condo. The time had been 1:00 a.m. Mrs. Afferton, no, *Meg,* he reminded himself—and he needed to remember to use her first name—had gotten up around three. He wished now that she'd had a full night's rest before they'd spoken, but she'd been insistent. The last thing he'd wanted to do was alienate the woman. He needed her trust and cooperation.

But how to handle her?

He made his way soundlessly to the kitchen and put on a pot of coffee, easily finding the filters and the coffee in the orderly cupboards and refrigerator.

After a mug of strong black coffee on the back deck, somewhat refreshed by the morning chatter of birds and the sigh of the gentle mountain wind in the cottonwoods, he went back inside and showered, putting on a clean blue shirt and clean blue jeans. In the city he would have worn khakis, but it was cooler here and far more casual.

He also might have carried his gun. Most DARPA agents did, especially in the field. But he chose to keep his handgun in his suitcase. He suspected Meg Afferton would go ballistic if she saw him packing a gun. He hoped he wouldn't need it.

Another cup of coffee, and he was ready to concentrate on Meg. To accomplish his job he really needed to gain her confidence. The trouble was that he was not very adept when it came to handling women. He didn't really understand them, and he was no good at faking it. Unfortunately, if his take on their first meeting was correct, he'd already made an unfavorable impression on her.

Okay, then, he'd remedy that. He'd become her new best friend and he'd pick her brain. Even if she were unaware of Afferton's whereabouts she subconsciously knew plenty. She had to. No one was *that* blind.

Mark paced the living room silently, mug in hand.

He did not want to wake Meg or her brother—though Brian Deverall was most likely down for the count after his night of carousing. Some help the kid was to his sister. Another facet of Mark's job that he hadn't factored in—dealing with the kid brother.

On the other hand, maybe by handling Brian, Mark could gain Meg's approval. It was worth a try.

So, Howie, where are you, he mused, *and how much does your pretty wife know?*

Did she suspect Afferton might be taking payoffs for updates on his research?

Mark pondered the situation. People didn't just vanish. Either Afferton had fled because he was afraid the U.S. government was already onto him, or he'd gotten cold feet and run before someone figured he'd sold his country out.

Another possibility, and one Mark was beginning to favor, was that Afferton had not taken off on his own volition, but had been abducted. Though perhaps not for the reason Mark had given his wife. Maybe Afferton had grown fearful of discovery and stopped feeding information to his money source. That would have pissed them off royally, and thus the kidnapping.

The more Mark considered the events of the past two days the more convinced he was that Afferton had been snatched. The man was in the middle of a seminar he'd put together at the elite Given Institute. Mark could not picture Afferton splitting before the completion of the lecture series he'd worked on so diligently.

Hell, the man would at least have waited till his colleagues flew home at the end of the week.

Whatever the scenario, Howard Afferton had to be found. This was now a matter of the highest level of national security. And to locate the man, Mark needed Meg's cooperation.

He heard someone stirring upstairs, water running, and then silence again. He refilled his mug, feeling the caffeine zing in his blood, and thought about all the mistakes he'd made with the women in his life.

A navy brat, he'd been raised all over the world, from the Philippines to the Mediterranean. Never in one place long enough to form close school ties, certainly there'd never been a steady girl.

Then he'd followed in his father's footsteps and gone to Annapolis. After that he'd made it through SEAL training and been given his own team. He'd been stationed in Florida for about two years, and there he'd met Carole, a navy nurse. Both military brats, they'd clung to each other, obviously confusing the need for a settled relationship for love. When the sex had cooled, so had their marriage. It had lasted a mere six months.

He never blamed Carole. As she had so accurately put it, he was not comfortable with intimacy.

"Mark," she'd said outside the divorce lawyer's office, "do yourself a favor and stick to playing drill sergeant to your recruits. You're just too repressed to be married. It's not your fault, still…"

He'd had to admit to himself that Carole had a point. *Better safe than sorry,* he'd decided.

And that brought him back to thoughts of Meg. How in hell to get close to the woman? If his assumptions about Afferton's disappearance were on target, the man would eventually contact his wife. Or his abductors would.

And Mark had to be right there beside her.

CHAPTER FIVE

SHE HADN'T SLEPT, not a wink. She was up and showered by eight, surprised to see that the coffee was already brewed, the pot half empty. Mark Fielder must have made coffee. Hadn't he slept, either?

He came out of the guest room a moment later. He was dressed in a light blue oxford-cloth shirt and jeans, and he didn't look a bit like a man who'd been up all night.

"You made coffee," she said, unable to think of a single clever thing to say.

"Yes, I hope you don't mind?" His gaze fixed on her, pinioned her, his question superfluous. He was in charge, and he wanted her to know it. But then Meg was used to a man directing her life, wasn't she?

"No, it's fine. Are you…I mean, how long do you plan to stay?"

"Until I decide you're no longer in danger." He hesitated, then went on. "I really need to stay right here. I know it's hard enough for you without having a stranger around, but in order for me to do my job, I have to be here."

"Yes, I understand," she said softly.

"Aren't you going to have a cup?"

"Ah, I, ah, don't drink coffee."

"Oh. Can I get you some tea?"

"Not right now, thanks."

"Well. Let me know how you want things done."

She looked at him. He sounded as if this was going to be a drawn-out arrangement. But he was wrong. Howie would come back. He *had* to come back.

"Did you get some sleep?" Mark was asking. "Has anyone suggested medication to you?" he added carefully.

"Yes."

"I see."

"I...I prefer not to take any."

"All right."

"Brian?" she said, remembering suddenly. "Is he...?"

"Your brother is still asleep."

She flushed. Of course he was.

"And there's nothing new regarding your husband."

"I figured. I would have heard the phone ring."

"I was going to fix myself something to eat. Toast, eggs? Cereal?"

"No, thanks." Her stomach curled.

"You have to eat, Mrs....Meg. You have to eat and sleep and try to stay healthy. I know it's hard, but..."

"You don't know anything," she said. "It isn't *your* husband who's missing."

Mark said nothing, turned his back on her and began searching the fridge. She saw immediately that he was no good in the kitchen. He broke the egg yolks, dropped part of a shell in the pan and muttered something under his breath. The English muffins came out of the toaster charred. He didn't seem to notice. He put them on a plate and pushed it across the counter toward her, then turned back to the stove where his own eggs were getting cold. He put another muffin in, undercooked this one, and then dumped the cold eggs on top of it. The only comment he made was "I usually grab fast food," then he ate the muffin and eggs without flinching.

He'd just finished when there was a knock on the front door. He swallowed and answered it, and she heard him speaking quietly to someone, couldn't make out the words. She felt disappointed at herself for letting him take over—she should have fixed breakfast; she should have answered the door. But she didn't have the energy, didn't care enough to put forth the effort to regain control.

Where was Howie? Could this man, Mark, be right? Could Howie have been kidnapped for his knowledge? Was he being held somewhere, starved, tortured?

She nibbled at the blackened muffin, thinking. Sure, she knew about bioterrorism. Anyone who worked in the biotech industry was well aware of the risks of researching the most dangerous diseases in the world. If one tiny vial of Ebola virus spilled, it could kill everyone who came into contact with it, then it could spread like wildfire. There was no cure and no preventative vaccine.

If a hostile nation or terrorist organization wanted to hold the entire planet hostage by threatening to let loose an incurable disease onto the world's population, it could do so.

Sure, Howie knew the dangers. So did his partner Jerry. Everyone in the lab was well aware of the risks. Elaborate precautions were taken. All employees were trained in safety measures. Warning signs were posted all over the lab.

Could someone have kidnapped Howie because of his research? Or, worse, could he have been duped by people who wanted the results of his research? My God, how easily the research could be turned to destructive use.

"…asked people not to…" Mark was saying.

She snapped back to attention. "What?"

"There's a police car posted outside. I've asked them to keep people from visiting," he said.

"You *what?*"

"It looks like meddling, but it's better if the place isn't full of visitors."

"But…"

"I realize you must have a lot of friends here. Concerned friends. The problem is that I don't know these people. We don't want a stranger to make his way in. Right?"

Everything he said made sense. But it was insane. She felt as if she'd fallen down a rabbit hole and everything was *off*.

"You should be aware that there's a tap on your phone now."

"There is?"

"Do you have a cell phone?"

"I…no. Howie does, though."

"Yes, I have that number. I've tried it. I only got his voice mail."

"How stupid…" she began. She'd never even thought of calling his cell phone.

"You didn't try it?" Mark raised a brow.

"No, I didn't think, I… God, I should have… Or the police. *Someone.*"

"It wouldn't have mattered."

"No, I suppose not."

The muffin seemed to have settled her stomach, but she felt so tired, so worn-out, she could barely function. Mark disappeared into his room. To work on his laptop, he'd explained. Brian was still asleep.

She stacked the dishes in the dishwasher. Routine, familiar chores. Cleaned up the kitchen, which had been overrun by too many people in the last two days. Washed platters left by well-wishers, by friends, by Howie's colleagues. Cleaned up the mess Mark Fielder had made.

She pulled the vacuum cleaner from the closet and began on the living room floor. All the while her brain spun, then jolted with a spasm of panic. Again and again.

Where was Howie? Was he even still alive? Wouldn't she know if he were dead? Wouldn't she *feel* it? Or had they grown so far apart there was no connection left at all? Cold dread filled her.

A hand came down on her arm, and the sound of the vacuum halted. Mark had switched the machine off, and he was standing over her, his eyes holding a reserved pity, his hand preventing her from continuing.

"Hey," he said softly.

"Can I finish? Do you mind if I finish vacuuming?"

"You're in no state to be cleaning house."

"Don't tell me what to do."

"You're overtired, Mrs....Meg, take it easy."

She dropped the vacuum and turned away, putting her face in her hands. Tears squeezed through her fingers.

"Go to bed," he said. "You'll feel better if you rest."

"I...I can't," she sobbed.

"Yes, you can. I'll finish up for you. I'll be here in case the phone rings. I'll take care of everything."

Something in his voice, in his words, was reassuring. Could she trust him? She'd trusted Howie, though, and look what had happened.

"Go upstairs. Close your door. Okay? Meg, do you hear me?"

"Yes," she mumbled through her fingers. Then she felt his hand on her again, this time on her back. Warm and, yes, unbearably comforting.

"Let me handle everything," he said.

SHE CAME FULLY AWAKE, instantly alert, knowing there was a crisis of some sort, knowing she had to react, but not quite remembering what it was. Then it all came flooding back—Howie, that man downstairs...

What time was it? Four-twenty-three. Dear God, she'd slept most of the day. She'd actually slept.

She sat up abruptly, felt a rush of dizziness, willed it away. She pulled on the same clothes she'd had on that morning, a blue T-shirt and the same khaki slacks as the day before—everything else was getting too tight for her.

Brian, she suddenly thought. What was *he* up to? In the bathroom, she ran a comb through her hair, brushed her teeth. Not that it mattered, not that anyone cared.

The condo was very quiet, the doors locked, even the windows were shut and latched. She looked around, feeling as if she were a prisoner. Someone— Mark?—had tidied up the magazines and newspapers on the coffee table. He'd said earlier he'd finish up the housework. Well, he had.

She noticed the glass doors to the back deck were open, and she found him out there on one of the lounges, reading a local paper, the *Aspen Times*. He heard her, turned as she walked out onto the deck and sat up.

"It's late," she said.

"That's okay. I'm glad you slept." He eyed her through the small round lenses. "You look better."

"Is there any news?"

"No." A pause. "I was just looking through the paper, trying to get a feel for Aspen. Interesting place." He held the paper up. "The only mention of your husband is on a back page. Which is good. I asked the local authorities to keep his disappearance under wraps from now on."

"And they agreed? Just like that? I'm surprised. Aspenites have a reputation for being very independent, not taking kindly to direction from the outside world."

He gazed at her impassively. "I explained to them that it might endanger Dr. Afferton if any more news got out. They agreed to cooperate, no problem."

She moved across the deck to sit in a chair at the round table. The sun was warm on her back. "Where's Brian? Did he…?"

"Oh, your brother. Well, he got up late and he, uh, packed his bag and told me to tell you he was going home to Denver."

She was stunned. "He's gone?"

"Yeah, he's gone. Oh, he also made a remark about getting out of Dodge before the sheriff shot him."

"And I'm the sheriff," she said dryly.

"Look, maybe it's better that he left. He was…upsetting you. You have enough on your mind right now."

She couldn't believe Brian's selfishness. Her husband was missing, and all her brother could think about was going out and drinking beer and God knows what else, and then avoiding admonishment for his behavior. But she clamped her lips and didn't say a word to Mark. She was too damn embarrassed. Looking down at her hands, feeling her cheeks flush, she said, "Maybe it is better."

Mark rose and stretched, and she saw his shirt pull tight against his flat stomach. She switched her eyes away. What was she doing? Looking at a man, a stranger, and admiring him, marking details that she should not notice: his corded neck, strong forearms with fine hairs that glistened with moisture, the al-

most-imperceptible cleft in his bristly chin, a mere
shadow. The artful carving of his lips.

What was wrong with her?

"You hungry?" he asked, then he smiled. "No, of
course you aren't, but I heated up some spaghetti
sauce with sausage I found in the freezer. I hope you
don't mind my ransacking your kitchen, but I figured..."

"It's okay. But I'm really not hungry."

"I'm a lousy cook," he said, "but I can boil pasta.
Well, usually," he added, and she saw a hint of a
self-deprecating smile touch his lips.

"I'm sure you do fine," she said.

"A guy's got to eat."

"You live alone, then?"

"Yes, I do."

"You're from Washington?"

"Did I say that?"

"I thought so. Or did I overhear you and the policeman last night?"

"I am from Washington."

"And you work for Merrick?"

"That's correct."

"But isn't Merrick based in Des Moines?" Howie
and Jerry had flown to Des Moines often enough for
meetings, she knew that.

"Well, yes, the corporate office is in Des Moines,
but the security division has a Washington branch."

"Oh." How odd, she thought.

He turned to enter the condo. "I'll boil up the
pasta. It's a little early for dinner, but you skipped
lunch, so..."

"Has anyone called?" she interrupted.

"Yes, a few people. I let the machine pick up the messages."

"I need to phone my mother," she said.

He turned to face her. "Careful what you tell her. Enough people know about this."

"I have to tell my *mother*. Besides, Brian's going to be home, and—"

"Don't go into any details."

"What details? I don't know anything," she pointed out.

He held up a hand. "Okay, fine."

She called her mother, knowing she had to tell Lucy about Howie and about Brian, who might be back in Denver already. Her poor mother—she'd be so upset when Brian showed up.

"Hello?" came her mom's voice.

"Oh, Mom."

"Meg?"

"Mom, I'm sorry, but Brian left here. He's on his way back to Denver."

"Oh, no. What on earth happened?"

Then Meg had to explain the whole thing, Howie missing, the police, this security guy from Merrick Pharmaceuticals...

"Oh, sweetie, how awful. But it's got to be a misunderstanding. I'm sure Howie would *never*, well, he'd never just go away. I hope, oh dear, I hope nothing's happened to him. Poor Meg. My goodness, in my day these things just didn't happen. People are so strange nowadays. I just don't understand, I simply don't... Oh dear, Meg, should I go up there when

Brian gets back with my car? Do you need me to do something?''

Meg sighed inwardly. ''No, Mom, I'm okay. I'll probably drive home in a while, a week or so, you know, when...when Howie's back.''

Mark had cooked the pasta while she was on the phone. She could smell garlic and tomato sauce, and it occurred to her that she was a little hungry. And she should eat, if not for herself then for the baby. If there *was* a baby. And if she was pregnant, how would she manage? Except for a small rainy-day savings account, she had no money. Everything was in Howie's name. He took care of all their finances, paid all the bills, gave her an allowance for anything she needed. But she had no idea where they stood money-wise—she'd never even paid the mortgage or the taxes.

''Meg?'' Mark said.

''Um,'' she replied, but her mind was elsewhere, drenched in fear and pulsing with questions.

She must have been crazy to let Howie manage everything.

''Meg?''

She walked toward the kitchen, forcing the thoughts from her head. Of course Howie would be found. This was all a mistake. Mark Fielder was jumping to wild conclusions. People like Howie didn't get kidnapped. Things like this just didn't happen.

''Sit down,'' Mark was saying. ''Try it. Salad?''

He'd overcooked the fresh pasta she'd bought the other day at the local grocery store. It was practically mush. The salad was better, though there was too much dressing for her taste. The only thing passable, really, was the sauce—garlic and basil and sausage— and only because it had come from her freezer.

"Spaghetti's a little overdone, huh?" he observed, but he ate heartily, anyway. When his plate was clean, she was still forcing herself to chew and swallow. The noodles might as well have been baby food, she thought, and then she recalled why she was eating in the first place—the baby.

Mark stayed seated at the counter and watched her. Like a mother hen.

"Don't you have something else to do?" she asked.

"Not at the moment." Calmly.

The phone rang then. He answered it, spoke quietly, hung up.

"Who was it?" she asked.

"A Dr. Nichols."

"Oh, Ted. Did you...?"

"I'm telling everyone the same thing. The authorities are on the case, you're unavailable. Don't worry, I'm polite."

"You should let me talk to my husband's friends."

"I think it's better right now if you don't."

"What if my mother calls back? Or Brian?" She wanted to say, *What if my own friends call?* but she realized she had few friends aside from Howie's, and none of them were more than acquaintances from her hospital volunteer work. But outside of the hospital, she never saw them. She was terribly alone; Howie had made certain he was the center of her life. She had, really, no life of her own at all.

"Then I'll give the call to you," he was saying.

When she finished eating, she put the dishes in the sink and turned the water on.

"Let me do that," he said.

"No," she said, her back to him. "I'm all right. Don't baby me." Standing firm for a change felt good. She'd handle this crisis, she could do it. She'd have to. Besides, he was worse than Howie in the kitchen, which was saying a lot.

The Aspen policeman who'd been on watch in his car knocked on her door when he was going off shift. "Just wanted to let you know my replacement will be here in a few minutes," he said to Mark. Did everyone recognize her lack of authority?

"Do you feel up to talking?" Mark asked when the cop left.

"About what?"

"About your husband. I need to know everything about him. About your life, his work. You might hold the key to his whereabouts without knowing it."

She paced the floor behind the tasteful beige leather sofas facing each other across a heavy, glass-topped coffee table. "I don't know anything. I'd tell you if I knew where he was."

"Sit down. Let me be the judge of what you know."

"Is this part of your job?"

"Yes."

"So you're really some kind of investigator? Not just in security?"

"Sit down, Meg."

She sat on a sofa; he lowered himself into the opposite one, his gaze on her. Something about his demeanor made her squirm. He possessed a distinct aura of authority that he seemed able to switch on and off at will. One minute he was unsmiling and direct to the point of intimidation, the next he was wryly noting his lack of culinary skills. But in either mode, she decided, he was uncomfortable around her. Or, perhaps, uncomfortable around women in general.

The notion flashed through her consciousness that a good-looking man like Mr. Fielder—*Mark*—should have his pick of available women. Yet her intuition told her that he was not loose with his feelings.

Was that why he made her so nervous?

But none of that mattered. He wanted to talk. He said she might unwittingly hold the key to Howie's whereabouts. She sighed and said, "Okay. What do you want to know?"

"Let's start at the beginning."

He never took his eyes off her. He asked questions at first, but then he fell silent and let her talk. She was surprised at how much she had to say, how easily it came after his first few queries. It was as if she'd been holding it all in, and now somebody wanted to know about *her*.

"So I met Howie when he hired me to work at his lab in Aurora. He was a little shy at first, but we started dating. We were worried, you know, it didn't look good, a lab technician dating her boss. But he, well—" she clasped her hands "—really swept me off my feet. Howie's so, he's so powerful. Brilliant.

Ambitious. Good-looking. So much more than I ever expected. I mean, he liked *me*.''

"You underestimate yourself," he said, then seemed to catch himself and said no more.

"No, no, I think I'm a realistic person," she felt it necessary to add.

"Go on."

"We got married, that was, um, six years ago. I stopped working at the lab. Howie didn't want me to work." She flushed.

"He sounds like a man who likes to be in control."

"Yes." She looked down. "He takes care of everything. At the lab, at home. He works very hard, he and Jerry both. They're both so smart, they were really getting somewhere with the vaccine."

"For Ebola?"

She looked up sharply. But of course Merrick would know. They were paying for the research in part, and they'd reap the profits marketing it. "Yes, Ebola. Other labs are working on a vaccine for it, too. It's a race, sort of."

"Is R and A Biotech a successful enterprise?"

"Well, yes, with the funding from Merrick. Howie was thrilled with the grant. He told me it gave them a step up on everybody else."

"Finances?"

"Is that your business?"

"Everything's my business."

"I'm not in charge of our finances. I have no idea, really, what Howie makes. He takes care of all that."

"But this condo. And your house in Denver."

"Well, yes, the lab's been doing well, and he

wanted a good life for us. Howie's childhood was not… Well, his family was poor. His dad was hurt in an accident." She refused to tell this stranger that Howie's father was an alcoholic. "We don't see his family. He told me he left when he got the scholarship to Harvard."

"And your family?"

"My dad died years ago. My mother is a school librarian in Wheat Ridge, a suburb of Denver. My brother…of course, you met him. He's a student at CU." She would *not* tell him that Brian was probably out on his ear after his last disastrous semester.

"Does Howie talk about his work with you?"

"Some. I don't understand the theoretical side of his research. I do know that what they were…*are* trying to do is very difficult—and dangerous. It's cutting-edge work." She shifted on the couch. Pulled a Navajo-patterned pillow to hold across her stomach. Hiding the telltale bulge? Defensive?

"He was a very… No, he *is,* he is a very intense person. Driven. He's been on edge lately, working long hours. Just last week I begged him to relax a little, take a break, but he said this was his break. Staying in Aspen. But, honestly, he set up the series of lectures here, and he had to prepare his own seminar, and he was…stressed out. It wasn't much of a time-off."

"Was this stress recent?"

She thought. "No, not really. It's been building for months." She felt a shock ripple through her. Her marital discontent had also been building for a long time. Was there a correlation between Howie's stress and her feelings of loneliness and rejection?

"How does he get along with his partner Jerry Riggs?"

She dragged her attention back to Mark. "Fine. They have their own areas of responsibility. Jerry does most of the fund-raising, the business end. Howie is the head of research. There aren't any problems at work, nothing bad between them. That's what you're fishing for, isn't it?"

He ignored her. "Someone is interviewing Dr. Riggs right now."

"Someone from Merrick?"

"That's right."

"Believe me, Jerry had nothing to do with Howie's disappearance."

"We have to look at every possibility." His voice remained mild. She wondered if he'd had experience with other distraught spouses. Did he handle them all with the same dispassion?

"Some of your *possibilities* seem pretty far-fetched, if you ask me." She met his gaze without flinching. "But you're not asking me, are you?"

"Tell me about Jerry Riggs and his family."

She related everything she knew. How Jerry and Howie had met in Boston, how they'd become partners. She described Joanna, Jerry's wife, their two children, Roy and Trudy. He listened, not interrupting, and he took no notes; she wondered if he would remember every word she said. She looked into his dark blue eyes and thought: *Yes, he just might recall it all.*

"This Joanna Riggs..."

"You can't think *she* had anything to do with Howie's disappearance?"

"It sounds like she's a friend."

Meg thought. "Well, we see each other a lot. Obviously. But she's got the kids and...oh, I don't know, maybe she's a good acquaintance, not quite a *friend*."

"Who are your friends?"

She blinked. "Well, some old school buddies." That was a lie. She hadn't kept in touch with any of them. "And friends of my mother's, you know, in the old neighborhood. And Howie's, um, colleagues and their wives. And there's a group of women I know through the volunteer work I do at a hospital."

"Anyone in particular?"

"No." Slowly. "Not really."

He changed the subject abruptly. "Your job at the lab... You said Howie didn't want you to work."

She got up then, tired of sitting, jittery, fed up with his relentless, emotionless questioning. Walking to the open sliding glass door to the deck, she stood on the threshold looking out at the darkening sky. Behind her she heard Mark's cell phone ring. He answered it, and she heard him say, "I'll call you back. It'll be late, yeah."

Who had that been? His boss, another *security* man from Merrick?

"So," she heard him say, "Howie didn't want you to work."

She turned, hugging herself. "He had this thing about women working. His mother had to support the family when his father was hurt, and apparently she was always exhausted. He wanted his wife to be a lady of leisure."

"Did you want to quit working?"

She said nothing for a minute, then asked, "What does this have to do with anything?"

"Please humor me. I need to understand your husband, and I need your help."

She sighed. Her phone rang, but he waved a hand, meaning, *Let the machine pick it up.* She heard the machine's electronic clicking, a man's voice—David—and her pulse settled. It was not Howie.

"I wanted to keep working. I even suggested that I'd get a job at another lab, so it didn't look so…awkward. But Howie was adamant."

"He's a pretty forceful guy."

"Yes, yes, he is. Not *physical,* I don't mean that, but emotionally, um, yes, he is."

"So you quit your job. This was six years ago."

"Yes."

"And then you did…what? You have no children."

Her heart gave a sick lurch. *No children.* "I…I took classes…at Metro College and…and…I take care of the house. When we moved, oh, eighteen months ago, it was hectic. I handled everything. And I had to buy furniture. I mean, we moved into a much bigger house."

"You mentioned that you do volunteer work? Like a blue lady?"

She nodded. "Yes. One day a week. But I'm usually available if one of our other ladies is sick or on vacation."

"Howie doesn't mind the volunteer work?"

She shrugged. "He did at first, but now, well, I suppose he thinks it's all right."

"Because it's a lady's job, and you don't get paid?"

"I guess so."

"I see."

Yes, he saw. That she was essentially a bored and useless housewife, who did nothing most of the week.

"And you took care of the move into this condo?"

"Oh, the condo." She glanced around. "Howie bought it like this. Completely furnished, right down to the toilet paper and dishes."

He looked at her. "Interesting."

"It was easier that way. And he figured it'd be rented out whenever we weren't in Aspen, so it wasn't worth fussing over."

"It's very...pleasant. I assumed you'd decorated it."

She gripped her upper arms with white fingers, tried to smile. "Not me. Someone with excellent taste."

He gave her a look, but she turned away from his gaze.

More questions. Outside, the racket of a treeful of blackbirds marked the setting of the sun. She noticed the lingering scent of garlic and basil tomato sauce and felt the air cooling on her bare arms. His cell phone rang once more; he replied quickly, then switched it off.

Where was Howie?

She told him about their life in Denver, entertaining

his colleagues. The dinners made her nervous—
Howie got angry if everything wasn't perfect. Once
the soufflé had fallen and he hadn't spoken to her for
two days.

"He's a perfectionist?" Mark asked.

"God, yes. And I'm, well, I'm more casual than
that. But Howie is so ambitious—he can't stand mistakes."

"He's impatient?"

"That, too. But he's a genius, you know. Geniuses
aren't always easy to live with. I'm very lucky. I'm
so lucky. I never dreamed a man like Howie…" Oh,
God, was she defending him?

"Did you and your husband plan on having a family?"

Out of the blue. A blow to the solar plexus. She
almost doubled over. "Uh…yes, sure…one day," she
managed to say.

He switched directions again, his expression sober,
his tone steady. No reaction, except for when he took
his glasses off and pinched the bridge of his nose.
Howie's college career, his manner with employees
at the lab. Friends, colleagues. Phone calls to foreign
countries on their home phone bills? Odd business
trips?

She moved back to the couch and sat down again.
"No, no phone calls to other countries that I'm aware
of. But he could have called from work or his cell
phone, and I wouldn't know. Howie kept…he kept
his work life completely separate. There were—" she
averted her eyes "—lots of little things I didn't know
about. Things that didn't matter."

She picked at a thread on the edge of a pillow. "I trusted Howie. He would never do anything to hurt me. He loved..." She put her hand up to her mouth, horrified. "He *loves* me. He gave me everything."

"Yes, he did."

She kept her glance down, but the words came of their own volition. "I sound like a pretty useless person, don't I? Spoiled and ineffectual. God, my husband is gone, and I have no idea, not a clue, no inkling of what happened to him. I can't even guess."

"I'm not here to judge you."

She raised her eyes. Was that carefully restrained pity she saw on his face? "Oh, yes, you are. You know more about me right now than anyone else in the world. Wonderful. You've laid me open, Mr. Fielder. Sliced me with your scalpel. Well, did it help you figure out where Howie is? Did it?" But he hadn't discovered the worst about her, that she'd been ready to leave her wonderful, generous, *loving* husband.

"My job doesn't work like that," he said patiently. "I'm merely gathering information. This is the first stage of the investigation. You're the most important person in your husband's life, and I need to know him through you."

"Do you know him now?"

"I'm beginning to."

"How nice."

"No need to be sarcastic. This is an ongoing process. I'll be sending in my report. So will the other agents. We'll pool it all—"

She interrupted him. "He could be with another woman, that's what you think, isn't it?"

"It's a possibility," he said without inflection.

"Go to hell," she said, and she got up and went upstairs, closing her door too hard behind her.

She hated Mark Fielder.

But she suddenly hated Howie even more for putting her in this position. Yes, she felt the pure cleansing flame of hatred, and she held it inside her.

It was better than abject fear.

CHAPTER SIX

WHEN SHE DRAGGED HERSELF from bed the following morning, she was determined to be more sensible. The long hours of the night had worn her down. She'd lain there, her heart racing, her mind going through one ugly scenario after another.

Mark Fielder was here to help, she told herself. He was doing his best. Okay, Merrick had a stake in her husband's safety. Maybe it was only a mercenary interest, but if Mark could find Howie, Merrick's motivation didn't matter.

She'd try to cooperate, she decided as she showered. But Mark would have to level with her. There were a lot of things that didn't quite add up.

He'd made coffee again. As she inhaled the aroma, she tried to deny the notion that, along with all her other problems, Mark Fielder had taken over her house.

It was cloudy out, one of those days that foreshadowed the Southwest monsoon season, she saw as she looked out the front window. The pewter sky suited her mood.

Where was Howie? What was he doing right now? Didn't he care what she was going through? Or was he past caring about anything at all?

"Oh, you're up," she heard from behind her.

"I suppose you could call it that." She turned. He had come in from the deck. He wore shorts, a T-shirt damp with sweat and running shoes. He had strong legs covered with light brown hair, a runner's legs.

"You went jogging?"

"The police have a man stationed out front," he was quick to say. "I wouldn't leave you here alone."

"That wasn't what I meant," she said. Then she realized that she was staring at him, observing his body, and that he'd noticed her doing it. She cringed and looked away.

"I do like to run, yeah, but it's hard up here. What's the altitude?"

"Around eight thousand feet."

"No wonder. There can't be any oxygen in the air." He took off his glasses and cleaned the lenses on his T-shirt.

"There's been no news," she said. It wasn't a question.

"No."

"Do you have *any* information I don't?" she asked.

He put his glasses on slowly, deliberately, as if biding time. "Some background stuff that was in our files," he finally answered.

"I don't believe you."

He shrugged, the T-shirt sticking to his damp torso. "That's your prerogative."

"Can we talk? And this time I'd like to ask the questions."

"Sure. Let me shower first. Why don't you eat some breakfast?"

"Will you please refrain from treating me like a child?"

"Sorry." The light from the window glinted off his glasses as he fixed his gaze on her. "I didn't realize you saw it that way."

She stood her ground, holding his eyes. "I do see it that way."

He raised a hand. "Okay. I'll take that under advisement."

She felt as if she'd made a point. The first point. A beginning.

He emerged from his room half an hour later, his hair still wet, wearing jeans and a white polo shirt. He hadn't shaved. He went straight to the kitchen, poured himself coffee, which had to be pure mud by now, and got out the cereal from a cupboard.

She sat on a stool at the counter and tried to swallow bites of toast as he ate. He seemed at ease in her domain, as if he had lived here for a long time. How did he do that?

He finished, put the dishes in the sink haphazardly, ran water over them.

"Leave the dishes, okay?" she said.

He turned.

"Can we have that talk now?"

He sat on one of the stools at the counter, too, settled himself so that he faced her. His expression revealed nothing, neither interest nor pity nor impatience.

She took a deep breath. "I'd like you to level with me."

"All right."

"I mean *really* level with me." She was suddenly nervous. "If you believe Howie was kidnapped for his research, shouldn't you know where to look?"

"We are looking," he said calmly.

"Who's *we?*"

"Other Merrick agents and certain firms that we hire to do that kind of work."

"Firms that Merrick hires?"

"Yes."

"Like private, um, investigators?"

"Something like that, yes."

"Shouldn't the FBI be involved by now?"

"Only when we're certain your husband was kidnapped."

"I see. I guess I see."

"I realize how difficult this must be," he offered.

"Difficult? I don't even know if my husband is alive. Yes, it's *difficult.*"

He did not respond.

"You told me there were people who would stop at nothing to get Howie's research. If that's what you really think and I've had no contact with him whatsoever, then you must believe something dreadful has happened." Cold washed over her like a shroud. Her teeth began to chatter.

"That was only a hypothesis. I have no idea yet why Howie disappeared. He could have gotten lost."

"Oh, please." She shook her head. "I know what

I look like to you, naive and spoiled. But I'm not stupid, and I want to know what you really think.''

"I have no opinion at this time."

"So, you've given up on the idea that he's run away with another woman?" she asked angrily.

"It's still on the list of possibilities. Not at the top, though."

She looked at him. "Well, I asked for the truth."

"Hey, Meg, you know your husband better than anyone. If you say he isn't with another woman, you're probably right."

"What did Jerry Riggs say?"

"Jerry Riggs?"

"You told me yesterday he was being questioned."

"I haven't received that information."

"But you will."

"Yes."

"Will you let me know when you get it?"

"I can't promise that."

"Oh, for God's sake, I'll just ask Jerry myself then!" She stood, frustrated, walked to the door to the deck, stood there for a minute, then whirled to face him again. "Tell me what *you* and your *bosses* and your *private investigators* think."

"We don't have enough information yet," he said impassively.

"Oh, God!" she cried. "You can't treat me like this. You can't... I'm his *wife*. I'm..." She'd been about to blurt out that she was carrying his baby. She clamped her mouth shut, put her hand over her lips. Tears burned behind her eyes.

"Meg," Mark said, "please, sit down. Come over

here and sit down. This is hard for you. But I really don't know much more than you do.''

She finally moved to the stool and sat, leaning on the counter, her head drooping.

"Okay," he said. He regarded her from behind his glasses, appeared to come to a decision. "If…*if* your husband has been abducted, then whoever has him may already have what they want."

"His research," she said dully.

"Yes. And if they do…"

"What?"

"If they do, there are two possible outcomes. One, they turn him loose when they're done with him. Two…"

"Don't say it," she whispered.

"It's always possible nothing sinister has happened to your husband. Maybe an accident, an emotional crisis… Yes, maybe even another woman. And the police and sheriff's office are still searching. The state police, too. Mountain Rescue is still on alert. Everything is being done to find him."

A tear trickled down her cheek. She brushed it away. *"But,"* she said.

"But," he repeated, his tone guarded, "you should prepare yourself for every eventuality."

She studied him, assessed his cold blue eyes camouflaged by glasses, his straight nose and high forehead, cheeks covered with stubble, strong chin, his mouth set in an implacable line. A mouth, she thought, that might smile or laugh. But she'd never see that.

He didn't shift his eyes from hers, and as she stared

at him, she sensed that he was telling the truth—Mark Fielder did not know where Howie was. But she also knew with certainty that he was not telling her everything. Why? What was he hiding?

"I'm going to make some phone calls," she said abruptly.

"To whom?"

"I don't think it's any of your business."

"I'm sorry, Meg, but I..."

"Am I a suspect? Tell me, am I? Do I need a lawyer?"

"No, of course not."

"Then I can call anyone I want," she said defiantly.

"It would be better..."

She slashed the air with a hand. "No, it wouldn't be *better*." And she went upstairs to use the phone in her bedroom. Shutting the door, she sank onto the edge of her bed and put her face in her hands.

Just now she'd lost it with Mark, openly displayed more anger than she'd thought possible—certainly more than she'd ever shown to Howie. But with her husband, she'd always felt so...she searched for the word...so *intimidated* that she never dared to show her true feelings.

But with Mark she was letting it all hang out. She supposed her irrational outbursts didn't matter with him. He'd be gone soon. Well, she hoped to God he'd be gone soon.

She finally called her mother. And after that, after talking to Brian and assuring her mother she was all right, she rang Joanna Riggs.

"Oh, Meg," Joanna said, "I didn't know whether to call you or what to do. Is there any news?"

"No, not a word. I feel so useless. And there's a man here from Merrick, who's glued himself to me, hoping either I'll confess to him where Howie is or Howie will phone while he's standing right there."

"We had a guy from Merrick, too. Asked a million questions, nosed all through Howie's office, his computer, the works, but I'm afraid neither Jerry nor I were much help." Her tone was cool.

"Joanna, I wanted to know—has Jerry said anything to you? I mean, did the man from Merrick give any hint of what they think might have happened?"

"Jerry is completely clueless. He told me the guy asked a lot of questions about the finances of the company. Jerry was upset by that."

"All Merrick cares about is its goddamn money," Meg said bitterly.

"Yes, I realize that."

She wanted to ask Joanna a lot more questions, but something in Joanna's voice told her to let it go. It occurred to Meg that R and A Biotech was in a precarious position now. How long would Merrick go on providing grant money when Howie, their top research scientist, might be in the hands of the enemy, turning over the very research Merrick had paid for?

This wasn't Howie's fault. But he'd be blamed. Forget that her husband might undergo physical torture or mind-altering drugs or might even lose his life, he'd still be blamed.

She knew as she held the phone to her ear that she wasn't going to get any sympathy from Joanna.

She said goodbye and hung up. She'd call someone else, someone who *could* help her, she thought. But *who?*

Then it occurred to her. There was no one else.

AFTER LUNCH—SUBS FROM Johnny McGuire's ordered in by Mark—Meg drove him to the Given Institute. A restrained Bauhaus-style structure very close to downtown, the institute was set among trees on a bluff overlooking the bucolic wildlife refuge of Hallam Lake. The building was constructed of concrete block, painted white, with sharp angles and curves and no external windows to speak of.

"It's mostly for meetings and conferences," she explained. "People come from all over the world to attend the seminars, and there are even free lectures for the public. It's called the Given Institute because the land was *given* to the city by the Paepke family."

"Paepke family?"

"Walter and Elizabeth Paepke practically created modern-day Aspen back in the forties. They had a vision and the money to make it happen. The Music Festival, the Given Institute. That was their house, but it's been completely rebuilt by developers." She pointed to a large, spanking-new Victorian. "Elizabeth died a couple years ago."

She pulled up under the tall spruce trees and parked. "Well, here we are."

He went to work immediately. As soon as she introduced him to Janet Fusaro, the director, Meg became superfluous. He asked a thousand questions, sitting there in Janet's office, then asked her to show him around the building. It was practically empty, because the conference on viral diseases and vaccines had come to a halt upon Howie's disappearance.

"So you never saw Dr. Afferton after his lecture?" Mark asked.

"No, I made sure the coffee and refreshments were set up. I waited until he'd begun speaking, I checked in with my secretary, then I left."

"And this was all routine procedure?"

"Absolutely," replied Janet, a pretty dark-haired woman, usually bubbly and enthusiastic. Somber today.

"And you know that Dr. Afferton finished his lecture as planned."

"Yes."

"You've asked your staff if they'd seen him?"

"Oh, yes. And the police were here questioning everybody."

"So, let me get a handle on the time frame. The lecture began at three. It was over at four. Then refreshments were served out there—" he gestured to the lobby "—and Dr. Afferton was expected to mingle, so to speak."

"Exactly."

"And you know he was there for half an hour, forty-five minutes?"

"Yes. The police interviewed as many attendees as they could find. He was there until he excused himself and said he had to get home. His wife—" Janet glanced at Meg "—was expecting him."

"And then he left, and no one has seen him since."

"Correct."

"Thank you, Miss Fusaro. Can I talk to the rest of your staff, please?"

Meg followed him around the building as he questioned Janet's secretary, then a doctor who was there picking up information on renting a conference room, then the one security guard on duty. Mark asked the same questions over and over, and she could see that he was memorizing the physical setup, the routine, the last sighting of Dr. Afferton.

If nothing else, Mark was thorough.

He examined the building, top to bottom, peering into every room, every office, every rest room and broom closet. Even the mechanical room that held the furnace and hot water heater.

Then Meg took him outside the rear of the building, to a broad green lawn shaded by towering blue spruce trees. He walked around the property, checking the decks, the tastefully situated benches, then he stood at the cliff edge looking down at Hallam Lake.

"Beautiful," he said.

"Yes, it is."

"A strange juxtaposition of resort and medical conference center," he mused.

"Hmm." She hugged herself. It was cool out here in the shade, the sun hidden by clouds. Mark, in a summer-weight tan sport coat over his white polo shirt, seemed impervious.

He moved to the wrought-iron table on the patio overlooking the lake and sat in one of the chairs, gesturing for her to join him.

It must have been the way he was sitting, elbows on the table, sport coat unbuttoned. She caught a glimpse of dull blue-gray metal in a shoulder holster, resting against his side below his armpit.

"You're...you're carrying a gun?" she breathed.

For a minute he didn't say a word or even blink. Then, finally, he said, "Yes."

"Just *yes?*"

"Look. Meg, all security agents carry weapons."

"But... It's been at my house, at the condo all this time?"

"Yes."

"My God."

"It's not a big deal. I haven't worn it until today, but I keep it close."

"Where? Where do you keep it?"

"My suitcase."

"God. In the guest room?"

"Yes, Meg, in the guest room. Now can we get over this moment and let me concentrate?"

She said nothing, simply stared at him in horror.

He changed the subject. "It seems that your husband's behavior was perfectly normal. He acted as if nothing was out of the ordinary. Therefore, I have to assume he didn't plan to disappear. He was not dressed for hiking, he had no traveling bag with him, he told everyone he had to go home." Mark paused, tapped his lip with a finger, and Meg thought about Howie. Had he behaved as if everything was normal? "But he never got home," Mark was saying. "So we've narrowed down the time of his disappearance. Okay."

She listened, not speaking. A breeze sighed through

the branches overhead. Below them, the surface of the lake rippled. It was going to rain, she thought.

He turned to her, intent, almost predatory. "How many ways are there out of this valley?"

"Well, you can drive out on Highway 82, either west toward Glenwood Springs and Interstate 70, or east over Independence Pass—" she gestured "—in the opposite direction. The pass is only open in the summer."

"One road in and out?"

"Yes, unless you take some back-country jeep road, but—"

"No, he wouldn't have done that. And there's the airport."

"Yes. A few direct flights to Los Angeles and Minneapolis. The rest are commuter flights to Denver."

"But there are private planes, charters and so on."

She nodded.

"All right. Access is pretty limited. Now, I take it Howie didn't have another car."

"No, we left the second car in Denver. He walked to the institute that day."

"So—" Mark ticked the possibilities off on his fingers "—either he rented a car or went in someone else's vehicle or boarded a plane. The car rental agencies are at the airport, I noticed. Are the air charter companies there, too?"

"Yes."

"Then that's my next stop. Could I drop you at home and use your car? I'll call for a policeman to meet us there."

"I'll drive you."

"That's not necessary."

She set her chin. "I said I'll drive you."

He studied her for a few beats then nodded his head. Reluctantly, she thought.

The Pitkin County Airport, or Sardy Field to Aspen locals, was only three miles outside of town. The third-largest airport in Colorado, it saw hundreds of thousands of tourist and travelers a year. United Express, connecting to Denver, supplied ninety-nine percent of the flights, and all the major car rental agencies had counters in the baggage collection area.

She pulled her Audi into the parking lot and turned it off. The weather had deteriorated, dark clouds building into thunderheads. The wind picked up dust and swirled it across the parking lot, pattering on her windshield.

"This shouldn't take long," Mark said.

"I'm coming with you."

"I don't think so."

"I can describe Howie to people."

"I have the photograph you gave me."

"I want to see what they say."

"I'll tell you what they say."

She twisted to face him. "How are you going to get this information from these people? They may have rules about giving out information to strangers. Privacy rules. I don't know how you think you can just go in there and demand..."

"Not your problem."

"Well, what about leaving me alone here?"

He nodded across the way to the airport security guard standing not twenty yards away. There were lots of people coming and going, too. "As you can see, you aren't alone. And I assure you, we weren't followed."

"And just how do you know that?"

He smiled without humor. "I know."

"But..."

"Wait here, Meg."

He was out of the car and gone before she could think of another reason she should go with him. And then she wondered why he hadn't taken a policeman or sheriff's deputy with him to facilitate his gathering of information. He hadn't even arranged for someone in authority to call ahead. Just who in hell did Mark Fielder think he was, anyway?

She sat there in the Audi, the windows open, growing more restless by the moment. People drove in and parked, emerged with suitcases or got into cars and drove away. A young woman in shorts and a halter-top came by with a man in a suit, jacket over his arm. Her husband or boyfriend, Meg figured, whom she'd picked up. The airport security guard walked up and down the sidewalk, over and over and over.

On the other side of the terminal planes taxied, their engines roaring, and took off, rising quickly into the dull sky, receding into specks and disappearing.

She sat there for an eternity, waiting, getting more and more jumpy. More resentful. Howie was her husband, dammit. She had a right to know if he'd left on a plane or rented a car.

How dare Mark Fielder, a perfect stranger, come barging into her life and tell her what to do?

She got out of the car and slammed the door. Wind

brushed against her, flinging dust in her eyes. A plane far down the valley banked, and she could see it turn and aim for the airport.

She marched across the lot, ignoring the cars and people. She passed the guard and strode toward the automatic glass doors.

This was about *her* husband, after all.

CHAPTER SEVEN

MARK FLASHED HIS DEFENSE Department ID at the United Express manager and asked to speak to the person who'd processed departing passengers on the afternoon of Howard Afferton's disappearance.

This was the last airline he could query. He'd been to the adjacent building where the private flights and charters were checked in and out. No luck there.

He'd spoken to the operations manager of the only other commercial airline that serviced Aspen in the summer. Same story when he'd shown Afferton's photo to the woman working the ticket counter.

"Sorry, but he's not familiar" had been her reply. She'd punched the name Howard Afferton into her computer terminal and come up with nothing. No Howard Afferton or H. Afferton that day—or any day since.

"Okay, thanks," Mark had said.

That had left United and the car rental agencies.

Nothing at United. All the car rentals were located in the baggage collection area. He spoke to three of the four managers and was ready to call it quits. Howie must have left town in a private vehicle. There was no other explanation. Well, there was one other possibility—Afferton was dead.

Mark walked the few feet to the fourth car-rental counter and showed his ID to the man on duty.

"Were you working on the afternoon of July 20?" Mark asked, pocketing his identification.

The man shrugged. "I own the franchise. I'm always on."

Mark produced Afferton's picture. "Have you seen this man?" he inquired. "Maybe rented a car to him or someone with him?"

The man shook his head. "I don't recall that face. And besides, I only did three rentals that day. When you own the business you remember the slow days." Then the man laughed humorlessly. "I wish it had just been two, if you really want to know."

"Oh?"

"Yeah. Some jerk, who could barely speak English. He rents a car that afternoon—supposed to be for a couple hours is all, and the next thing I know, the idiot's dropped it in Grand Junction."

"Really," Mark said, his interest sharpening. "I take it that's unusual?"

"Hell, it happens. But most people make arrangements, you know? Not this character, though."

"Um. You said he could barely speak English?"

"That's right. Actually, there were two of them. I'd say Russian or maybe Eastern European."

"I see. Any particular reason you thought that?"

"Well, the guy who rented the car had an international driver's license, and if I recall correctly, it was issued in some weird country I never heard of."

"Could you look it up for me?"

"Sure, why not," he said, and he disappeared into

a tiny office behind the counter then returned. "Yep. Just like I recalled, it was issued in Turghistan. Credit card was generic, you know, a Visa card."

The man handed Mark a slip of paper with the car renter's name on it. "Figured you might want this."

Mark read it—Boris Lebedev—then put the paper in his pocket. His instincts told him this could be a lead. The first break in the case. He would run the man's name through his database as soon as he got back to Meg's.

"Tell me something," Mark said. "Why would someone dump a car in Grand Junction?"

"Sometimes the weather here has all flights grounded, but Junction's airport is usually open and operational, so folks drive down there. It's about a hundred-twenty miles to Walker Field, not all that far, but the altitude is way lower than here and the weather is usually much better."

"But the weather wasn't a factor that afternoon," Mark pointed out, recalling the initial Aspen Police report.

"No, it wasn't. So my guess is these guys came in on a private plane that dropped them then flew on down to Junction."

Mark raised a brow.

"Happens all the time. There's only so much parking here for private planes, and when it's full the pilots drop their passengers then fly to Junction and park."

"Wouldn't they fly back into Aspen to pick up their clients?" Mark asked.

"Sometimes. But it's cheaper for everyone involved to drive down to Junction. Less jet fuel, less landing and takeoff fees.''

And less exposure, Mark was thinking. No one in Aspen had seen Howard Afferton since his 3:00 p.m. lecture, and this could be the explanation. Afferton had been in that rented car on his way to Grand Junction. It *felt* right.

There remained one big question, however. Had the good doctor gone along willingly?

''My son had to drive me, in fact, because I couldn't drive two cars back myself, right?'' the man was saying. ''It was a real pain. I'm still trying to get a drop-off charge posted on the guy's credit card, but—''

Meg appeared at Mark's elbow just then. ''I asked you to stay in the car,'' he said quietly. ''Did something happen?'' He was certain she'd been fine. He'd poked his head outside every few minutes and seen her sitting in her car, the airport security guard still marching up and down the sidewalk.

''I was going crazy out there.''

''Dammit, Meg, can't you follow instructions?''

''I am not a child,'' she began.

''Hey, look, sorry,'' he said, cutting her off.

But she waved a hand. ''Well, did you find anything out?''

He took her arm and smiled at the man behind the counter. ''Thanks for the information,'' Mark said.

''What information?'' Meg implored, as he led her toward the automatic doors. *''Mark?''*

But he was thinking, calculating just how much he could afford to reveal.

"My husband is missing and you may know something that you won't tell me," she said. "I'm not an idiot. And I..."

"All right, all right," he said as he ducked his head against a dust-laden gust of wind, "in the car, okay?"

He opened the door for her, then got in on the passenger side. He couldn't tell her that her husband might have gone voluntarily with a man from a foreign country. If he opened that can of worms she might have a meltdown. And he had no proof Afferton had gone without a struggle, much less sold out his country. Hell, he had no proof Afferton wasn't lying undiscovered on a hiking trail somewhere. Mark was working on best guesses. And his assumptions could be completely wrong.

"Well?" She ran an impatient hand through her windblown, reddish-brown curls, then gripped the steering wheel tightly.

"I'll tell you what I know. It isn't much, and I've got a lot of checking to do, but..."

"Just tell me, for God's sake."

He told her all that he knew so far, leaving out his own interpretation—that her husband was on the run. "So I need to drive to Grand Junction and talk to the airport personnel there," he was saying, when he noticed that Meg had a hand clamped over her mouth, her eyes were wide, and her shoulders were quaking.

"Hey," he said, realizing he had just given her reason to believe that her husband was still alive.

"Look," he began again, "this *could* be a wild-goose chase."

But she was shaking her head, obviously trying to

collect herself. "I know it's crazy to get my hopes up with so little to go on. But *you* must think it's something or you wouldn't drive all the way to Grand Junction."

"It's routine. My job is to check every lead."

"But you think it was him, don't you?"

He wanted to make her feel better; he was tempted to tell her, "Sure, it's your husband, safe and sound," but he couldn't do that. "I have no opinion," he said without inflection. "It's too soon."

"You're trying to prepare me in case it isn't him, I know you are," she said shyly. "Is that part of your job, too?"

"You're dead wrong about that," he said too quickly. *Shit,* he thought, meeting her eyes, and that was when a fire roared through his gut, a reaction so unexpected that he had to turn away to compose himself. But she was talking to him, and he couldn't finish the thought, much less analyze it.

"Still, I appreciate everything you're doing, Mark. I can't tell you how much this means to me."

They were quiet on the drive back to Meg's condo. He assumed she was making an effort to process the new information—he would do exactly the same in her shoes. For his part, he stared out the window at the magnificent scenery. As they crossed the Maroon Creek bridge he could see Pyramid Peak up a narrow verdant valley. Overhead it was still gray, but the sun had broken through in a dazzling shaft of golden light that hit the pyramid-shaped mountain standing sentinel in the distance, still snow-capped despite midsummer temperatures. Of course, at fourteen thousand feet, the snow would hold all year, he surmised, and he had the sudden urge to drive up the valley, stand at the base of the mountain and ponder the grandeur of nature.

But there was no time for that. He cleared the pleasantries from his head and realized he'd been taken off guard back at the airport by Meg's sudden shift in attitude toward him. Hell, he'd been wondering for two days how he was going to get on her good side, and stay there, when the answer had been so easy—appear to be the man, the *only* man, capable of finding her husband for her. The local cops had thus far failed to help. Even Howie's longtime business partner was out of theories. But not Mark, Meg's white knight. He only prayed this glimmer of a lead in Grand Junction panned out.

In his years with the SEALs he'd learned to win the trust of the men under his command. Their trust and their unquestioning willingness to follow his orders. Now, if he played his cards correctly, and if Afferton eventually contacted Meg, she'd confide in Mark. Her trusted friend Mark.

So don't be an ass and blow it, he told himself.

Meg started dinner that night while he ran a computer check on the name Boris Lebedev. As luck would have it, the man was in one of his files. He was Russian, an ex-Soviet official who'd had to flee when the Iron Curtain fell. It was suspected that he'd had ties to Biopreparat, the shadowy organization that had once directed the germ warfare program for the Soviet Union.

Mark was well aware that the Kremlin had signed

the 1972 Biological Weapons Convention, as had the States and most European countries, but he also knew that Russia had secretly continued biological warfare research. Hell, Mark thought, who hadn't?

Now it would seem that Lebedev had found an important position with the fledgling Turghistan government—a government that, perhaps, had paid Afferton for his research with the intent of turning the potential Ebola vaccine into a biological weapon. Much cheaper than procuring a nuclear arsenal. Cheaper and equally as lethal.

"Afferton," he muttered, "you goddamn moron, what have you done?"

He finished reading the information on Lebedev, switched off the computer and went to see how Meg was doing.

"Did you find out anything on that man who rented the car?" she was quick to ask, a big wooden spoon in hand.

"Not really," he replied.

"And what exactly does that mean? Was he in one of your databases?"

Of course, Mark recalled, Meg would know all about security files and databases—she'd worked as a lab technician and must have been on the computer a lot, researching or exchanging data with other labs on secured sites. Meg Afferton might be naive and pampered, but she was not dumb.

"I found him, yes, but it was an old file, an army record."

"Army? What army?"

Mark smiled and shook his head at her. "Hey, it

was nothing,'' he said evasively. "If I'd found anything significant, Meg, I'd tell you. Okay?''

"Well... I guess.''

He stood next to the refrigerator, one shoulder casually leaning against the wall, his arms folded, and he watched her as she went back to preparing dinner.

She had changed her clothes, he noticed, from the khaki pants and white blouse she'd been wearing all day. Tonight she wore a black V-neck cardigan over black designer jeans and an eggplant-colored camisole. The deep purple hue was striking against the dark red in her hair and the fine texture of her pale skin.

She was really quite a beautiful woman, he mused, wasted on the likes of Afferton. And yet she believed she was fortunate that the good doctor had picked her.

Man, did she have that backward, he was thinking, unabashedly studying her when she nicked her thumb with a knife.

"Oh, dammit,'' she gasped, stiffening, looking for something to staunch the blood.

He was there, the white knight with his white handkerchief.

"Oh, no, you'll ruin it,'' she began, but he took her hand, wrapped her thumb in the hanky, then applied pressure.

She was flustered. "Oh, how stupid of me. I must slice a thousand tomatoes a year and I've never cut myself before.'' Her embarrassment was written all over her face in hectic spots of red.

She was blushing.

He should have backed off. Instead he kept his

hand on hers, pressing, and stood over her, playing his role to the hilt—her protector, her new best friend.

"Just hold still and give it time to clot," he suggested, so near he could smell her perfume and feel her warmth. So she'd dabbed on perfume. Was she expecting her husband to miraculously walk in the door? "Are there Band-Aids in the kitchen?"

"Ah, no, upstairs, in the bathroom cabinet, I think. Howie…well, he keeps an emergency medical kit there."

Yes, he would, Mark thought. "Okay then," he said, "I'll get you a Band-Aid. You better hold the handkerchief on it for another minute."

"All right," she replied, and she cleared her throat. "Thanks."

"No problem," he said, finally letting her go.

"I'll, ah, wash your handkerchief, some cold water and then bleach and…"

"I have plenty," he said at the foot of the stairs. "Throw it out."

"A dyed-in-the-wool bachelor," she reflected, and he did nothing to alter her opinion. He was a bachelor. Sure. But he had been married. And loused it up. He only hoped he didn't screw up this relationship as well. There was too much riding on it.

The master bedroom was spacious and tidy. He entered the bathroom and wondered if she was always so orderly. Or maybe she stayed awake at night straightening and cleaning, as his mother had done when Mark had graduated from Annapolis and his father had died of a sudden heart attack right in their spanking-new Naples, Florida, home. His mother still lived there, but she'd long since gotten over the death of her husband. She had her card games and even a new boyfriend, a widower. With a forty-seven-foot Sport Fisherman. Housekeeping was the last thing on her mind these days.

Mark paused and wondered if Meg wouldn't be better off in the long run if Afferton were dead. If Mark's assumption about the man was correct, the knowledge was going to wound her deeply.

He moved to the wall cabinet and noted damp black panties and a lacy bra hung to dry on an empty towel rack. A woman's world. Perfume and makeup and a glass shelf, scented soaps and bath oils lined up on the ledge above a Jacuzzi tub.

He opened the cabinet and found the medical kit and two Band-Aids. He was putting the plastic box back next to a perfectly folded set of sage-green towels, when his eye caught sight of a home pregnancy test kit. His mind registered two things. One, the kit was unopened, and two, all young women probably kept the things handy.

He closed the door, not giving the pregnancy kit a second thought.

Dinner was pork chops and mashed potatoes. She'd also made a fresh salad with iceberg lettuce. "I don't like all those baby field greens in my salads," she said, sitting across from him at the small round table that divided the kitchen from the living room. "They're bitter. I hope you don't mind. Howie always…" Then she put her fork down, and her eyes filled with sudden moisture. "I'm sorry. God, I just…

My whole life was…is…my husband. I'm trying to be brave, but sometimes…''

"Perfectly understandable," he offered, but he was thinking, *Howie, that asshole.*

Then she dabbed at her eyes with her Southwest-patterned napkin. "Mark?" she began.

"Uh-huh." His mouth was full of salad.

"If this man who rented the car has something to do with Howie…I mean, if he forced Howie to go with him, how will you get him back? If some foreign government is holding my husband, how do you negotiate his release?"

She certainly asked tough questions, he thought, tough and pointed. But she needed to believe he was capable of the job.

He swallowed and took a drink of water. "First I have to determine if this Boris Lebedev has anything to do with Howard's, Howie's, disappearance. Then I get concrete proof as to who has him and *where* he's being held."

"Then you go to the government? The State Department?"

"That's one option."

She regarded him, her head tilted. "One option? Well, who else could you go to?"

Careful, he thought. "Let's say Howie is being held to gain access to his vaccine research. I've already explained your husband's welfare is a matter of the highest level of national security. There are several agencies…"

"The CIA?"

"And the Defense Department."

"Not the *military*," she breathed, no doubt envisioning a full-fledged attack of some sort to extricate her husband.

Mark shook his head. "The Defense Department has its own intelligence community apart from the armed forces."

"They do?"

He shrugged. "Sure. It's safe to assume one of the government entities will step in to negotiate Howie's release."

"I see," she said, nodding. "That's good then." She looked up. "But what would happen to you if some hotshot government agents get called in?"

She was getting too close for comfort. He took his glasses off and rubbed the bridge of his nose, framing his reply. "There's no evidence yet warranting government intervention."

"But *you* think something happened to him."

"I suspect so."

"Then if you're right, and if you get proof Howie is being held against his will, do they let you stay on the case?"

"We'll cross that bridge when we come to it."

"So they'd send other men to question me and watch me," she said in sudden alarm.

"Now, Meg."

"God, I hope you find him soon."

All right, he thought. She was beginning to identify with him, depend on him. He was manipulating her exactly as he'd hoped to.

Why then did he feel like such a bastard?

DESPITE MEG'S DISAPPOINTMENT that Mark was going to leave her in Aspen under police protection, he borrowed her Audi and made the two-hour drive to Walker Field in Grand Junction the next day.

Usually he wasn't much for road trips, but the landscape along the corridor of Interstate 70 was breathtaking. And the lack of traffic in the sparsely populated valley afforded him plenty of time to gaze around.

The highway followed the Colorado River, and for miles outside the resort town of Glenwood Springs, dozens of white-water rafters could be seen bobbing along in their bright orange vests. It looked like fun. Maybe someday he'd come back to the Rockies and try rafting. On vacation. When his mind wasn't in overdrive.

Past Glenwood Springs and beyond Six-Mile Canyon, the valley widened as he passed hamlets with names like Silt and New Castle, and what looked to be a large ranching town called Rifle.

The landscape changed magically as he drove. Now on both sides of the highway the mountains showed their age. Eroded red shale walls rose to flat tops. Mesas, he thought. Other mountains had been so scoured by wind and rushing water and countless eons that there was little left but twisted pinnacles of rock.

The colors of western Colorado were stunning. Desert colors. Browns and oranges and reds and ochres against a pellucid blue sky. Green irrigated acreage on the riverbanks met dry brown sagebrush prairie. Few trees. Some cottonwoods and aspens close to the river and then emptiness save for a lone scrub oak or two. Absolutely nothing grew on the mountainside here, nothing but naked rock. He saw a hawk wheeling and wondered what the hell it was hunting. Strange, hard land. To Mark's eyes it was as alien as another planet.

He liked it. The openness, the freedom. A far cry from a drive along the humid, overcrowded Beltway at home.

He reached the eastern edge of Grand Junction, a sprawling city that spanned both sides of the Colorado River, and there it was—Walker Field.

The airport was larger than he'd assumed, and it took him a few minutes to locate the manager. But once he found Ted Holloway, his investigation proceeded swiftly. Mark's DARPA credentials—as always—worked wonders.

Holloway walked him out to the private plane hangar and introduced him to the on-duty crew. Mark spoke to flight control and to the ground personnel.

He showed them Afferton's photo, one after another, asking the same question: "Did you see this man boarding a plane with a couple of foreigners?"

"Yeah, he was here," one of the men in grease-stained overalls said.

Another mechanic: "Sure, we saw him. I remember because the other ones, they had accents and were rude as hell. In a big hurry."

And Mark asked each one another question. "Did Dr. Afferton appear nervous or frightened? Was he under restraint?"

No, no and no. "He was like friendly with the

Boris guy. Like they were, uh—'' he thought
''—professional colleagues.''

Mark left Grand Junction satisfied that Afferton had
gone with Lebedev and gone of his own free will.
The man had sold out his own country. What he
couldn't yet be positive of was why. Why had Afferton run at that particular time? And what was the
man's next move? Did he think he could miraculously
reappear with a cock-and-bull story and resume his
former life? Was he mending fences right now with
his foreign pals after some sort of a fallout, or had
the man disappeared because he knew he'd gone too
far and he was terrified of imminent discovery?

Mark drove back to Aspen with the questions
heavy on his mind. And another problem—what to
tell Meg. He now had eyewitnesses to her husband
boarding a private jet. Voluntarily. He even had the
number of the plane—NC3921. And the destination—
Seattle. Mark had already filed a request with his boss
at DARPA to trace the plane from Seattle, where the
pilot most likely would have refueled and filed another flight plan before taking off again.

Mark guessed the jet had gone on to Canada at that
point, and maybe met with other men there. Perhaps
Afferton was still in Canada, or perhaps he'd ended
up in Turghistan by now. DARPA could trace him
through his passport if he'd left Canada. *Maybe.* It
would depend on how friendly the governments were
with the U.S. If Afferton hadn't left Canada, or if the
Seattle route had been used to throw off anyone trying
to track him, then the man could be anywhere.

By the time he walked into the condo and relieved

the policeman who was there, Mark had decided how much he was going to tell Meg. The closer he stayed to the truth, the better. But not the whole truth.

She was waiting for him anxiously, her cheeks the color of milk. There was something so lovely about her, so delicate and vulnerable, that he would have gone straight over to her and pulled her into his arms and held her until her trembling subsided. Yeah, he would have reacted without thinking and probably messed up their fragile relationship. Fortunately, the cop wasn't quite out the door. What luck.

Rather than touch her, he allowed himself another stab of loathing for her husband. What bastard would do this to his wife?

"Did you…did you find out anything?" she asked.

"At least two ground crew personnel identified Howie's photo."

"Oh, my God," she breathed. "He *is* alive. I knew it. But…but if they saw him, why didn't they help him? Call the police? Oh, God, I don't know, hold the plane?"

Mark thought of a dozen lies he could tell her, but somehow he couldn't bring himself to do that.

"I don't understand," she was saying, and she moved to him and put a hand on his arm. "I don't…"

"Look," he said, acutely aware of her cool, shaking fingers, "I don't have an answer. All I know is the ground crew didn't notice anything unusual. Maybe your husband didn't have a chance to signal anyone that he was in trouble. I don't know, Meg." Then, carefully, he said, "For all we know, Howie went voluntarily."

He'd let the notion rest with her, a seed germinating.

"That just doesn't make any sense," she said after a long interval. "First…first, Howie would never go off with some strange men like that. And not in the middle of his conference. It was so important to him. All the bigwigs here, Howie's friends… No. He wouldn't do that." She paused and her brow furrowed. "And he wouldn't have left me sitting here going out of my mind with worry. Howie can be…self-absorbed, I know that, but he isn't cruel. The ground crew just didn't understand what was going on. I mean, how many kidnappings have they witnessed? Howie was forced to go with those men. That's the only thing that makes sense."

It never ceased to amaze him how deeply denial was imbedded in some people. Here she stood in the middle of an Aspen condo that her husband couldn't possibly afford, blindly insisting he'd been kidnapped.

He wondered how long it was going to take her to put two and two together. He could tell her. But then she would turn on him—typical kill-the-messenger psychology—and he couldn't risk that.

She seemed to realize she was gripping his arm and she jerked her hand away. "I'm sorry," she said, "I didn't know I was doing that."

"No problem."

She walked into the living room and began to pace. Then came the inevitable questions. Could he trace her husband from Grand Junction? What if those men who had Howie were…torturing him? Shouldn't they contact the State Department or the FBI or CIA now?

Finally she collapsed in a chair. "Goddamn you, Howie," she cried, "why couldn't you have done normal research? Cancer, Alzheimer's. Something—*anything*—less dangerous."

Mark let her vent. The release was good for her. He leaned his shoulder on the wall near the staircase, watching her shift from one emotion to the next—fear to anger to confusion and back. And again he felt a strong dislike for Afferton. But, more to the point, he was afraid DARPA might come up empty-handed on the trace of the plane once it had left the country.

Howard Afferton, along with his vital research, might have vanished for good.

CHAPTER EIGHT

SHE AWOKE IN THE MORNING, the decision made. She was going back to Denver. As for Howie's belongings—she'd leave them here. Just in case. Just in case he walked in the door.

But in her heart she was beginning to believe that Howie was not coming home. Not to Aspen and not to Denver. For two days she'd been slowly approaching this knowledge, and a new seed of fear was growing by the hour that her husband might have done something terribly wrong.

She needed to leave here. Needed to be back in Denver to talk to Jerry Riggs face-to-face. Jerry would level with her. If nothing else, her husband's partner was an honest man.

At 8:00 a.m. she descended the stairs lugging her suitcase. She had another reason to go home to Denver, one that was as important in her mind as speaking to Jerry. She had to see her gynecologist.

She spotted Mark on the deck, the early rays of sun lighting his hair as he stood admiring the morning, the ubiquitous mug in hand.

He was going to give her an argument. Tell her that it wasn't advisable for her to go back to Denver. Well, to hell with what he thought, she decided, dumping her suitcase by the front door. He could stay right here if he wanted. She no longer cared. And if by some outside chance Howie called or showed up, Mark Fielder could deal with him.

A bubble of anger rose in her chest. How could her husband put her through this nightmare? She lived in fear each waking moment, trying to convince herself this state of affairs would somehow turn out all right. And with every breath she took she was sure she could feel the life growing inside her. Joy surfaced a hundred times a day only to be pressed down by dread.

But she couldn't succumb today. Today she was driving home. It was time for the baby.

"Good morning," she said to Mark.

He turned and nodded, then adjusted his glasses. "You're, ah, up and dressed awfully early," he observed.

"Yes. And packed. Mark, I'm going back to Denver. I can't stay here any longer. There are things at home that won't wait."

He started to say something, but she mustered her courage and held up a hand. "Please," she continued. "I can't handle an argument."

"Hey," he cut in, "I think Denver is a good idea. I was going to suggest it myself."

"You were?"

"Yes. I'd like to talk to Howie's partner and get a look at the lab. I'm sure you want to talk to Jerry Riggs, too. I'll drive in with you."

She let out the breath she'd been holding. "Sure. But what about the phone here?"

"I can have all the calls transferred directly to your Denver number and my cell phone, if that's all right."

"Well, I guess so," she said.

"I'll have to stay at your house," he added. "As far as you needing protection, Meg, nothing has changed. I hope you understand that."

"I suppose," she said, trying to envision dangerous men coming for her when her husband refused to co-operate with them. The scenario was too unreal, and she simply couldn't consider anything right now except the baby's welfare.

And yet, she had to admit to a sense of relief that Mark would be with her. She wasn't sure if the relief was due to his easy acquiescence or something else, a slippery feeling that made her uncomfortable, that she couldn't quite put her finger on, a feeling she banished as quickly as she could.

Mark made a single call—to whom, she never knew—and miraculously all contacts were switched to his cell phone.

She tidied the kitchen and checked light switches and window and door locks, while he packed and phoned the Aspen police to inform them of their plans. He also left his cell phone number with the cops, and Meg heard him promise to keep in close contact. After all, the police and local rescue services were still on high alert.

Then she wrote a note for Howie and left it by the front door. She wouldn't cry, though, she thought as she set it down. Enough tears.

Mark offered to drive, and she let him. She did,

however, caution him about the road over twelve-thousand-foot Independence Pass just east of Aspen.

"I'm not being a back seat driver," she said. "But you're in the outside lane going over the pass to Denver. The road drops off on that side, and sometimes oncoming cars get too far into your lane, and it's scary."

"I get it," he said. "You'd appreciate my not driving you over the edge of a cliff."

"Well, you need to watch the road."

"Trust me," he said, and, as they drove past the hillside subdivision of Mountain Valley and began the long climb, he cast her a quick sidelong glance that caused her stomach to shift.

"God," he said at ten thousand feet as they passed the old ghost town of Independence, which had sprouted during the silver-boom days a century ago. "How did anyone survive up here?"

She looked out the passenger window. They were almost at the timberline. "Well, the town only survived for one, or maybe it was two years."

"I'm not surprised."

"But we're following the old stage coach route right now. Think of *that*."

"I can't. The paved road's bad enough."

Then the frighteningly narrow road narrowed even further and began to make switchbacks along a rocky cliff up to the summit. The drop on her side was more than two thousand feet.

"I can see why," Mark said, his attention fixed on the road, "this is closed in winter."

It was her suggestion they stop at the summit. "But

bring your jacket," she said, opening the door. "It's going to be cold up here."

They walked side by side along the trail to the observation area at the twelve-thousand-foot summit. It was cold, as she'd predicted. But neither of them noticed the temperature when they saw the view.

"It's spectacular," Mark said.

They were both breathing hard in the oxygen-thin air.

"Yes, it is," she said. "It's the Continental Divide, you know." And she stole a glance at his profile. The wind pulled at his short, unruly hair and the brilliant sunlight played on his strong features.

He was a good-looking man, she decided, inordinately good-looking. She wondered if he knew the effect his bedroom-mussed hair and unshaven face had on women. She wondered if he had a girlfriend, and if that girlfriend had taken charge of his haircuts and shaving habits. Or maybe his appearance was natural—his hair was permanently unruly and he hated to shave. Maybe he didn't care at all about his looks. Some men didn't.

She had to drag her thoughts back to reality, though, because he'd said something to her. Had he caught her staring? My God. What was he thinking? What was *she* thinking?

"Excuse me?" she said.

"I asked if you and Howie stop here on your trips to Aspen."

"Oh. Oh, sometimes. Actually, we *used* to. But you get jaded, I suppose, and always in a rush. You know."

"Well, it was worth it," he declared, and he touched her arm.

She was taken aback, but he was only indicating that it was time to go.

They drove down the other side of the pass and through the mountain hamlet of Twin Lakes, then climbed again to Leadville, the home of the infamous Molly Brown and some of the richest gold deposits ever found in the Rockies. Of course, it was too expensive to mine gold nowadays or, as Mcg explained to Mark, "It's refining the ore that's so costly. Unless it reaches more than five hundred dollars an ounce on the world market it isn't profitable. I don't think there's a working gold mine left in Colorado."

"You're quite the tour guide," Mark observed.

"Ah, but I'm a native Coloradan. All this stuff was drilled into our little heads in school. Didn't you learn your state's history?"

"Not really."

"But I thought every school—"

"I was a military brat."

"So you were never in one place long enough?"

He shrugged, and she realized she didn't know the first thing about him. Not his age, his roots, his education, not even exactly where he lived. In a condo, apartment, house? Did he have pets? Plants someone was watering for him? My God, she thought, he'd lived in her house for nearly a week, and she knew absolutely nothing about him except his employer and his name. And maybe not even that much. Did security men use their real names?

"How did you get into security?" she blurted out.

"It's a long story," he said, and that was the end of that.

Past Vail and the Eisenhower Tunnel, they grabbed a sandwich and soda in Georgetown at a gas station minimart, and then Meg drove the rest of the way into Denver.

Her house—hers and *Howie's*—was located in a new upscale development in the suburb of Cherry Hills. It was a gated community of large, custom-built homes on half-acre lots. Their house was single-story gray brick with a Federal-style columned entryway that led inside to a great room with a vaulted ceiling, and a circular staircase leading up to an open library. To the right of the entry were three bedrooms. To the left of the large living room were the dining room and the kitchen, the utility and laundry room beyond, leading to an oversize two-car garage.

When they pulled into the garage, Mark said, "That's your husband's car." As if he already knew.

Howie's big black SUV, his pride and joy, sat there in its space, gleaming. "Yes." She sighed.

"New?"

"Yes, it's new."

"Nice."

She showed him into the kitchen, then slid open the door to the patio. He looked out, squinting into the bright sun.

The pearly gray flagstone patio was surrounded by Meg's garden. The truth was she didn't much like the house. It was too pretentious for her tastes. The place never felt warm to her. But her garden she loved; it was colorful, a variety of flowering perennials and annuals that she tended lovingly. She'd even installed the underground sprinklers and automatic timer herself.

When Howie had found her outside on her hands and knees just after they'd moved in, her old shirt mud-splattered, dirt on her face, her hair dripping sweat, he'd been appalled.

"God, Meg," he'd said, "we hire people to do this kind of work. First off, you don't have a clue what you're doing. You can't buy sprinkler systems at those cheap do-it-yourself places and install them. And what the hell will the neighbors think?"

It was one of the few times she had prevailed against her husband. "Don't be such a snob, Howie," she'd said, wiping sweat from her brow. "The instructions are really simple and I know I can do this. It's *my* garden. I'm enjoying it."

He'd growled something, then said, "Fine. Just tell me when you want me to call the landscaper and get him to fix it, okay?"

Well, she'd dug the trenches and installed the sprinklers and planted her flowers and the garden was the envy of the whole street.

And Howie had never said a word.

"Beautiful flowers," Mark said.

They were standing at the big double doors leading to the patio. She smiled. "Thanks. I did the garden myself. Even the sprinkler system."

"You're kidding. You did that?"

"Just followed the instructions." She was boasting, she realized.

"Well," he said, "I live in a condo complex and

we pay a fortune for the landscaping, and yours looks a hundred times better. I'm very impressed.''

"Thank you," she said, and she wondered why Howie couldn't have acknowledged her success just once.

Howie.

Frowning, she turned away from the patio and led Mark to the guest room down the hall from the master bedroom. "There are separate controls for the air-conditioning." She showed him. "Now, I've got to make a few calls and run to the grocery store, so…"

"Meg," he said.

"What? I really need to…" But then she remembered. She wasn't going anywhere by herself. She nearly burst into tears. She'd had a good day. Well, almost. She'd practically forgotten the ordeal of the past week. Just leaving Aspen, the scene of the crime, had been a relief. But it wasn't over. Not by a long shot. She squeezed her eyes shut and took a deep breath. *It isn't forever,* she told herself. This would all pass. One way or another. And she'd live through it.

"Hey," she heard Mark say, and she opened her eyes. "You okay?"

"Oh, sure, I'm fine." She faked a smile. "I was just thinking. Howie will be home soon, won't he? This isn't forever, right?"

"Of course not," he said.

She phoned her mother and let her know she was safely home in Denver. Lucy asked a dozen questions about Howie and what could have happened and didn't this Mark Fielder have an idea what was going on?

"What are you going to do if Howie isn't found?"

"God, Mom, I haven't thought that far. Howie *will* be found. This will all seem like a terrible nightmare."

"I don't know how you can be so sure of that, honey. It seems to me your husband is gone. It's that research he does. Fooling around with nature. It's no wonder he's gotten himself in trouble."

"He works on vaccines, Mom. He's no different from, say, Dr. Salk. Do you think the man who discovered the polio vaccine was fooling around with nature?" She was doing it again, she realized, defending Howie. Good Lord. "Sometimes you make me so... Oh, never mind. I'm sorry, I don't want to fight. How's Brian?"

"Drinking." Her mother's tone was brittle.

"That's it? Just drinking?"

"He stays out till all hours. I hear him stumbling around. I'm at my wit's end."

"You should throw him out on his butt, Mom. Tough love. You're enabling him now. Has he contributed anything toward the house bills?"

"Some."

"I'll bet."

"Now, don't you take that tone, Meg."

"All right, all right." Meg sighed. She didn't have the energy for this, anyway. Between Howie and Brian and Mark and her pregnancy she felt as if her brain were on a nonstop roller-coaster ride. "I'll try to drop by tomorrow, okay?" she said.

"Will that man be with you?"

"I don't know." But she knew he would.

"Well, I'd like to talk to you without some stranger horning in."

"Okay, Mom," Meg said, and hung up.

She called her gynecologist and got an appointment for the next day at 11:00 a.m. Her breath seemed to flutter in her breast when she was off the phone. The pregnancy was suddenly terrifyingly real. By avoiding going to the doctor, by avoiding telling Howie until they were in Aspen, her condition had been only a possibility. Now she *knew* she was pregnant....

She'd be alone with a new baby in a house she could never afford to maintain. Except for her small savings account, the bank accounts were in Howie's name, most of the credit cards, too. She had a Visa of her own, one she used at the gas station and grocery store, but Howie paid the monthly bill. How much credit did she have on the card? Could she get the credit line increased? And where did he keep the checkbook? She couldn't even recall signing a signature card at the bank. Or had she, years ago?

Pregnant, she thought, sitting on the side of the king-size bed, her hands on her stomach. She felt as if she had no safety net. No job. No real money of her own. Bills she'd collected from the mailbox just this afternoon were stacked on the kitchen counter for Howie. But there was no Howie.

My fault ran through her head. She'd gone along with her husband's every directive. She'd never complained. She'd rarely questioned him. Even when he'd bought the house and she'd wondered how on earth they could afford it, she'd barely said a word. And when he'd purchased the condo in Aspen she'd remained quiet, though at the time she had thought how odd it was that Howie's partner lived such a modest lifestyle compared to theirs. Should she have asked Howie, stood up to him for once, and asked where the money was coming from?

In hindsight she should have questioned him, she thought glumly. Too late now.

Where *had* the money come from? There was no mortgage that she knew of on the Aspen condo, only a small one on this house, no unpaid credit card bills or auto loans. Could the lab be this profitable? Could Jerry and Joanna simply be more careful, saving up for college educations for their kids and maybe early retirement?

On the other hand, *could* Howie have done something unspeakable, something treacherous, just to get ahead?

She felt as if she were going insane. She was contemplating the worst about her missing husband, while another part of her brain reminded her she needed to do laundry and run to the grocery store and think about maternity clothes and names for the baby and even things like Lamaze classes.

She wanted to scream. She stared at the big empty bed and thought about a stranger living in her house, a man who'd said he was there to protect her.

She realized that she'd fallen into the same behavior pattern with Mark as she had with Howie. She was dependent on him, trying subconsciously to please him. Afraid of speaking her own mind. *Weak.*

She was weak. And the truth was, she didn't entirely trust Mark. He had his own agenda. Nor did she trust her own husband any longer, the man she'd lived with for six years and whose child she was carrying. He might not even be alive. A widow. She might be a pregnant widow.

The grocery store, she thought, forcing herself to focus on the present. She couldn't do a thing about Howie at the moment, and she had to stop projecting and concocting wild scenarios. *Calm down, calm down.*

The store. Milk, eggs, bread, lettuce, vegetables, meat…

She walked to her bedroom door, concentrating on the mundane. Then she nearly burst into hysterical laughter. Howie had never gone shopping with her. Over the years she'd seen thousands of husbands and wives shopping together, and she'd always felt envious. Well, she had a man to go to the store with now. A good-looking man who could carry the bags for her. Would some lonely female shopper see them and feel envy?

My God, she thought, the scream again welling in her breast.

CHAPTER NINE

"WE CAN GO TO THE LAB this morning," Meg said, "and then I'll drop you off here or you can stay there."

Mark regarded her over the rim of his coffee mug.

"I...ah—" she looked out the kitchen window at her garden "—I have a doctor's appointment at eleven."

"A doctor's appointment," he said. Her DARPA file said nothing about health problems.

"Just a routine checkup," she added hastily.

"I have to go with you."

"Oh, please, can't I just..."

But he was shaking his head.

"I wonder," she said slowly, "I wonder how real this is?"

"This?"

"This supposed threat to me. I know what you think, but you haven't seen anyone following us, and no one has tried to break down the door. I just don't know. Maybe..."

"Maybe what?"

"Maybe you've exaggerated the danger?"

"Why would I do that?" He set his coffee mug

down on the polished granite counter. Gray, like everything else in the house.

She pivoted and stared him in the eye. "I don't know. Why *would* you do that?"

"Meg, you're upset. You're not thinking straight. Just let me do my job, okay?"

She turned her back to him and resumed rinsing the breakfast dishes and stacking them in the dishwasher.

"I'll go to the doctor's with you, but I'll stay in the car. How's that?" he offered.

She mumbled something. He thought it was "all right," but he decided not to press the point.

She drove him to the lab, past the houses of the subdivision, east toward the suburb of Aurora, to the University of Colorado Health Sciences Center at the old Fitzsimons Army Medical Center. R and A Biotech was situated in a new building in the Aurora Bioscience Park, where the private research companies were located.

She pulled up in front of the one-story cement-block building, into a parking space marked H. Afferton.

"Well, we're here," she said.

"The place looks brand-new."

"It's only a few years old. R and A was one of the first tenants."

He got out of the Audi and followed her into the building. There was a receptionist at a modernistic Plexiglas desk, and she smiled when she saw Meg.

"Hi, Ruthie," Meg said.

"It's so good to see you," Ruthie replied. "And we're all so worried about Dr. Afferton."

"I know, me too. Ruthie, this is Mark Fielder. He's from Merrick."

"Hello," Ruthie said, her smile fading. "Your co-worker Richard Parker was already here."

"I take it he was thorough," Mark said, knowing Parker had probably turned the lab inside out.

"Oh, yes, he was that."

"Is Jerry here?" Meg asked.

"In his office." Ruthie nodded.

Meg led the way down a sterile corridor past the reception area. The walls were white, the floors spotless beige tile, blown-up photos of *things*—viruses, Mark guessed—on the walls. She knocked lightly on a door and then entered.

"Oh, God, Meg," the man behind the desk said, standing instantly.

"Hi, Jerry."

"How are you doing?"

"As well as can be expected."

"I can't believe...I just can't believe he's gone." He came around the desk, clasping Meg's hands in his. "He'll come back. I know he will. This is just—"

"Jerry," she said softly, "this is Mark Fielder, from Merrick."

"Another one?"

"I'm afraid so," Mark said.

Jerry Riggs held out his hand, and Mark shook it. Jerry was a wiry man of medium height. Dark hair, dark eyes that didn't come across as piercing in a photograph, although they certainly did in person. He was in his late thirties, thirty-eight, Mark recalled. From Boston, the same as Afferton.

"Look, I can't say I like what your associate Parker did when he was here. I'm just now getting everything back in order. But, believe me, if you can find out what happened to Howie, I'll help you in any way I can," Jerry said.

"I'm not going to rip the place apart, Dr. Riggs. I'm only here to find out what you do, get a feel for things. There may be something here, something you can't see."

"Well, Parker couldn't see it, either. He left here with all our computer records, everything in Howie's desk. Maybe he's got an idea by now."

"He'll contact me with any information," Mark said.

"Mark wants to look around," Meg said. "Can you show him the lab?"

"Do I have any choice?" Jerry smiled ruefully.

"I'll wait in Howie's office," she said. "There're a few things I wanted to look for in his desk."

"I'm sorry, Meg. Mr. Fielder's associate took almost everything."

"Oh."

"Go on, though. Ask Ruthie if you want coffee or something."

Mark followed Riggs into the hallway, watching Meg open another door—Afferton's office—and go in. She left the door ajar, and he leaned in and said, "I'll try not to be too long," but she just waved a hand. He guessed she didn't care as long as she made her doctor's appointment.

Riggs led him to a wide metal door at the end of the hall, opened it, and they were in an alien world.

There were long counters, microscopes, dozens of white-coated lab techs on stools. There were walk-in refrigerators and doors leading off the large room, doors marked Caution Biohazard, Electron Microscope, Decontamination. Scary stuff. A bank of computers lined one wall.

"Hey, everybody," Riggs said. "This is another Merrick investigator. Please cooperate. As you know, he's trying to find Dr. Afferton."

Dozens of faces swiveled toward him. No welcoming smiles, no greetings. Then they turned back to their microscopes and computers and petri dishes.

Riggs led him up and down the aisles, trying to explain what the technicians were doing.

"We're trying to find a way to produce a vaccine for the Ebola virus and other hemorrhagic fevers. The way Jenner discovered the smallpox vaccine," he explained. "It would be a major breakthrough. Then Merrick will market the product. Just think, you could vaccinate all the children in the Ebola-prone areas. You see, the fear is, with no place in the world more than an airplane flight from any other place, a person who didn't present any symptoms could get on a flight in, say, Nairobi, and the next day be in New York or London or Tokyo. And then... Well, we've avoided that so far, but it'll happen one day."

"Yes, I imagine so."

"That's how AIDs got out of Africa. One man, that was all it took. It's inevitable. Here we are, a huge and growing population, *food* to a virus. And trust me on this, a virus is more dangerous than nuclear radiation because viruses can replicate.''

''And how close are you to finding this vaccine?''

''We're getting there. It's difficult. And dangerous.'' He pointed to the door with the Biohazard sign on it. ''We don't do research on animals here. We do mostly theoretical work. We've been trying to decipher the virus's DNA and analyze the skin of the virus cells. Proteins, complicated proteins. But we do handle a small amount of the actual virus, and so we need a Biosafety Level 4 lab.''

''I take it Parker took a look at everything?''

''Every nook and cranny. If you want to see Level 4, you can, but it requires putting on a space suit, a chemical shower, then decon.''

''I'll pass, thanks,'' Mark said. ''I'll read Parker's report.''

Riggs then ushered him into a darkened room, in which stood a metal tower taller than a man.

''Our electron microscope,'' Riggs said proudly.

There was a console covered with dials and digital readouts and a viewing screen. The monstrous apparatus could have been a prop from *Star Trek*, Mark decided.

''We can look inside cells with this. It's like gazing into infinity,'' he said with a kind of wonder in his voice.

''Did Afferton use this?''

''Yes, sometimes. He did more of the actual research than I did. I'm sort of the business partner. But when there was something really fascinating under the scope, he'd call me in.''

Mark phrased his next question carefully. "Dr. Riggs, is it possible your partner is closer to developing a vaccine than you think?"

He could practically see the sweat pop on Riggs's brow. "Oh, no, no, I don't think that's possible. Why…why do you ask?"

"Just curious." Mark shrugged.

They walked back through the lab. There was a low buzz of conversation, people discussing problems, solutions, esoteric subjects. The place smelled of alcohol and disinfectant and the very faint, coppery odor of fresh blood.

Through the heavy metal door, the *airlock,* Mark thought, back into the more ordinary world. He saw Meg sitting behind her husband's desk; she was bent over, pulling out drawers, looking for something. A memento of her husband? A clue as to his whereabouts? Or maybe just a photograph she wanted to take home. She looked young and lost behind the wide pale wood desk. A desk with nothing whatsoever on its surface but a telephone and a computer. No paperweights or blotter or photo, no books or Post-its or pink memo pads.

Had Parker removed it all, or had Afferton been obsessively neat?

"Can I do anything else for you?" Riggs asked anxiously.

"Not right now. I think I'll take a look in Dr. Afferton's office. Thanks."

"I hope you find him. I hope nothing's happened. I don't understand. Howie's not like that, not irresponsible, you know. In fact, he's totally anal.'' Riggs pursed his lips. ''Which makes him a great scientist.''

''We're trying our best.''

''Look—'' Riggs lowered his voice ''—I know why you guys are all over the lab. I know what you're afraid of. Our research, it's pretty tricky. It could be used, well, it could be dangerous in the wrong hands. I'm aware of that. But, believe me—and I told your associate this, too—Howie would *never* endanger anyone. He isn't like that. He'd never—''

''I understand, Dr. Riggs. And I'll certainly take that into consideration.''

Jerry Riggs disappeared into his office, and Mark stepped into Howie Afferton's.

Meg glanced up. ''Find anything?''

''Nothing that I could possibly understand.''

''It's a very specialized area.''

''It certainly is. From what I could tell, the lab is impressive.''

''Yes.''

''Did you find what you were looking for?'' He nodded at the desk.

''Most everything's gone. I was looking for, well, I thought Howie might have some bank statements here, and our insurance. Even a checkbook. I...''

''Wouldn't all that be at home?''

''I looked.''

''Well, would you mind if I take a stab at it?''

''Be my guest.'' She rose and walked past him, so close he could smell the shampoo scent of her hair. And he wondered, *again,* how Afferton could have left this woman.

Not much in the drawers. Parker must have it all. Some business stationery, computer manuals, a bottle of aspirin, a roll of antacids. Eyedrops. Kleenex.

He tried to get a feel for Afferton, tried to imagine him sitting in the upholstered office chair, answering his phone, scribbling notes about complicated proteins or DNA sequences. But the room was bare, the windows covered by blinds, nothing here that gave him a hint about the man or his underlying motives.

Jerry Riggs's office had been cluttered, plants and photos on the windowsill, notes stuck to his computer, papers, books leaning on a shelf, lots of family snapshots and prints of animals on the wall. A calendar on his desk, covered with writing. Phone numbers scratched around the dates.

Sure, Parker had removed a lot of Afferton's belongings, but not the personal touches. Mark guessed there hadn't been any. Howie Afferton had left no trail whatsoever.

Riggs was probably unaware of his partner's activities. There had never been a single odd or questionable entry on him in DARPA's files. No red flags. Nonetheless, his company had been compromised, and he could take a fall along with Afferton.

Mark turned on Afferton's computer, spent fifteen minutes trying to access files, but the lab-related data was password-encrypted, as Mark already knew. Copies of the files were in Washington right now, having been removed by Parker. But as of last night no one had broken the encryption. In time DARPA's computer department would gain access. Nevertheless, the files might not explain why Afferton had vanished.

He checked the Lotus personal accounting files, which were not password-protected. These, too, had been copied and taken to DARPA headquarters. Mark saw the same thing the experts in Washington had: a lot of money coming and going.

Interesting, he thought, scrolling down the database, all debit entries were categorized and defined, while few of the credit entries were. Surely Afferton knew exactly what this would look like—a lot of unaccounted-for income. Why hadn't he deleted these files? If he'd known he was going to have to disappear he would have gotten rid of this damning evidence. Did that mean Afferton had taken off abruptly? Had he expected to return before the bloodhounds were called in? Or maybe, just maybe, Afferton had truly been abducted.

But Mark still didn't believe that. Afferton had left the country voluntarily. The man was working with another entity, and it looked like Turghistan.

He made a printout of the Lotus data for Meg and was ready to shut down the hard drive when it occurred to him that Meg still had not found a checkbook.

He logged onto the Internet, clicked Afferton's Favorites list and found what he was looking for, the online bill-payment program. He tried to access it, but no go. The service required a log-in password. That meant that Afferton had left his wife with no means whatsoever to pay their bills.

The jerk.

He could hear Meg talking to the receptionist Ruthie through the open door. Soft female voices in anxious conversation. Of course, they must have known each other when Meg had been a lab tech here. Before she married Afferton, who wouldn't let his wife work.

There was a closet in the office. He opened its door and saw empty hangers. Nothing like a favorite old sweater to work in. On the shelf above the hangers were neat piles of technical publications. Howard Afferton did not reside anywhere in the room—he'd left no mark on it.

He was aware that Meg was at the door, watching him. How long had she been there?

"Are you done?" she asked. "It's almost time for my appointment."

He glanced at his watch. "Give me a few minutes."

"There's nothing in the room."

"Not much." He went through the books on a shelf near the window. *Molecular Biology; Genetic Engineering—the Puzzle of DNA; The Human Genome.*

Then he remembered and turned to Meg. "Here," he said, handing her the printout of Afferton's expenditures. "It's a list of all the checks your husband wrote."

"No checkbook?"

"Sorry. He used an online bill-payment service."

"Can you access it?"

Mark shook his head. Not without removing the entire hard drive, he thought. Of course, that would be the next step if DARPA didn't break the code soon.

She was putting the folded printout in her purse. "Well, then," she said, "I'll wait for you outside."

"Okay." He felt her gaze on him, the weight of her questions and her worry. What a crappy job he had. No matter the nobility of his intentions, the significance of his work, innocents like Meg always suffered. But that was Afferton's fault, not his, he reminded himself.

"BUT I DON'T WANT YOU TO come to the doctor's with me," she said.

"I told you, I'll wait in the car."

"Oh, for God's sake, I can't function like this."

"Would you prefer I come in and wait in the doctor's office?"

"*No.*"

"You're not going alone."

"Why can't you give me some breathing space?" she asked in a pleading tone.

"You know why."

"I don't know anything anymore," she said, taking a turn onto University Avenue. "You have no idea what I'm going through, and all I'm asking for is an hour of privacy."

"Sorry" was all he could offer.

She left the car keys with him, dropping them defiantly in his lap after they'd parked at the clinic. He almost asked if she wasn't planning on returning, but he figured he'd pushed his luck as far as he dared today.

A checkup, she'd said. He sure as hell hoped it wasn't anything more.

He backed the car into the shade of the next-door building, rolled the windows down and waited. After half an hour he got out and stretched. He looked longingly toward the air-conditioned waiting room of the clinic, but he'd promised Meg. After all, the doctor, the nurses, the desk personnel probably knew Afferton or had seen him. Mark would be a curiosity, and he didn't want to draw attention to himself.

He waited, then he opened the glove compartment and idly leafed through the papers there. A map of Denver, one of Colorado, registration for a 2002 Audi sedan. Mark whistled at the registration fee. Insurance papers from Prudential. Owner's manual, and records of servicing done to the car. Oil changes, new snow tires, a broken taillight replaced. Very neat.

Women came and went. A few very pregnant ones, some with their boyfriends or husbands. The car was hot, even in the shade, and the air smelled of melted asphalt. On University Avenue traffic whizzed by, stopped at intervals for lights, started up again. The sun beat down on the parking lot.

He was practically lulled into a doze when she emerged from the smoked-glass door. He sat up straight behind the steering wheel and saw her walk toward him, her face expressionless. But she moved oddly, too carefully, as if she was terribly fragile and some part of her might break if she didn't take care.

Damn, he thought. She's sick. She's got some complicated female trouble, the kind that scared and baffled men. *Hell.*

She didn't argue with him being in the driver's

seat. She opened the passenger door and slid in, then sat there silently.

"Are you all right, Meg?" he finally asked. "Are you sick? Did the doctor tell you something wasn't right?"

No response.

"Meg, come on, something's wrong." He wanted to touch her, reassure her, but no way. "Meg."

She burst into tears, putting her hands up to cover her face. "Oh God, oh God."

"What is it?" And he laid his hand on her arm.

"What great timing," she sobbed, her words muffled by her hands.

He was reaching for his handkerchief, hitching up his hip to get at his back pocket, when the knowledge bludgeoned him. That pregnancy test kit in her bathroom.

Of course.

He was stunned, abruptly pushed against the seat back as if by a hand. *Of course.*

She was pregnant.

Shit. Then, despite the heat of the summer day, the sweat that dampened the back of his shirt, he went cold with anger. Afferton had left her alone and pregnant. Did the bastard *know?*

"Oh, God," she said again, but less violently.

He fished his handkerchief out and put it into her hand. She grasped it, her knuckles white. Then she dabbed at her eyes, sighed and took a shaky, quavering breath.

"It's okay," he ventured.

She sat up, blew her nose on his handkerchief and made a valiant attempt at a laugh. "Stupid, aren't I?"

"No, Meg."

"Knocked up like a dumb high-school kid."

"Meg—"

"Oh, don't say a word. To hell with you. To hell with Howie and…everybody. I'll make it somehow."

He felt a flash of admiration for her then. He put the keys in the ignition and turned the car on, reversing out into the parking lot. *Pregnant.*

"Let's go home," she said.

And right then, sitting next to Meg in the hot car outside of the OB-GYN clinic, Mark despised Howard Afferton. And he envied the hell out of him.

CHAPTER TEN

OVER THE NEXT FEW DAYS her life took on the semblance of normalcy. She shopped, cooked, ran loads of laundry—even washed some of Mark's clothes, though he was more of a dry-cleaner-type guy, lots of starch in his shirts. She gardened, took Mark to the hardware store and Home Depot countless times. He didn't appear to mind. Howie, on the other hand, detested the hardware store and had told her more than once how unladylike it was for her to shop for screwdrivers, lumber and nails. She supposed she worked on her garden and the low fences and trellises herself in part to stick it to her husband for his constant criticism of her. It was a stab at independence. Besides, being her own landscape artist lent her a tiny measure of self-worth.

When Mark wasn't on the phone with colleagues or tapping at his computer keyboard, he watched over her like a mother hen. Especially when she was gardening in front of the house, where she was exposed.

His reasons were twofold. ''I know you don't really believe you could be in danger,'' he told her one day when she was rummaging around the garage, the double doors open to the road, ''but better safe than sorry. Right?''

"Sure," she said, distracted.

"So you'll let me know when you leave the house? Even to get the mail?"

"Sure, sure."

And that same afternoon, when she was repositioning one of her fences, he took her by the elbow and brought her to her feet. "You shouldn't be doing this heavy work," he announced.

A shot of anxiety drilled into her. Howie would have said the exact same words. And it all came flooding back, the dozens of times her husband had criticized her for doing manual labor.

Howie. Her husband. Her mind whirled with sudden fear. *Was* he all right? Was he in dire need of rescue? Was he even alive? The father of her baby. How could she for an instant put him at the back of her mind? And here was a stranger in her garden, her house, her guest room, gripping her arm.

She almost screamed. But Meg never screamed, not in public, not even in front of Howie. Ever. Instead, she said, "I *like* doing this work. I need to do it."

"I'm just thinking about your condition," he said.

"My...oh, you mean my pregnancy?" She laughed abruptly, a breath of release straight from her heart. "I thought you meant...well, I thought you were going to say...oh, never mind."

"What?"

"No, it's not important. Really. And as for the baby, it's fine. The doctor said I could do anything I wanted."

"You're sure?"

"Yes, Mark, I'm sure." *And thank you for caring,*

she nearly added, but thought better of it. Still, she had to wonder: would Howie care? Would he have been embarrassed that she was crawling around in the dirt for the neighbors to see?

Mark also didn't like her insistence that she put in her volunteer day at Presbyterian-St. Luke's Hospital. But again, not for the same reasons as Howie.

He dropped her at the hospital's sweeping circular entrance at 9:00 a.m. sharp that Wednesday, a dark expression cloaking his features. "This is a lousy idea," he said.

"We've been through this a hundred times," she insisted. "I'll be right on the tenth floor in the women's surgical wing all day. The place is always busy. There are nurses and lab techs and aides and doctors, orderlies and the cleaning crew… Mark, I'll be fine. I have to do something to keep busy. I'm sorry if you're stuck here all day, but I need to work."

"Bad idea," he repeated.

"I'll tell you what," she said, opening the passenger door to the Audi, "I'll meet you at one in the cafeteria. I get a half hour for lunch. It's to the right of the main lobby, down this long corridor…"

"I imagine—" he cut her off "—that I'll have plenty of time to find it. Just do me one favor, don't go running any errands in some goddamn remote area. Stay right in the women's wing and stay in sight of the nurses' station. Okay?"

"Sure," she said.

The morning flew. The women's surgery wing was always busy, but this week it seemed there wasn't a single unoccupied bed. There were six women who'd had hysterectomies, three breast cancer patients, twelve surgeries for various female troubles such as ectopic pregnancies and ovarian cysts and overactive bladders. There were a dozen other patients checking out and a dozen more pre-ops due in right behind them.

Meg had been at a dead run all morning. She emptied bedpans, filled water jugs, fetched ice and bandages and cleared breakfast trays. She fed two elderly women and played shrink to a lady whose bladder had been nicked during a hysterectomy. She cried with another woman who'd just lost a third baby at eight months and whose doctor had told her there could be no more attempts to have a child—the woman was forty-six years old. Meg said nothing about her own pregnancy, but her blue lady uniform bulged in front and a safety pin held it together at her waist.

Everyone at the nurses' station exclaimed over her pregnancy and had to hear all the details. When was the baby due? ''The middle of January,'' she said over and over. Was it a boy or girl? ''I haven't had an ultrasound yet, but I don't think I want to know.'' What does your husband think? ''Oh, he's happy,'' Meg replied, hating the lie.

She served lunch trays at noon and fed eighty-year-old Mrs. Albers her meal. At twelve-forty-five she began clearing trays, restacking them neatly onto a big stainless-steel caddy sitting in the center of the hall. She cleaned up a few spills. Adjusted beds and pillows, called for an orderly when Fran Nelson accidentally pulled out her IV and blood spurted onto the bed and the floor and wall.

Meg reassured Fran and made her comfortable, then she checked her wristwatch. Uh-oh, just five minutes to get downstairs to meet Mark.

But the nurses' aide waylaid her. "Mrs. Afferton? Could you get Mrs. Nelson a change of sheets?" the woman asked.

Damn. The linen supplies were on the same floor, but a million miles away in another wing. "Sure, I'll get them," Meg said.

She thought about phoning the cafeteria and having Mark paged, but five minutes wasn't going to matter one way or the other. She hurried past the nurses' station, past one bank of elevators, around an ell in the building, past a visitors' waiting room and a patients' gym and down a long corridor. Supplies were kept in a large storage room at the end of the corridor near another bank of elevators used mostly by hospital staff.

Using the key she'd grabbed at the nurses' station, she let herself in and switched on the light.

Rubberized bed pads, blankets, towels, wash cloths... She spotted the sheets and pillowcases. Had Mrs. Nelson's pillowcases been stained, too? *And* the thin, loose-weave white blanket?

Well, better bring it all. She was just pulling a sheet from a rack when she felt something clamp down on her shoulder.

She gasped and tried to spin around, but fingers, thick men's fingers, tightened on her like a vise.

She let out a yelp as fear tore through her.

"You be quiet, Mrs. Afferton," a voice murmured in her ear, a man, yes, a foreigner. "And do not attempt to turn around."

"I..." She wet her lips. "I..."

"I am telling you to shut up. Shut up and listen."

She could hardly breathe much less listen. *Mark.* His name rang in her brain. Mark would find her and...

"This is a warning, *Meg*," the voice rasped next to her ear, so close she could smell the man's breath. She registered in a panicked instinct that the breath was hot and animallike. A scream formed in her throat.

"A warning. You understand? Do not speak. Nod your head if you understand."

She thought she moved her head.

"We can get to you, Meg. We can get to you whenever we wish. Do you understand?"

She nodded. The scream moved up to her lips.

"You will tell your husband you are in danger unless he comes out of hiding. Yes?"

"Ye...yes," she moaned.

"Shut up. Now, do not turn around. Do not move for five minutes. I will kill you if you move. You and the baby," the gravelly voice said, and then suddenly the hand was gone from her shoulder.

She sagged in horror to her knees. She had no idea how she'd gotten on the floor or how long she remained frozen there on the hard linoleum. She couldn't breathe. It was as if all the air had been sucked from the room. She didn't recognize the sound emerging from her throat as she clutched the cold metal rack next to her shoulder and pulled herself up. In a daze, she ran down the hall, one hand over her chest, the other in front of her as if for balance.

Find Mark raced through her brain, and then there he was, his back to her at the nurses' station in the women's wing, badgering a nurse, his voice loud enough so that heads were turning.

"Mark," she gasped.

He swung around, and she nearly collapsed in his arms. "Mark," she sobbed.

THE AFTERNOON WENT BADLY. By the time Mark drove her home, she didn't know who frightened her more—the faceless man behind that horrible voice or Mark. The tension was unbearable. When he turned the engine off in the garage, he pounded the steering wheel with the palm of his hand and swore.

She finally asked him to stop. "Please, I'm upset enough as it is. You're swearing and…"

"What goddamn swearing?" he ground out.

"It's not helping. You're only upsetting me more than I already am. That man…that man…his voice…"

Mark pivoted to her. "What about his voice?"

"He had an accent. A foreign accent."

"Could you recognize it? On tape? We have hundreds of tapes you could review."

"No." She put her face in her hands. "*No*, I won't listen to any tapes. I can't…"

"All right. But you must have gotten a glimpse of him."

"I've told you I didn't. Why won't you believe me?" she cried.

He muttered something, then turned and shoved opened his door. "We'll talk about it when you're calm," he finally said, his tone low and dangerous.

"What about when you're calm?" she shot back, pushing open her own door and slamming it.

A half hour after they were inside, after Mark had made at least ten phone calls, he was still in a barely controlled rage.

"I've got every goddamn base covered within a thousand miles of Denver," he said, more to himself than her. "The airports, car rentals, even the goddamn trains. But without some idea of what this jerk looks like... You didn't even see his clothes?"

"No, I told you no, no, no. Don't ask me again. Please don't even mention it again. You can lock me in the basement if you want, I don't care, but just please don't ever mention that man to me again."

"Look," he began.

But she held up a hand. "You were right. Okay? You were right and I was wrong. I hope that makes you feel better."

"Are you kidding?"

"No," she said without thinking. "Howie would rub it in my face till I choked. So I'm sure you must be feeling vindicated."

"You aren't serious," he said, suddenly very still, his gaze pinning her as if she were an insect.

"I'm quite serious," she said loftily, her stomach churning, sweat breaking out of every pore in her body. "Now I'm going to take a bath. I'm going to sit in the Jacuzzi till I can at least get my breath. I hope *that's* all right?''

He didn't answer. She strode to her bedroom and closed the door hard, then stripped off her clothes. She decided to burn them or throw them away, because that man had touched them. Had he touched her flesh? *Had he?* She remembered his breath, the heat, the odor. She'd never forget that breath.

She soaked for an hour and grew furious at her own stupidity, at Howie for putting her and the baby in this untenable situation and at Mark for being so *right*.

She was a shriveled prune by the time she put on gray sweatpants and an old oxford-cloth shirt of Howie's, the hem reaching down to her thighs, the sleeves rolled up to her elbows. She towel-dried her hair, and the curls stuck out in dark red clumps. Her eyes were red and swollen, her cheeks splotched when she walked out of the bedroom.

Mark was in the kitchen. Making some sort of a stew. Destroying the kitchen was more like it. At least he wasn't yelling at her. Or swearing.

She sat on a stool in the dining room on the opposite side of the counter. She was drained. Exhausted and numb. She knew only one thing for certain, she couldn't, she *wouldn't* discuss that…incident. Not tonight. Maybe not tomorrow. Hopefully never again.

''What are you making?'' she finally said, her voice level.

''Stew. I think.''

''Um. Sounds good.''

''I doubt it.''

"I'm trying to be polite."

"I know."

He turned a moment later. He, too, was wearing an oxford-cloth shirt, a yellow one, starched, the tails neatly tucked in. He looked as if he'd showered. He seemed calmer, she decided, and she whispered up a prayer of thanks.

The chef's knife was in his right hand; in the other was a potato. "I know you don't want to talk about this," he started.

"Mark, I really, really…"

"And we won't. I promise," he said.

"Okay, good."

"But I am going to say one last thing."

"Oh, God," she moaned.

"I want you to know how I felt today."

She looked up. "I can imagine. You don't have to say anything."

"Just let me say this, okay? I want you to know, you need to understand, that if anything had happened to you. If…"

"At least you wouldn't be stuck here with a fat pregnant woman," she said in a sudden attempt at levity.

"Is *that* what you think?"

"Well, I…"

"For God's sake, Meg," he said, and then he showed her his back and started chopping at the potato. "Goddamn," she heard him growl.

CHAPTER ELEVEN

THE WEEKS PASSED at an erratic pace for Meg. When Mark was on duty at the house, the hours miraculously flew. But he wasn't always there. Twice between the end of July and mid-September, he'd been relieved by different security agents from Merrick.

She'd had Richard Parker hovering over her for a week and another agent, a woman named Janie Weathers, for ten days. The company of the woman was nice for a change, and Meg had finally done a little shopping for maternity clothes, but the hours had still seemed to drag. Then Mark was back one evening and the time settled into a livable rhythm.

She thought a lot about that. She resented these people in her house. She resented every aspect of her protected life, of the necessity for it, and yet seeing Mark again at her door caused her heart to lighten. She told herself her elation stemmed from the familiarity of his presence and the sense of safety he provided. A hundred times a day she convinced herself there was nothing more to her emotional reaction. What else could it be?

When he'd reappeared that September evening she had also become acutely aware of another reality. No one could miss her pregnancy now. At twenty weeks her stomach was undeniable.

"It's a boy," Lucy had announced one day. Then she'd said, "You aren't going to name him Howard, I hope."

Meg had retorted, "No. And if it's a boy, I'm not naming him Brian, either." She didn't mention that a few short months ago Howie had been her mother's hero.

Her brother had been a real problem in the early autumn. Because he'd taken conditionals on so many of his courses last year at CU, he was not allowed to begin his junior year.

Typical of Brian, he'd shrugged and said, "So what? CU was Mom's idea, anyway."

And he still didn't have a job.

But Brian and her mother played secondary roles to her own worries. Even after the incident at the hospital, there still was no word from Howie. The Aspen police had long since given up the search for her husband, and the Merrick security team had run into a cold trail once the plane that had supposedly carried Howie had left U.S. airspace north of Seattle. Mark had learned through Canadian authorities that the plane had landed in Vancouver, B.C., but from there no one knew where it had flown—or no one was saying, Meg often thought in moments of hysterical paranoia.

There were hours when she did not think about Howie at all. Then she'd be folding laundry or brushing her teeth, and she'd turned around to say something to him, and she'd remember and she'd tremble.

The worst was not knowing. If Mark one day told her they'd found Howie—even his body, for God's sake—at least she'd have some closure.

After what she'd come to think of as the "incident" in the storage room at the hospital, she'd had horrific nightmares for weeks. But they, too, subsided with time. And Mark—or Parker or Janie—was always close by. She knew they were carrying guns. She never said a word. And so far she'd been safe. How long, though, she tried not to think, how long before that man came for her again?

There was now an even more pressing problem. She was practically out of money in her personal savings account, had no access to Howie's online checking account, her credit cards were full. In mid-August she'd filled out an application for a new card, and she'd gotten the plastic quickly, but the bank had only allowed her a couple thousand dollars in credit. Which was nearly gone. She tried desperately to keep the panic at bay, but it was always there, just beneath the surface.

It occurred to her to ask Jerry for her old job back, but the lab was struggling. Merrick and the government agency were breathing down Jerry's neck. All the grant money was in jeopardy. The very existence of the lab was in jeopardy.

She thought about working for real at the hospital or taking a temporary job at the nearby mall. Now that the kids were all back in school, there were certainly openings for counter help in the department stores and shops, but Mark was dead set against that idea.

"I don't think so, Meg. We can't protect you. Bad idea."

And she was very pregnant. Who would give her a job when she'd obviously be quitting in a couple of months? Certainly before the Christmas rush when she'd be most needed.

January, she thought constantly. By mid-January she'd be a mother. The doctor had asked her after a routine ultrasound if she wanted to know the baby's sex. She'd mulled the idea over, then shaken her head. She wanted it to be a surprise. And any healthy baby, no matter the sex, was going to be fine by her.

On the last day of September, she was barbecuing salmon steaks she'd purchased on sale. She stood there with the long spatula in hand staring into the middle distance. The salmon was burning, but all she could think was that her life was in limbo. Five months pregnant and she didn't know from day to day where the next meal was coming from. She tried to plan the future, envisioning Howie's return. He could have this monstrosity of a house and she'd get an apartment for herself and the baby. Maybe even have a man in her life again—someday—and he would make love to her. No one had told her about *that* part of pregnancy. Her desire to be held and caressed had been put aside for the most part, but there were startling moments when strong need consumed her. She fought her longings, though her struggle only seemed to lend them more power.

It was awful. She didn't know if she were a wife or a widow. If the man she was married to was a victim or some kind of spy. Her body was misshapen.

Yet she still had the urge to be with a man. Was she ill, deranged?

She looked down at her hands and at the ruined salmon and burst into tears.

Mark was endlessly patient with her. Being an old hand at fixing ruined food, he scraped the steaks and put them on plates along with a salad and said, "They're a little well done. They'll be perfect."

He was always understanding. He seemed to accept her highs and lows as if they were an old married couple. When she couldn't sleep, tossing and turning, afraid of her nightmares, he played cards with her. He always went to the grocery store with her, and sometimes he paid. "Hey, just keeping up my end," he'd say. There were other things, too. Such as the electric bill, which he'd snatched from her and said Merrick would pay. "Consider it part of my rent, okay?" He'd left no room for argument.

She watched him put the plates on the table and wondered what he really thought about her. She was in her usual outfit—the maternity jeans she'd bought with Janie and one of Howie's pinstriped shirts. Her hair needed coloring, and it was too long; spiky red tendrils fell in her eyes half the time and curled up on her collar. She'd trimmed it herself twice since Howie's disappearance, but she was overdue for a professional cut. How could she afford *that,* when she couldn't squeeze another dime out of her credit cards as it was?

They were going to eat on the patio, but a stiff, cold wind tore down out of the Rockies and whipped across the Front Range, scattering leaves and lifting dust from the garden soil she'd just turned.

"Let's move inside," Mark said, picking up the plates.

"Fine," she said, following him in, wondering—and she always did of late—why she was allowing yet another man to run her life. Look where the first man had taken her.

Yet Mark was very different from Howie. He was at her side when she needed support, but he never directed her work, disapproved of her or even verbally discouraged her, aside from the time she'd mentioned getting a job. After the "incident," she couldn't blame him. He never ordered her around or argued with her. Yet she knew he observed. Always. She sometimes wanted to shake him and ask what he really thought, but that would mean touching him. Touching Mark. Even the notion was taboo.

"Sorry about the fish," she said when they were seated at the dining room table, she in her spot, Mark occupying Howie's chair.

"I told you, it's perfect. Besides, I hate anything resembling sushi."

She couldn't contain a smile. "And how do I know that's true, Mark? I think you say whatever it takes to please the poor little fragile lady. The pregnant lady."

"Would I lie to you?" he said.

"Oh, I don't know. Why don't we see how honest you can be?"

He regarded her soberly through his stylish glasses.

"You know," she continued, "you're still practically a stranger. We've lived under the same roof for almost three months, and I don't know the first thing about you. Oh. That's not quite true. I know you're an Army brat.''

"Navy, actually.''

"So tell me.''

"My life story is boring as hell, I promise you that.''

"You're ducking the question. Where were you born?''

He took a mouth full of salad, chewed, swallowed. "The Philippines.''

"What was your father? An admiral?''

"Is this important?''

"Yes. Vital.''

He muttered something, and then he said, "A captain. Submarines. We went weeks, sometimes months without hearing from him. It was the Cold War, remember?''

"I see. And you said *we*. Who is we?''

"My mother. She lives in Florida now, and a brother.''

"Older?''

"Younger.''

"What does he do?''

"Silicon Valley. He was the brain of the outfit.''

"And your father?''

"Dad passed away years ago.''

"I'm sorry. So did my dad.''

He nodded. Of course he knew. He knew all about her and her mother and Brian. Knew every sordid detail.

She cocked her head. "So you lived all over. Did you go to college?"

"Yes. Followed in Dad's footsteps. Annapolis."

"My. Then what? The navy?"

"Uh-huh."

"Were you a captain? Oh, no, I bet you were military police and that's how you got into security."

"Actually," he said, giving her a slow smile, "in the navy it's called sp—Shore Patrol. But I joined the SEALs."

"Oh. A tough guy."

Then he laughed. "No. Just dedicated."

"But you left."

"Hey," he said, "enough about me. Your food's getting cold."

"I'm not hungry. Tell me why you aren't still in the SEALs."

"You're not giving up, are you, Meg."

"Humor me."

"Because I got too old. Couldn't keep up with the recruits, and in the SEALs that's no good. I retired before I *was* retired. Now enough, okay?"

She was nowhere near done, however. "Just one more question?"

"Okay, one more."

"Were you ever married? Children?"

He seemed to decide something then. She knew his expressions so well. His brows drew together and his jaw tightened, his lips thinning. Oh, she knew that face.

"Mark," she pressed.

"Yes, I was married and no, no children. Satisfied?"

"Not entirely, but for now it will do."

"Thank God," he uttered.

She thought about these revelations all night. She pictured Mark and his brother playing in strange playgrounds in strange lands, their mother probably lonely, their father living in a submarine deep beneath the ocean, maybe on a nuclear submarine. Were the terrifying stories in *The Hunt for Red October* true?

Was that why Mark's marriage had not lasted—problems with intimacy? Because of an insecure childhood, no father figure around?

She certainly knew about loss and feelings of insecurity. And since Howie's mysterious disappearance, she'd been forced to examine that lack of a safety net. She supposed that her father's premature death had ultimately led her to a man such as Howie. She'd mothered her brother. Sure. But when it had come to her own needs, she'd fallen on her face. She'd subconsciously sought a man who could replace her father, a man to take care of her and her every desire.

She lay in the darkness of her bedroom and asked herself if that was what attracted her to Mark. He was steady and competent and there for her. Even when she railed at his presence he turned the other cheek. He hadn't abandoned her. Like her father had? Like her *husband* had.

So Mark hadn't abandoned her *yet*. But as soon as Merrick located Howie, wouldn't Mark leave?

She bit her fist and curled up into a ball, her stomach hard against her knees. She had to admit to herself just how much she was attracted to him. When that curious and humiliating desire for a man crept up on her it was not Howie's arms she longed for. For many months her dreams had not been of her husband, the father of her baby. The man of her secret desires had been pure fantasy. But now... God, now he had a face.

She lay there in the darkness and allowed herself to imagine how it could be. She would be asleep, and she would hear a knock on her door. A light tap, which would wake her, and she wouldn't be sure she'd really heard anything. But, yes, it would be Mark. Opening her door and saying her name softly. *Meg.*

"Yes," she'd breathe.

He'd push the door open and come in, a figure detaching itself from the shadows. He'd be wearing sweatpants, and his torso would be bare, with the sprinkles of light brown hair she'd imagined for weeks. He'd approach and sit on the edge of her bed, and he'd lean down and kiss her, and she'd put her arms around his neck and pull him close.

She'd stroke his skin and kiss his lips and rub herself against him as if she were a cat. And he'd run his hands all over her, and they'd sink together into the fragrant sheets of her marital bed.

She nearly laughed into the darkness. As if a good-looking man such as Mark would even give her a second glance. What a joke. If Merrick weren't paying him to baby-sit her, Mark would be gone.

She was to wonder about her assumptions that next afternoon, however.

The sun had come back out, and it was a perfect Indian summer day. She went out to the yard early in the morning, avoiding the too-warm afternoon hours. She raked leaves, bagged them and spread fertilizer on the front lawn.

Mark had offered to help a dozen times, but she wanted the exercise. "Besides," she said, "I feel terrific lately." Then she caught herself. "Oh, God, that sounds dreadful, doesn't it? I *mean* I feel physically good. I didn't mean about Howie…"

"I know that."

She was tilting her head, leaning against the painted fence that separated her property from the neighbor's, eyeing the fertilizer she'd scattered. There was one area she'd overdone. Howie, she was thinking, was going to be mad, and that was when she felt the queerest sensation in her belly, like a flicker or a tick of a muscle.

Mark was looking at the overfed spot on the lawn. "You're going to have crop circles. The neighbors will think spaceships landed."

But she didn't hear him. She straightened up, feeling the sensations again.

"Oh," she gasped. Then a strong nerve twitch rose from her stomach, and she chewed her lip and laughed. "Oh, my God," she said, "I think, I think…"

"What?" Concern spread across his features. "Meg?"

"I think the baby just kicked. Oh. There it is again. *Oh,* wow, it's so strange, the baby is *kicking.*"

He stared at her wordlessly, and she instantly felt herself flushing. How embarrassing, a strange man, a bachelor, and here she was telling him about her baby kicking. She turned from him, collecting tools and putting things away in the garage.

What a fool she was, just like Howie had always told her. She never thought about what she was going to say; it just came out of her mouth. *Idiot.*

Mark was standing at the garage door when she turned to leave, a silhouette against the brightness outside. She stopped short and held her breath.

"Is that okay?" he asked.

"Is what okay?"

"The baby...moving."

"It's fine. It's supposed to."

He approached and stood close to her. "Should you call the doctor?"

"No. Everything's fine."

He was too close, his concern evident on his face. She wanted to take a step back but she couldn't, and he didn't move, either, and the moment became charged with a kind of sweet danger.

She was suddenly overwhelmed by the urge to lean into him, to feel those ever-present whiskers rub against her cheek and neck. She could almost taste his mouth, feel his hands move along her full stomach and hips.

Heat pulsed through her veins, searing heat, and she was dizzy, breathless with longing.

He must have sensed the shift in her, because he

swayed closer and raised his arm. He never said a word. Somehow his hand was on her neck, his fingers brushing her hair.

She lifted her eyes to him. Terror and confusion and yearning leaped along her limbs and her brain cried yes, then no, then yes.

How long the moment lasted she never knew. She only remembered backing away and stammering, "I-I'm sorry. Oh, God, I'm so sorry," then rushing toward the house. The next cognizant moment she had was when she was stretched out on her bed, humiliated. How could she face him again?

It was ages before she dared to leave her room. She'd made up a thousand lame excuses to tell him and settled on one. She'd say she was overcome by nausea and had gotten sick, and oh, gosh, how embarrassing, and hopefully he'd let it go.

Mark was nowhere to be seen. She heard him, though, down the hall in the spare room on his cell phone. Then a few minutes later she could hear the sound of him connecting to the Internet, which he did frequently, checking sites for news of Howie—a credit card charge, an e-mail to somewhere. Mark had admitted a fellow security agent had tapped into Howie's personal e-mail program.

She waited all afternoon to unburden herself, but when he finally appeared, his nonchalant demeanor warned her to say nothing.

Then the phone rang. He took the call. "It's for you, your mother," he said, handing her the phone.

She was still trying to decide whether or not to say something to Mark when her mother sobbed, "It's

Brian, honey. I'm about at my wits' end. He went for a job interview at this place and they called and wanted to see him again but he blew off the appointment. And the other day there was one hundred dollars missing from my wallet. Oh, Meg, I know you have awful troubles of your own, but…''

There wasn't a lot Meg could say. Just the same old litany. ''Mom, kick him out. You aren't helping. You're making it easy for him to screw up.''

They talked for a half hour. In the end Meg felt as if they might as well not have talked at all. Lucy didn't have the courage to throw her son out and that was that.

When she got off the phone, Mark was in the kitchen, reheating that morning's coffee. She thought again about saying something, but she held her counsel, reminding herself that in the end he was going to be gone from her life. He was there for one reason, to protect Merrick's interests.

I don't give a damn what he thinks, she told herself, and the words became her mantra.

Joanna Riggs called two days later. Meg hadn't spoken to Jerry's wife in weeks, and she was surprised when Mark handed her the phone.

''Joanna? Have you heard anything? Is everything—''

But Joanna was abrupt with her. ''I'd like to see you, Meg, in person,'' she said.

''Well, we could—''

''I need to do it today. But not at your house or the lab. Can you meet me at Panchito's in Cherry Creek at noon?''

"Ah, well, sure. Is there something—"

"I'll see you at noon," Joanna cut in sharply, "and alone. No goddamn watchdog, or lunch is off." She hung up without another word.

Meg took the receiver from her ear, held it and stared at it. Wow, she thought. The only motive she could come up with for Joanna's rudeness was that the lab was in more financial difficulty and perhaps Jerry wanted an update on Howie.

She met Joanna at noon at the outdoor café on First Street. Mark had driven her, and she could see him parked a half block away, still in her line of sight as she put her linen napkin over her protruding stomach.

Joanna seemed agitated, and Meg said little before they ordered, allowing her friend—well, she *had* been Meg's friend—to take the initiative.

They both decided on taco salads with the works, and soda pop. Meg had been laying off caffeine, not to mention alcohol, but occasionally she longed for a Coke.

Joanna handed the waitress her menu and looked at Meg. "How are you, ah, feeling?"

"I feel really good. I haven't been sick in the mornings for weeks now, and I usually have a healthy appetite."

"It's been…difficult, I'm sure," Joanna allowed.

"Yes. It sure has." Then Meg thought, what the hell? "I know how hard it's been for you and Jerry and the kids, too," she said. "Mark keeps me abreast as much as he can. I know the funding is in jeopardy. It's all Howie's fault. I realize that. Even if he hadn't disappeared…voluntarily," she said carefully, "I have to believe he isn't a completely innocent victim." My God, this was difficult, she thought, her gaze shifting away.

Joanna was studying her. She could feel the tremendous burden of the woman's stare. Why didn't she say something?

Meg tried again. "It's been hard on everyone. I just wish—"

But Joanna interrupted. "Is that Mark Fielder in your car down the street?" She surreptitiously nodded toward the Audi. "Don't *look,* for the love of God, Meg, just say so."

"Ah, yes, that's him. He—"

"All right. Okay." Joanna took a quavering breath. "I don't want you to react when I tell you this. I mean it, Meg, just keep your cool. And you can't tell anyone, either. *No one.* You owe Jerry. You owe me and the kids, so no matter what it takes, stay silent. Do you understand?"

A bubble of trepidation welled in her throat. Howie. Joanna knew something. There was no other explanation for...

"Meg. Promise me?"

"Ah—" she swallowed "—yes. Of course."

"All right. Now, don't jump up or faint or anything. Just smile and pretend we're chatting."

"Sure," she muttered, the bubble rising again.

"Howie contacted me."

Meg could barely move a muscle. Somehow she pulled her lips into a smile that must have resembled a grimace.

"You're doing fine. Now, listen. Howie is going

to be at the Mariner Hotel on Marine Street at the docks in Vancouver, British Columbia, for the next three days. That's the Mariner on Marine Street. Have you got that?''

''Yes,'' Meg whispered, just as the two plates of salads were set down in front of them. ''The Mariner. Vancouver. Joanna, did he…is he…?''

''He didn't say anything to me, okay? But I'll tell you, he sounded totally stressed out.''

''I wonder, oh God, did someone hurt him?''

Joanna stiffened. ''How naive can you be,'' she muttered. ''Your husband's in trouble, that's for goddamn sure, but not because someone tried to extract information from him.'' Joanna stopped then and caught her breath. ''Never mind. Ask him yourself. Nothing I say can be proved, anyway. But where the hell do you think your house and condo in *Aspen* came from? Think about *that*.''

Meg could barely breathe. She kept the sick smile on her lips because her face was frozen. All she could do was nod and think: *He's alive. He's in Canada at a hotel and he needs me. He's alive.*

''Three days, he said. And don't tell anyone. You're going to have to ditch that government watchdog, too. I have no idea how. But you have to pull this off, Meg, and you have to tell that son of a bitch husband of yours to clear Jerry and the lab. Do you understand?''

''Yes, yes, I know what I have to do.'' Then it hit her. She blinked and gazed at Joanna. ''You just said…you said I had to ditch that government watchdog. You didn't mean *government*…''

"You really are blind," Joanna said as she rose to her feet, tossed a few bills on the table and began to turn away.

"Joanna?" Meg pleaded.

"What?"

"You're sure about Mark? I mean..."

"Yes, I'm sure. Jerry said he's either National Security Agency or Defense Department. Either way, Meg, he's dangerous. Not just to Howie, but to all of us. He can drag us down anytime he wants. So be careful. Get rid of him and get on a plane. And for God's sake convince Howie to do the right thing. Meg, I'm sorry for you. I really am. But I'm sorrier for me and my family," she said, and she made her way through the tables and disappeared inside the restaurant.

Meg couldn't even feel her legs, and her mind was reeling. Howie... Mark... Howie... Howie waiting for her in some hotel in Canada. The *government* after him. Not Merrick. It had *never* been Merrick.

Her blood turned to sludge.

It took a long time for her to move. She never ate a bite of lunch, hoping Mark could not see her from his position. And what was she going to tell him about Joanna suddenly leaving without eating her lunch? How was she going to evade him and get to the airport? Pay for a ticket? Was there enough credit left on her card? If not...what? Borrow from her mother. Lie and borrow the plane fare. And what if that faceless man was watching the house? What if he followed her?

Okay okay okay, she thought, *you can do this. You can do it because you have no choice.*

Eventually she found her legs and stood. The napkin fell to the brick patio, and she managed to bend over and retrieve it.

Act normal.

No, she thought wildly, act sick. If she told Mark she felt nauseous, then maybe he wouldn't notice her near-hysteria.

Howie was alive. Alive and awaiting her.

Her story about feeling ill and about Joanna having to leave early to pick up one of her kids must have passed muster with Mark, because he only said, "Well, then, I'll get you home as fast as possible," and he drove off without another word.

She went straight to her bedroom when she got home, closed the door and plotted her getaway. She desperately tried to convince herself that the faceless man had long since given up watching her because she was so closely guarded. But what if he hadn't?

It all seemed overwhelming, but she had no choice now, did she?

Mark. A government agent.

She longed to confront him. But what if Joanna was wrong?

She told him through her bedroom door later that afternoon that she still felt sick. Then she had an idea. "Would you mind doing me a favor?" she asked.

"Sure."

"There's a bottle of Tums in the garage somewhere. It's either in the SUV or on those shelves near the entrance to the laundry room."

"The Tums are in the garage?"

"Ah, yes, I had them the other day, when I was planting those bulbs and... I just know they're out there."

"I'll look. No problem."

"Thank you," she said sweetly.

The minute she heard the garage door open and close she rushed to his room and rifled through his things. Nothing. She thought about turning on his computer and scanning his files—if she could get access—but there wasn't time.

And then she had a flash of genius. His cell phone. The unit was recharging by the bedside.

She snatched it up, her heart beating a crazy rhythm against her ribs. She hit redial and put the small mobile phone to her ear. The number rang once, twice. Then a voice, "Defense Department, how may I direct your call?"

She nearly dropped the handset. But she lowered it very carefully, pressed Off and replaced it on the charger. She walked out of his room hugging herself, wondering if she could keep from vomiting.

For almost three months she'd lived under the same roof with this man. He had seen to her every need. Driven her to the store, to her mom's, to the doctor's. He'd been with her when the baby had first kicked inside her womb. He'd befriended her, gained her trust and even her sympathy. Was his father really dead or had that been a lie, too? And he'd done it all for one reason—he believed she'd lead him to Howie. So that he could arrest her husband for some awful breach of national security.

Mark Fielder had betrayed her. He'd used her and lied to her. Just like her own husband had done—*was* doing.

But worse. The very worst was that she'd leaned on him shamelessly. Leaned on him and even... fantasized about him. Mark and her and the baby.

The garage door opened and closed. *You stupid fool,* she thought, but somehow she managed to walk toward him. *Never again,* she promised herself. *Never again.*

CHAPTER TWELVE

BY SEVEN THE NEXT MORNING her bag was packed and hidden in her closet. As far as she knew Mark had never been in her bedroom, but after his lies and deceptions, she wasn't about to take any chances.

She'd had another night from hell. She was a wreck, a hag, her hands trembling, her appetite gone. *Howie.* Her brain spun.

Most mornings Mark went jogging. Early, before she was up. He always made sure the doors and windows were locked when he left, the house alarm armed. She paced in her bedroom, waiting for him to leave, her heart beating at every sound. *Please, go for a run,* she begged silently.

The bastard. Lying to her. Merrick security. *Right.* The Defense Department had sent him, and she knew exactly why he'd lied to her, why such an elaborate setup had been required. The government suspected *her* of being involved in Howie's disappearance.

Shortly after seven she heard the alarm being set, then the front door open and close softly. Her heart began to pound. He was going for his run.

Breathe, for God's sake, she told herself, taking her bag from its hiding place.

At her bedroom door she paused again. Sweat

broke out on her upper lip. What if he returned to get his sunglasses or something? What if he kept her house in view for his entire run? Her heart beat furiously, the baby kicked, probably feeling Meg's tension.

You're doing this for your husband, she told herself, *for the father of your child. You can do it.*

She took a breath and opened her door, reset the alarm to give her time to get out the kitchen door, then she raced to the garage, remembering to throw the bag in the trunk of the Audi—just in case she ran into Mark. In that event, she had a story planned. She needed milk and eggs—which was true—and she was only going to the corner minimarket. She'd be right back. Five minutes.

But she didn't run into Mark, and thirty minutes later she was pulling into a long-term parking lot at Denver International Airport, where she caught the shuttle to the terminal, still worrying about what she'd do if her credit card didn't go through when she tried to pay for a plane ticket.

MARK TOOK HIS SUNGLASSES off, pulled the tail of his T-shirt up and wiped his face. Stood there perspiring, breathing hard, looking around the living room, the kitchen, noting she hadn't eaten a bite, feeling her absence as keenly as her presence.

"You're a rotten son of a bitch, Fielder," he said to the empty house, and then he phoned Bollinger, instructing the other agent to pick him up right away.

He didn't have to tail her; another team was already doing that. But he wanted to be at the airport, anyway.

man. Had she been so concerned about not wanting Mark to see her drive off that she'd failed to notice a car following her?

Desperately, she cast her eyes around the terminal. There were hundreds of people milling everywhere. Waiting in check-in lines. Any one of them could be that man, or an associate of his.

The paranoia returned full force. Dear God, what if she was leading that foreigner to Howie?

But it was too late now. She was committed to this insane trip. Committed to finally knowing the truth.

You'll make it, she thought frantically. *You have to make it.*

"Here we are, Mrs., ah, Afferton," the agent said, handing her the ticket. "Flight 404, eleven-forty. Gate B-34. Lunch on board."

She walked toward Security and the lower-level train that would take her to the concourse from which her flight would leave. Had Mark discovered her absence? Of course he had. But he'd think she was running errands. For a while, anyway. He'd be mad, sure. Good, she thought. Then she remembered the faceless man and her moment of triumph fled.

She bought a newspaper in a shop so that she'd have something to read while she waited for the flight. But when she sat by the gate, she found she couldn't concentrate. Howie was all she could think about. Howie in Vancouver for three days. And then what? Where did he plan to go in three days? What had he been doing for the last three months? He'd never even phoned. Not even a quick call to say he was alive. How could a person do that to someone?

Where had he been? Giving away classified information to his captors? Or were they his business colleagues? Had he planned this? Planned to escape with his ill-gotten gains?

And what had he thought would happen to his wife? *Howie, how could you have done this to me?*

But he was alive. At least she knew that. She'd see him, ask him all those questions. Maybe he was innocent. Maybe there were answers, logical answers.

And he'd see her. She closed her eyes and imagined the look on his face. Surprise, yes, and shock, then the image dimmed and she had no idea what his reaction would be.

SHE TOOK THE BUS FROM the Vancouver airport because it was cheaper than a cab, and she only had eighty U.S. dollars left in cash from her own account. The tidy suburbs of the city flowed by, but she barely noticed. Far off in the distance she once caught sight of snowcapped peaks, and for a moment she was confused and thought she was back in Denver.

At the downtown bus station, she hefted her overnight bag and went outside to look for a cab. She'd splurge this one time because she had no idea where the hotel was, and she was simply too weary to try to figure out how to get there by public transportation.

"The Mariner Hotel on Marine Drive, please," she said to the driver, and he nodded.

She settled back in the seat and tried to calm herself. What if Howie wasn't there? She should have called him from the airport. What if she had been followed? Not by Mark—she was almost positive she'd evaded him—but by a colleague of his, another government agent, or even the faceless man?

She turned a dozen times in the seat trying to scan the faces in the cars around them, but no one was the least bit familiar. Of course, how could a faceless man be familiar?

The taxi took her past the port, past buildings and docks and glimpses of green parks, and then proceeded into a dingy area, bars and run-down buildings and hotels advertising cheap rooms.

Howie, she thought, staying here?

The cabbie stopped in front of the careworn brick building. The Mariner Hotel. Was this it? Was her husband inside that ugly place? Howie, who complained to the management if there was fuzz on the rug or wrinkles in the sheet in a hotel room.

She paid the man, giving him a small tip. He took American dollars without a word; she guessed this close to the border it didn't matter. Then she slung her strap over her shoulder, checked a last time to try to spot a tail, took a deep breath and walked toward the entrance to the hotel.

At the desk she asked if Dr. Howard Afferton was registered. Only then did it occur to her in a flash of panic he might be registered under another name. But wouldn't he have told Joanna that?

"Yes, Dr. Afferton is registered. You can call him from the house phone," the man behind the desk told her.

"Can I just go up to his room? I'm his wife, and—"

"Our policy," the man said apologetically.

She went to the wall where a single old-fashioned beige phone sat on a counter. Dialed 0 as directed, asked for Howie. The phone rang, and she stood there, trembling, terrified, excited.

"Hello?"

She was stunned into stillness. Howie, yes, his voice. Familiar, once beloved, his voice, tinny over the phone but unmistakably his.

"Hello?" A hint of fear in his tone.

"Howie," she managed to say.

"Meg, is that you?"

"I'm in the lobby, oh, Howie, oh my God..." Her tears overflowed.

"Come up," he said. "Room 314."

"Yes," she whispered.

The hallway smelled of disinfectant and old sweat. There was a fake patina of shiny brown on each door. Flakes had come off in places, displaying other colors, and around the locks were gouges and scratches. She followed the numbers on the doors: 310, 312, 314. There it was, and Howie was behind it. Waiting for her. She put a hand to her mouth and closed her eyes for a moment.

Then she knocked.

Instantly the door swung open. He reached out, then took her arm and pulled her into the room. And then they both stood there, wordlessly, and stared at each other.

His shirt was wrinkled, his pants baggy. He looked thinner, almost gaunt, and a nervous tic pulled at his left eyelid.

"Howie," she finally said.

"Meg." His voice was hoarse.

She didn't know what to do then. Hug him? Hold his hand? Ask him the thousand questions that crowded her brain?

He made no move to touch her, to welcome her after so long an absence. Her skin crawled with anxiety, the baby kicked.

His gaze took her in, searching, devouring her. He, too, had questions, she realized. Then his stare swept her again, and he stepped back, his eyes widening. She heard the quick intake of his breath.

"Yes, I'm pregnant," she said.

"My God."

"I was going to tell you that night, Howie, but you never...you didn't come home."

"How far along?"

"Five months."

"So it's too late to..." He swallowed his words.

She stared at him. "I want this baby," she said softly.

"Well, I don't," he said, his apathetic tone abruptly turning harsh. "You know I never wanted children. Why in hell didn't you take care of it when you found out?"

"Take care of it?"

"You know what I'm talking about."

"It's my baby. *Our* child. Howie, you can't think..."

"Oh, yes I can."

"Howie..."

He looked at her, his expression hard. "Good God, how do I know it's even mine?"

She went rigid with shock, felt the blood drain from her face. *No,* her mind said, *he can't believe that. He can't, he can't.*

Then he sagged, all his temper draining. "Oh, God, Meg, I'm sorry. I didn't mean that. I know you wouldn't... I'm half out of my mind. It's been so terrible, you have no idea." He moved close to her and held his hands out to embrace her. She moved away from him, subtly but purposefully, and he dropped his hands.

"I'm sorry," he whispered brokenly.

She found an inner strength that she hadn't known was there. "Let's sit down. I'm very tired. I didn't sleep much last night. Can we sit? And I'd love a glass of water."

He went into the bathroom, and she could hear water running. She wasn't really thirsty, but she wanted the time to think, to decide, to judge the man to whom she was married but who now was a stranger.

He came out and handed her a glass. She took it and went to sit on a chair in the corner of the room. A brown chair, its vinyl seat slashed as if someone had been in some kind of inarticulate rage. A brown speckled carpet, cheap prints of ships on the walls, a faded striped spread on the sagging bed.

Howie sat on the edge of the bed. She noticed that his fingernails were quite long, and without a bridging thought, she saw Mark's hands in her mind's eye—square and strong, with short nails and light brown hairs on the backs. She blocked out the picture.

"Meg," Howie began.

"Start at the beginning," she said. "I want to know

everything." She spoke in a severe tone of voice, quite uncharacteristic of her, but he didn't seem to notice.

"Oh, God, it's been so awful. I didn't know, I didn't realize... And it was all for you, too. I wanted you to have a good life, not like my mother. You know that."

A cold chill ran up her spine. What had he done?

He leaned forward, elbows on his knees. His hair, the dark straight hair she had so often run her fingers through, was unkempt. His cheeks were hollow with black stubble. Not like Mark's. No, different.

"About two years ago a research scientist from a former Soviet state contacted me. He was very flattering. We e-mailed each other, you know, talking about this and that. He was Russian, but he lived in Turghistan and was the head of their National Medical Academy. Sort of like our centers for disease control. Well, this man, his name was Boris Lebedev...."

Wasn't that the man who'd rented the car in Aspen and the plane in Grand Junction? Yes, Meg thought. Could he have been the faceless man?

But Howie was talking. "He told me he was very interested in our Ebola vaccine research, because there had been incidents in Turghistan, some outbreaks of a similar hemorrhagic fever, and he wanted... Well, he said it would help him out if he could take advantage of what we've done so far. You know, Meg, they're far behind us in research and Russia can't help fund them anymore, and..." He put his head in his hands and scrubbed his hair.

"Go on, Howie."

"So...so...he asked me to keep them up to date on our research, and if I did..." He raised his head and regarded her with bloodshot eyes. "If I did, then his government...would compensate me."

Ah, she thought. The crux. Money.

"Meg," he said, "please understand. It was a humanitarian gesture. To save lives. You understand, don't you? Meg?"

She nodded.

"I sent Boris my disks. And he was as good as his word. He paid me. Very well. It was for you."

"The new house," she said. "And the condo in Aspen."

"Yes, yes."

"And the car and the bracelet."

"I wanted those things for you. Beautiful things. The lab, well, you know, it isn't going to show a profit for years. *Years.*"

"You lied to me."

"No, no."

"You told me you'd given yourself a raise because you'd gotten more funding." She was amazed at her own calmness.

"I...but, Meg, I thought you would be so happy."

"Finish your story."

He looked at her. "I kept sending Boris the disks, and everything was going along fine. Fine. And then, well, I got a little suspicious. I kept asking about his progress, and about the fevers in Turghistan. Had he isolated the virus yet? Was it a retrovirus? Was it similar to Ebola or Marburg? What were the symptoms? The death rate?" Howie stood and began to pace, and she recognized his body language. He was lying. He'd known all along why Boris had wanted the disks. Howie was not this stupid. "And I realized that there had never been mention of a hemorrhagic virus outside of Africa. I scoured the professional journals, searched on the Internet."

She took a sip of water. Now she knew for sure he was lying. Howie was an expert on hemorrhage viruses. He'd have known there were none recorded in Turghistan.

Howie went to the window, pulling aside the dingy drape, looking out. Then he turned. "It occurred to me that my friend might be using my research for something else. Not a vaccine for a deadly virus, but a biological warfare agent."

"Yes," she whispered. Mark had told her that, hinted at it, but she hadn't believed him. Hadn't wanted to believe him.

"I stopped sending the disks, Meg. The minute I thought he might be using it for biological warfare, I stopped. I ended it.

"And then, just before the seminar at the Given Institute, Boris e-mailed me. I didn't reply. He phoned me. He wouldn't leave me alone. He kept offering money, but I couldn't continue. I couldn't."

You would have kept right on, Meg thought, *but you got scared.*

He paced and ran a hand through his hair again. "But Boris wouldn't give up. He told me he would leak my arrangement with him to my government. And I'd be arrested as a spy."

"I see," she said.

"Then he called one day, when we were in Aspen. He called and said he had to see me in person, and that he knew where I was and I better cooperate or he'd feed me to the sharks. I had no choice. You can see, Meg, that I had no choice?"

She didn't move a muscle. Even the baby was utterly still.

"So he picked me up at the lecture that day. He picked me up, we drove to Grand Junction then flew to Canada.

"He threatened me. I had to promise to send more of my research. He even threatened you, Meg. But then he told me the government had a man guarding you, and I...I couldn't... Oh, God, I couldn't do anything right. I didn't know what to do. I didn't dare call you or write you. That man was there.

"You don't know, Meg, you don't know what I've been through. I got away one night and I've been running. Scared to death. Running and hiding from Boris and from my own government. I knew the government suspected me, or they wouldn't have sent that man..."

"Mark Fielder," she said.

Howie shot her a hate-filled look. "And I couldn't come home. I didn't want you to get involved and I couldn't let Boris find me."

She straightened. "Howie, how could I not be involved? My husband disappears, and everyone in Aspen is looking for you, Howie. In the river, for God's sake."

"I know, I know. I tried, but...everything went wrong."

"And he attacked me," she finally said.

"He…? Who attacked you?"

"I didn't see his face, but his accent was foreign, probably Russian. Probably *your* Boris."

"Oh, God. Did he…hurt you?"

"No, not physically. But he said you had to come out of hiding and that he could get to me anytime."

"Well." Howie waved dismissively. "I'm sure that was just to scare me. They're not after you." Then suddenly his eyes widened. "You weren't followed?"

"I don't think so." He didn't even care what she'd suffered. Or about the threats. He never even asked how or where she'd been accosted. He didn't care.

"So what now?" she asked, numb with sorrow and disappointment.

"I don't know. I have money. I can get hold of it. I've been afraid, though. DARPA's probably watching my accounts."

"DARPA…"

"Defense Advanced Research Projects Agency. Part of the Defense Department. Where that man is from."

"Mark," she said again.

"Yes, *Mark,*" Howie hissed. "In *my* house, right there with you every second."

"He's helping out, Howie. You disappeared. I didn't know if you were dead or alive. And after Boris attacked me, it was dangerous for me to be alone. Do you realize you didn't leave me any money? No checkbook. I can't even pay the mortgage…."

"It's not important."

"It's important to *me*," she said with heat.

"I have money. I saved a lot. I'll...I'll take care of you."

"Howie, you don't know how humiliating it's been. I barely have enough to buy groceries."

"Meg, calm down."

She closed her eyes for a moment, fighting her anger. "Where's all this money you say you have?"

He looked pleased with himself, an incongruous expression. "In a bank on Grand Cayman. The First British Limited Bank. I have an account there. See, Boris wired the payments there, and I had them wired to me. It was his idea."

"So no one knew you were getting these... payments."

"No one."

"Not even me," she said to herself.

"I'll get however much you want, Meg. If you just wait until tomorrow."

But she was shaking her head. "How could you have done this? You're a spy. Like...like the FBI man they caught selling information to the Russians."

"No, I'm not. It's not the same. You see the difference, don't you? I made a mistake. Boris lied to me, he misled me. That's why I ran away and hid from him. I never would have..."

"Oh, Howie" was all she could say.

He stopped in front of her, his eyes red rimmed, the one lid twitching. "I want you to come with me. Right now. Don't even go back to Denver. I'll get the money. We can take a plane, we'll be gone before anyone knows it."

"What about my mother, Howie? And Brian?"
And our baby, she thought.

He waved his hand. "You can contact them later. When it's safe."

"And you'd give up your research, the lab, everything you've worked for?"

"I have no choice."

It wouldn't do any good to argue, she knew. Logic wasn't part of his reasoning any longer. Fear held him hostage.

"Come with me."

"Howie, even if this wasn't insane, I don't have a passport."

That stopped him. Obviously he had one, and then she remembered Mark asking her if Howie had his passport with him. So long ago. And she'd had no idea if Howie possessed one or not. There was a lot she hadn't known about her husband.

"We'll go to the U.S. embassy here or the consulate, whatever. Say you lost your passport, have them issue you one. They can do that. I think. Or maybe they'd search their records for your old passport number and…I don't know. We'll find out. It can't be that hard." He spoke quickly, words tumbling over themselves. His hands gestured nervously.

She shook her head.

"What?"

Suddenly she felt very sad for him. He'd ruined his career, his life. He'd done it not because he was inherently evil, but because he was morally weak. Had she noticed that about him before?

"What about the baby, Howie?"

"The baby."

"Our *child*. What kind of life…?"

"You did this, Meg. You could have prevented it. It's your fault."

Abruptly, as she was sitting there in the ripped chair watching her husband, a strange serenity came over her. She saw her choices clearly. If she went with Howie, this would happen. If she went home, that would happen. If she turned him in—

He was staring at her, and she could smell fear emanating from him. *My God.*

She sat quietly watching him.

"Argentina," he began. "I hear Buenos Aires is nice. Or Chile. Ecuador? Not Venezuela or Colombia."

"I think I should go home now," she said.

"Home? But…"

"Yes, home."

He was shaking his head. "I don't know. If you go home, that government man…what if he—?"

"He *won't.*"

"But what will you tell him? I mean, where does he think you are right now?"

She looked up sharply. Blood was pounding in her ears. She knew she had to tell Howie something. "I'll take care of all that."

Her husband considered her words. Before this terrible mess he'd made of their lives, he would have been stunned at the conviction in her voice. But now he was too weak, too stressed to notice. He was a stranger.

He finally nodded and wrung his hands as he paced.

"All right. You take care of things in Denver. Then you can join me. You're a smart girl, Meg, you can handle it."

Girl, she thought.

"Yes, and I'll set everything up in South America. I'll have my money wired in, decide where to settle. Maybe I'll go there first. Take a look around. Yes, it's probably better that way, isn't it, Meg? Maybe I'll buy a house."

"Sure," she said.

"But you need money now, don't you? I didn't think… Here, Meg, here. Is it enough?"

He pulled money out of his pocket, a fat wad of American bills. Hundred dollar bills. He peeled a handful off, held them out.

She stared at the cash. Dirty money. She shook her head again. "I have some cash. You keep it," she said.

"Okay, sure, okay. And I'll keep in touch through Joanna," he said eagerly, as if their plans were finalized.

"Joanna's furious at you," Meg said.

"Yes, yes, I know, but I'm sure she'll give you the messages."

"You left Jerry in a bad position."

"It couldn't be helped."

She was at a loss. She couldn't deal with Howie; he wasn't the man she had married. But she had to try. Even though all her instincts screamed at her to leave, to run away from this wreck of a person who'd made all the wrong choices.

"Howie, listen to me. Sit down, will you?"

He sat on the bed facing her, hands on his knees, bony shoulders hunched defensively.

"There's another option. You could come back to Denver with me and turn yourself in." She held a hand up to stop him from talking. "No, wait. You said it yourself. You made a mistake. They'll listen to you."

"Oh, sure," he scoffed. "Turn myself in? To that guy who's been staying in my house?"

"Yes. He'd be fair. I know him. He'd listen to you."

"I'll bet you know him."

She bent her head and took a deep breath, ignoring his remark.

"No," Howie said.

"If you tell them all you know about Boris and what he's doing and that country…"

"Turghistan."

"Yes, tell them all about it. Trade information for leniency. Howie, what they want is information, and you can provide it."

"They'll put me in jail. I'm a traitor to them. You're fooling yourself. Just because you trust this guy, this…"

"Mark Fielder."

Howie grimaced.

"Please, for me and for our child."

He slashed the air with a hand. "Out of the question."

She'd known he wouldn't listen to her. She wasn't even disappointed.

"All right, Howie. I disagree, but you're going to do what you think is right for yourself, I know that."

"Valparaiso is supposed to be nice, in the mountains, not too hot. What do you think?"

"Valparaiso?"

"Chile."

"Oh."

"I'll take a look."

"Sure, you check it out." She stood and picked up her overnight bag. She thought she was going to vomit.

"You're going?" he asked, sounding like a lost child.

"I think I should. If I'm gone too long, Mark will get suspicious." What a fine liar she was turning out to be.

"Well, we sure don't want that, do we?"

"No, we don't. I'll probably be able to catch a flight back this evening."

Howie stood, too close to her. She felt as if she were suffocating. She had to leave, she had to get out of that stuffy little brown room or she'd die.

"I'll be in touch," he said.

"Okay."

"I'm sorry, Meg."

"I'm sure you are."

"You won't say anything to Boris if he contacts you again?"

"What?"

"About where I am."

"Boris didn't contact me, Howie, he attacked me."

"But he didn't hurt you."

"Oh, God."

"Meg, just don't mention Vancouver."

"No, of course not," she said, her lips stiff.

Howie wanted to embrace her, to kiss her. She could sense his need. She moved toward the door. "Goodbye, Howie."

"I wish you could stay. I'm so lonely here. No one to talk to."

"I can't."

"Right, *Mark* will get suspicious."

"Take care of yourself."

He tried to smile, a twitch of his lips. But it didn't work. "Bye, Meg."

She went through the door and took a rasping breath when it closed behind her. She felt her hands trembling, her heart pounding like a jackhammer. And the baby moved restlessly inside her. She weaved down the hall to the elevator and pushed the button. She'd get a cab to the airport, then catch the first plane to Denver. If she had to wait all night in the airport she would. It didn't matter; she had to get as far away from him as possible.

BY 4:00 p.m. MARK'S HEAD ached. He'd spent hours after the coup at Denver International Airport on the phone with Washington and Vancouver, coordinating and manipulating. His head shouldn't have hurt. He should have been riding high, because Lebedev had been foiled, and Mark's plan, after weeks and weeks of preparation, was finally coming to fruition.

The plan was known to DARPA as Project Setup.

So dubbed by Janie Weathers after she'd done her shift with Meg at the Denver house last month.

Mark hated the moniker. He hated thinking that he was setting Meg up. But she was the unsuspecting star of the carefully orchestrated show. And he thought of the Riggses as co-stars, although definitely central to the plot. Jerry and Joanna had not been willing players, and had only agreed to their roles after much pressure had been placed on them. Either cooperate with their government and help nail Dr. Afferton or they'd lose their funding and the entire lab would go down. At first Jerry had been loyal to his partner, but last month he'd capitulated.

"All right, all right," he'd said, practically in tears. "I'll call you, Mr. Fielder, if Howie contacts me. I'll goddamn do it because of my wife and children."

The only player without a script was Meg. Of necessity she'd had to be kept in the dark.

Then the waiting had begun. Mark knew Afferton was eventually going to try to get in touch with his wife. He also believed the good doctor would not make contact directly. And the logical contact person was Jerry Riggs.

The trouble was, as it had been since the day of Afferton's disappearance, that the government did not have enough on the man for an arrest, much less a conviction. The attorney general would demand hard evidence on Afferton, and thus DARPA needed Afferton's confession. The next best thing would be if Afferton spilled his guts to his wife, named names and, more to the point, named banks, so that Mark could follow the money trail and connect the dots: Afferton to Turghistan.

There were holes in Project Setup, one of them being the possibility that Meg would opt to stay in Canada with her husband. In that event, the two DARPA agents who'd been on her tail since she'd left the house would pick up both her and her husband. Meg would be escorted home. The extradition process on Dr. Afferton would begin.

Not a good scenario; forcing a confession might be messy.

So Mark was banking on his investment in Meg. She'd return to the States with a head full of details, names, dates, places and bank accounts, and hopefully a need to clear her conscience.

"Don't coerce her," Mark's boss had said on the phone today. "*If* she returns, let her come forward on her own. Don't scare her off."

Mark worried all afternoon that he might have misread Meg entirely. What the hell did he know about women? Plus she was pregnant. She might elect to stay with her husband, despite everything, for the sake of the baby.

Though when Mark spoke to Joanna Riggs, who'd been a key player in Project Setup, Joanna had been positive Meg would not run off with Howard.

Joanna had said, "Meg? Take off with Howie? No way. First, she'd never leave her mother and brother. But second, Meg's pregnant. I know she'd rather raise the baby herself then live on the run with that... asshole she's married to."

Pacing Meg's house shortly past 4:00 p.m., Mark

wished the DARPA agents in Canada would check in. Of course, Meg might decide to stay a night or two with Afferton. Hell, the man was her husband, the father of her baby. But still Mark wanted to believe she'd see Afferton for what he was: a goddamn traitor. She'd finally realize the truth and she'd come straight back.

His cell phone rang at four-thirty-five. It was Janie in Washington, relaying a message that had come in on a secured line from Vancouver. "Well, Mark," Janie said, "you lucked out and Project Setup is still on track."

"Meg's coming home?"

"Now, don't *we* sound excited?"

"Get to the point, Janie."

"Bollinger just touched base and Mrs. Afferton boarded a flight twenty minutes ago."

"Roger that," Mark said.

"You just better hope the Riggses don't spill the beans."

"I think they're secure."

"As far as the setup, maybe. But that doesn't mean Mrs. Afferton won't learn who you really work for. Too many people know."

"Hmm," he said.

"And if your lady friend does find out, then you're sunk."

"I believe she'll do the right thing."

"Maybe yes. And maybe no. You've been cooped up with her for an awfully long time. Maybe you can't judge her any longer."

"I'm judging her just fine," he said.

"She's a pretty lady. And she isn't an idiot," Janie said. "Well, I'm out of here for the day. Good luck with Meg."

"Sure," he said, and he clicked off. He allowed himself a moment to consider Janie's warning about Meg, then dismissed it. He'd simply be cautious. Hell, the last thing he wanted was to bring down the curtain on the whole show.

CHAPTER THIRTEEN

SHE PARKED THE AUDI in the garage, stepped wearily out onto the concrete slab and looked at the door leading to the kitchen.

She knew Mark had heard her drive in. Even from the bedrooms one could hear the garage door opening and closing. And she was sure he'd be waiting just on the other side of that door.

How would he react when he saw her? Would he be worried, furious? Or would he be sickly sweet and concerned, playing his role to the hilt in the hope that she'd fall in his arms—her handsome protector—and confess all?

She shrugged and hauled her overnight bag out of the car. She told herself she didn't give a damn what Mark Fielder thought or how he'd react. She was too beaten up to care. Beaten up by her husband. By his dreadful downfall, the state of his health, the terrible decisions he'd made over the past two years.

And he'd even tried to blame her—saying he'd sold out his country for *her*. What crap. She'd never once asked for a thing from Howie. She'd told him the house was too big, too extravagant. And the Aspen condo. She'd asked him over and over if it wouldn't

have been more sensible to rent when they visited the
Given Institute.

She closed the car door and walked toward the
kitchen entrance. Howie, Mark, Howie. The *creeps*.
The *liars*. They'd both used her. To hell with both of
them.

As expected, he was in the kitchen. He was dressed
in a blue shirt and tan cashmere V-neck sweater and
jeans, loafers. Mr. Casual. But his expression wasn't
casual. He looked very serious. For a moment her
nerve fled, but she retrieved it and held it close.

He was leaning against the counter, arms folded
across his chest, ankles crossed. Behind his glasses
his eyes were the color of a storm-tossed sea.

"Mind telling me where you were for the last fourteen hours?" he said, his tone quiet and even. But she
could hear the edge of anger just beneath the surface.

She stared at him. Had he really not traced her
whereabouts? If he was acting—pretending he had no
idea where she'd gone—he was putting on a good
show.

"Family problems," she said, setting her suitcase
down.

"Really."

"Yes, really."

"Your mother? Brian?"

She sighed matter-of-factly.

"Or maybe your husband?"

"Listen," she said. "I'm very tired. I've hardly
had a bite to eat and I'm done in. I'm going to bed."

"Come on," he said, uncrossing his legs as if he
might move toward her. "Don't you think it's about

time you put a little trust in me? Meg, I'm here to
help you."

The lying bastard, she thought, flashing him a look.
Merrick Pharmaceuticals. Oh, right, he was here to
help her. Trust him. When hell froze over she'd trust
him.

Still, as exhausted and disgusted as she felt, she
had enough sense left to know it wouldn't do any
good to antagonize him. He was playing a game.
Well, she could play, too.

"Can we talk in the morning?" she said, and she
even managed a thin, weary smile.

"I'd rather talk now."

"I wouldn't. I told you—"

"Why don't I heat up something to eat? You said
you haven't eaten all day."

"I'm not hungry."

"Maybe not. But do you think it's wise, not eating?"

How dare he behave as if he gave two hoots about
her or the baby?

"Meg. Look. I'm not...lying to you," he said with
care. "I've been worried about you all day."

"Um," she said. "Why didn't you call Mom's,
then?" She felt like laughing hysterically. He hadn't
called to look for her because he probably knew exactly where she'd gone.

"Well?" she pressed.

He didn't answer. Instead he nodded, as if conced-
ing this round, and then he opened the refrigerator
door and took out a couple of white cardboard con-

tainers. She recognized them. Chinese. From Hunan House, a few miles away on University.

"I'm going to eat," he said, searching for pans to reheat the food.

He hadn't been frantically searching for her or phoning all over God's creation, because he had *known*. He had probably had her followed since early that morning, she suddenly realized. Had her followed all the way to Vancouver. And he'd probably gotten word when she had taken the afternoon flight back to Denver. He'd gotten the take-out then. *Her* favorites.

"I've got twice-cooked pork and that Imperial shrimp you like," he said. "Join me?"

But she barely heard. If Mark had people on her tail all day, then why hadn't they picked up Howie at the hotel?

Or maybe she was misreading the entire situation. Maybe Mark had no idea where she'd been. Maybe he'd gotten back from his jog and seen that the Audi was missing and figured she had merely stolen a day to herself. If someone had kidnapped her, he might have reasoned, the Audi would still have been in the garage.

She didn't know what to think. She didn't even know if it mattered anymore. Between Howie and his insane talk about South America and this man right here, she no longer knew day from night. Too many lies, too many games and deceptions. It was a wonder she hadn't lost her mind.

She finally ate with him at the dining room table. As much as she hated to admit it, he was right—she needed to eat for the baby's sake.

He didn't say another word about where she'd been or about her mother or Brian or anything else. His silence on the subject was frustrating because she couldn't read him. Did he know she'd been with Howie, been with his quarry of the past months? Was there some reason—which she didn't understand— why he hadn't had her husband arrested? Surely the U.S. government could have arranged Howie's arrest despite his being in Canada.

By the time she fell into bed, exhausted, he had her completely bewildered. He knew everything. No, she kept reasoning, he couldn't have known. And he'd erased the anger she'd read in his eyes when she walked in the door. Erased his frustration and re- placed it with infuriating goodwill. He was so good at that. A chameleon. An expert. Maybe the Defense Department always sent Mark Fielder on assignments involving married, *pregnant* women. And maybe every one of the pathetic women fantasized that it was Mark they were married to, Mark who had planted his seed in their wombs, Mark who held them and cared for them in their darkest hours.

She fell asleep with that thought foremost in her brain. She dreamed, however, of an Argentinean beach. A white, crescent-shaped beach shaded by tall pines and splashed by turquoise-and-sapphire waters. She was there, trim and sexy and tan. The baby was there. Fat and happy. Filling sand buckets. And Mark was there. Emerging from azure water, his perfect body shimmering with a thousand droplets of mois- ture, and he was smiling and waving proudly to his family.

SHE WAS IN THE SHOWER when she heard his voice.

Good God, she thought, automatically grabbing at the towel outside the glass shower doors, had he come into her bedroom? Surely he'd heard the water running?

"Meg?" she heard again. "I'm sorry, but there's a call for you, and I think you better—"

"I'm in the shower," she called back. "Tell them to—"

"You better take this" came his voice, and shockingly he stuck his hand in the slightly ajar bathroom door. "Here," he said, handing her the phone. "If you need me I'll be right outside, okay?"

She muttered something and snatched it, then slammed the door shut. "Hello?" she grated out, angry, embarrassed.

It was her mother. Sobbing.

"Mom? Mom, I can't understand a word you're saying. Will you please calm down and tell me what's going on?"

Lucy sniffed and stifled her sobs. "It's…it's Brian. He was…in a car accident. Oh, Meg."

She felt as if she'd been struck. She sagged, trembling, onto the wet bath mat. Brian was dead. She knew it. She had *always* known this was going to happen.

"And he's… They arrested him, Meg."

It took her a long moment before she grasped Lucy's words. Brian…arrested. "Give me a second, Mom," she breathed. "You said, you're saying, Brian was in an accident and the police arrested him?"

"Yes, yes. Oh, God, my baby is in jail."

"But…"

"They won't tell me much. Some woman, a policewoman, phoned and said my car was wrecked and Brian was under arrest."

He'd been drinking. Meg knew that immediately. He'd been drinking and driving and crashed the car. Lucy's car.

"Mom," she said abruptly, "was anyone hurt? Was anyone else…?"

"No, no, I don't think so. Oh, Meg, what am I going to do? Can you…can you come over?"

Meg sighed and took a shaky breath. "Yes, Mom, I'll be there as soon as I can. Twenty minutes." Now there were three names spinning in her head—Howie, Mark, *Brian.*

Mark drove. She gave him no argument. Insane people didn't argue, she thought. No. They ranted and raved.

But she couldn't even do that. As the baby kicked in her belly, she felt that she was running on a treadmill that wouldn't stop, and if she didn't focus completely on each step and each breath, she'd fall off and tumble into some great dark hole.

Mark, Howie, Brian, Mark…

Her mother was thoroughly undone when they arrived at the modest Wheat Ridge house where Meg and Brian had been raised. Lucy was waiting on the white-painted porch as they drove into the narrow gravel drive. She had been sitting in her wicker rocker, and she rose and hurried to the car, her usually perfectly styled hair standing on end at the back, her brown eyes swollen. She was still in pink-striped pajamas, an oversize Irish knit cardigan thrown on and half buttoned.

"Mom," Meg said, "oh, Mom, I could kill Brian. Look at you. Come on. Come inside and get warm. Have you had coffee yet?"

Lucy mumbled something and gave Meg and Mark a sad, apologetic smile, pulling the sweater more tightly around her. As Meg walked her mother inside she met Mark's eyes. Humiliation tore through her. What a pathetic family she had. An ineffectual mother, an out-of-control brother, a husband who was a spy. And what must Mark think of *her?* But she knew. He thought she was an easily manipulated, hysterical, *stupid* female.

She made a pot of coffee, and the three of them sat in the small, square, tidy living room on the same couch and chairs Meg recalled from childhood. The upholstery had been changed several times over the years—from flowers to stripes to flowers again, but now it was plain, a knobby beige, with throw pillows to match the green-patterned rug. But it was the same furniture. "You can't buy frames and springs like this anymore," Lucy always said. "I may be poor as a church mouse, but I know nice things when I see them." Her mother's badge of honor: the poor widow.

Right now she was the poor *frantic* widow. "I don't even know if my son is hurt. They won't tell me a thing. Why are the police like that? And my car. What am I going to do without a car?"

Meg was sitting next to her. She had no answers. If Howie were here, he'd... But Howie wasn't here.

And he'd never be here again. Meg had no money for an expensive lawyer. Brian had nothing. Not a dime. Still, she had to think of something. Get a public defender?

"Now, Mom," she said, "aren't you the one who always told us that things have a way of working out?"

Lucy held her coffee cup and glanced timidly across to Mark. "Mr. Fielder," she began.

"It's Mark. Remember?"

She nodded shyly. "Of course. Mark. I always taught my children the right things. I took them to church on Sundays, and we never used bad language in our house. We may have been poor, but I raised my children the best I could after their father passed away."

Meg felt like crawling in a hole.

"And Brian never missed a day of school. Did you know he was a basketball player? Well. Not now, of course, but—"

"Mom," Meg cut in, "I'm sure Mark isn't interested in ancient history. The point is, Brian's in trouble, and we need to come up with a plan. Either that," she said cautiously, "or we can let him get out of it himself. He's the one who got himself in this fix and—"

"How could you even say such a thing? He's your brother. Sometimes I think you're heartless, Meg. All your talk of tough love. Well, those things just don't work. Your brother needs our support right now."

Meg sat up straight. "Your son needs a kick in the pants," she began, ready to remind Lucy that Howie had disappeared and that Meg was alone, pregnant and penniless, but Mark cleared his throat and met her eyes. He shook his head ever so slightly, as if to say, *Don't go there.*

She pressed her lips together.

Mark cleared his throat again and set his flowered cup back on its flowered saucer and put both on the perfectly polished oak coffee table. "I realize this is none of my business," he said. "But maybe, if you'll allow me, I could drive over to the police station and assess the situation."

"Oh," Lucy gasped, a hand to her chest, "we couldn't let you do that. It's too much of an imposition."

"Mom's right," Meg began.

But he took charge. He stood up, shrugged on his sport coat and smiled. "It's no imposition at all. I'd be glad to help."

Meg started to say something. She couldn't let him get involved. This was too embarrassing, too personal. Yet a tiny voice of reason whispered inside her head: *What other choice do you have, you idiot?*

Then Mark was saying, "Which police station, Mrs. Deverall?"

"Oh, my. Oh, yes. It's a big one in downtown Denver. I know it's near Broadway, but—"

"I think I've passed it a few times," he put in. Then he nodded at Meg. "Talk to you outside for a minute?"

She followed him. A maelstrom of emotion whirled inside her. She felt humiliated. Deflated. *Angry.*

"Listen," he said, pulling the Audi keys, *her* keys,

out of his jacket pocket. "Please stay here with your mother till I get back, okay? Will you promise me you'll—"

"I'll be right here. You don't have to worry about me." She knew she was being nasty and silly, and she should thank her stars he was here to help. But she couldn't. The old Meg had died and gone to wherever gullible women went.

"All right," he said.

She looked up and met his eyes, sober and very dark behind the lenses. "Can you really do anything? I mean…"

He grinned then. A kind of feral twist of his mouth she'd never seen before, and she had no idea how to read him. All he said was "Don't worry, Meg, this I can handle," and he turned and left her there.

MARK PARKED ACROSS the street from the downtown Denver police complex and darted in between a couple cars, jaywalking toward the buildings. He entered a courtyard that separated two tall gray structures and stood and read the signs. One structure housed the jail and related offices, the other the Visitor's Information Center and general police departments: Vice, Traffic, Homicide. He could head to the jail, see what he could accomplish there, or he could go straight to the top, ask to speak to the police chief.

He opted for the top.

The power behind his Defense Department ID never ceased to amaze him. Whenever he flashed the fancy embossed badge people sat up, and he was an instant VIP. He always figured if folks thought about it they'd conclude the ID meant zilch. Hell, he could be a janitor at the Pentagon for all anyone knew. But people seldom thought. They reacted.

The chief was there today and yes, Mr. Fielder could go right up. Mark was given a visitor's ID to clip on his jacket and shown to a bank of elevators.

"When you get off," the sergeant told him, "take a left. His office is straight ahead."

"Thanks," Mark said.

Chief of Police Cole Marino greeted Mark in his outer office and led him into his inner sanctum. He was a good-looking man. In his early forties, trim build, full head of salt-and-pepper hair, a mustache to match. He wore a uniform, the navy-blue shirt crisp and starched. He also wore a sidearm.

Chief Marino was direct and spared no words. Which was fine by Mark. "So, Mr. Fielder, exactly what do you do for the Defense Department?"

Mark leveled with him and was mildly surprised to learn Marino knew of DARPA—most people didn't.

"DARPA, eh? Interesting. Can't imagine what I can do for you, Mr. Fielder, but I'm sure you'll get to the point."

All right, Mark thought, the man really did get down to business in a hurry. *Good.* "It's like this," Mark began, "I need to get a kid, he's twenty, I believe, out of your jail. I don't know the entire story, but the kid DUIed last night sometime, wrecked a car, his mother's, though I don't think there was anyone else or another vehicle involved. I might add, *sir*," Mark emphasized the sir to show his respect, "that I can't tell you the exact reason I need to do this kid a favor, but I can tell you it's connected to a matter of national security. The kid isn't a player, he's related to one, though, the star player, in fact."

"Interesting," the chief said. "You can't tell me more?"

Mark shook his head.

"Okay, I accept that. And I'll let you take custody of this kid as long as you accept responsibility for getting him to his hearing, which I assume will be tomorrow or the following day. They'll have that info at the jail. Now, what's the kid's name? And I'd like a number I can call in Washington to verify your ID, if you don't mind?"

Mark smiled. He took a piece of paper the chief handed him and wrote down a number. He liked this man. Cole Marino was military through and through, direct and exacting.

A half hour after arriving at police headquarters, Mark was crossing the courtyard again, heading to the jail. He was glad he'd made the decision to go to the top. That had worked out nicely. Now he only hoped things worked out as well with Brian.

The kid was a mess. The first thing Mark noted when the jailer led Brian through the release process was how hungover he was. Then there was the kid's broken wrist. Apparently the arresting cops had taken him to the hospital, where he'd spent half the night getting a cast. His clothes reeked of booze; his hair and scruffy beard had a few flakes of blood glued to them from a cut on his forehead. His eyes were swollen and lobster red, his breath so bad Mark backed up.

"I don't want to ever see you in here again, son," said the officer who'd completed the release forms.

Brian did not answer. He took his billfold and pocket change and dropped them in a jacket pocket without even checking, then followed Mark out into the gloriously bright autumn day.

When the sun struck his pasty face, he groaned. "Shit. Oh, man, do I feel like shit."

Mark started toward the Audi, which was still parked across the street, but Brian was lagging. The kid finally slumped onto a bench across a side road from a row of bail bond offices, and he dry heaved, hanging his head between his knees.

Mark stood next to the bench and studied him. He'd seen worse. A few months in the military usually straightened their sorry asses up, though. That much was fact. The trouble was, Brian was a civilian and there wasn't a whole lot Mark could do right now to put the fear of God in the kid.

"You done?" Mark shook his head.

"My goddamn wrist hurts, man, and I'm dizzy. Give me a minute."

"Sure." He sat next to Meg's brother and pondered the situation. The boy needed a strong hand. Hell, obviously no one had had any control over him since his father had died.

Meg had said she tried for years to discipline Brian, but Lucy always gave in the minute Meg turned her back. There was no consistent message being sent to him. Mark knew his situation too well. He'd dealt with hundreds of young men exactly like Brian. In the military it was a snap dealing with them. You lay down the law and informed them of the consequences if they broke that law. The kids got the point real quick. Most did well in the highly structured system. On the few occasions when a man had screwed up, the penalty had been swift and just, and seldom had that person repeated the offense. More often than not, in Mark's experience, these wayward youngsters sucked up the heavy discipline and thrived on it.

But, again, Brian was a civilian.

Mark regarded him as he sat with his head in his hands, swallowing convulsively to keep from vomiting again.

"So, where is your mother's car?" he finally asked, although he already knew the answer. It had been towed to an impound lot.

"I dunno."

"Don't you think you ought to find out before you see your mother?"

"Who gives a shit?"

"I imagine your mother does. It's her only means of transportation to work. And if she doesn't work, kid, who will support your sorry ass?"

Brian looked up. Tried to focus. "Screw you. Who the hell asked your opinion?"

"No one. But I'm telling you like I see it because you owe me."

"I *owe* you?"

"Oh, yeah, I had to pull strings to get you out of jail. Now I owe for those strings and you owe me. That's how it works."

"No one asked for your help."

"Then you want to go back to jail? Is that what you're telling me?"

Brian swore at him again.

"You use that language around me one more time, kid, and I'll march you right back to where I found you."

Brian started to say something, but Mark poked a finger in his chest. "Don't try me, Brian, I never make idle threats."

"Real tough guy."

"Yes, I am when I need to be. I have a lot of experience with guys like you."

"Oh, really?"

So Mark made a decision and explained exactly why he knew how to handle the Brians of the world.

"I'm real impressed," Brian said, "a navy SEAL. *Wow*."

"I'm only telling you so you'll get the point, kid. I put myself on the line for you, and now you have to own up to your actions. It's the way it works in the real world. At some point a judge is probably going to take your driver's license and sentence you to at least some community service, and there may even be more jail time. You'll for sure have mandatory counseling."

"Great!"

"I'm just telling you to face it like a man. You screwed up. Now you pay the price. Your mother and your sister can't help you on this one."

"Like they ever did."

"Whatever. That's your opinion. You're entitled to

it. But don't you think it's time you took responsibility for your actions?''

Brian snorted and looked as if he might dry heave again. When he finally glanced up, he said, "I don't have to put up with this crap. I'll split. Big deal."

Mark didn't mean to lose it. On the other hand, the kid was begging for it. He grabbed the front of Brian's shirt and half crushed him against the back of the bench. He barked, "No, Brian, you won't split on this. You won't do that to your mother and you won't do that to your sister who, in case you failed to notice, is up to her ears in her own problems. But mostly you won't do that because I'll find you." He let go of the shirt and took Brian's chin in his hand, forcing the young man to look him in the eyes. "And believe this," Mark said in a low whisper, "when I find you I'll break your neck."

Brian was silent. He didn't even struggle against Mark's grip.

Mark said, "You believe me, don't you?"

And slowly, barely able to move against the force of Mark's hand, Brian nodded. He was scared. For once in his life someone had gotten through to him.

Good, Mark thought, and he released him. "Now, let's take you home," he said, and Brian lurched to his feet.

CHAPTER FOURTEEN

MARK PULLED OUT OF LUCY'S driveway and Meg sighed. "I can't deal with this. I just can't handle any more."

"You don't have to deal with it." The voice of reason.

"Sure I do. My mother isn't any help at all. She only makes it worse by bailing him out. You know, he's a smart kid," she said. "But he never applied himself—that overused word, but in Brian's case it's true. He squeaked into CU, probably because he was in-state. But all he ever did was party. I tried, but it never did any good. He needs structure. He *needed* structure, and my mother couldn't provide it, I guess. And now…" Her voice faded.

"You shouldn't have been in the position of taking care of him in the first place."

"Well, you know what, Mark? You can't always choose what *position* you're in."

"I realize that." He hesitated, and then said, "Did your husband help you out with your brother?"

"No." She looked out the side window of the car. "They didn't like each other very much." She wondered why she was being so damn nice to this man, why she was conversing with him in such a civilized manner. She'd been so angry in the shower that morning, ready to fly off the handle the minute she saw him. Then the news about Brian had come.

And now... Well, now she couldn't seem to dredge up the energy to be mad. And he'd handled Brian's problems like magic, she had to admit that. Maybe gratitude offset anger. For the time being.

At some point, though, she was going to have to deal with Mark, with the lies and betrayal. And Howie. He was going to get in touch through Joanna. Howie expected her to join him in South America. Live in a foreign country. Just walk away from her whole life and live not as expatriates but as fugitives. Raise their child... How? With lies? Always looking over their shoulders? No, she couldn't.

She felt as if she was on that treadmill again, and it was moving faster and faster and she couldn't keep up. Either the machine was going to self-destruct or she would.

That afternoon the situation came to a head.

"I've been giving Brian some thought," Mark announced.

She was in the kitchen and she turned and sighed. She didn't want to talk about Brian or anything else. What she needed to do was think. Think about herself and the baby and Howie. She needed to think about survival.

"I believe I can help with him, if you'd like, that is."

"You'd like to help." The words escaped without any volition on her part. "Oh, you sure have helped, haven't you? You think I don't know who you are and why you're here?''

His eyes narrowed slightly and one of his hands curled into a fist.

She went on heedlessly. "I know all about you, and I don't believe a word you say. You're a liar. You're not from Merrick at all. You're from the Defense Department. You pretended to be my friend, to *protect* me, when you were really using me to find Howie.''

"Meg.''

"Oh, stop. Don't do that. You're so goddamn reasonable. I hate you!'' As she said the words, as her mind tested them for veracity, she knew she was no better than Mark—she, too, was a liar.

"What makes you think I'm from the Defense Department?'' he asked in a guarded tone.

"Because Joanna told me. And because when you left your cell phone here, I pressed Redial and someone at the Defense Department answered.'' She jutted her chin out defiantly and crossed her arms on her chest.

"That was pretty clever, Meg,'' he said. "I guess I underestimated you.''

She glared at him.

He pulled out a dining room chair; it seemed to take a very long time, as if he was doing it in slow motion, and the chair legs scraped across the wood floor like fingernails on a blackboard. The air was fraught with tension. Finally he sat in the chair and looked at her.

"You're right," he said. "I did…mislead you. But let me explain exactly why I did it that way."

"Why should I listen? You'll just lie some more."

"I will not lie to you, Meg," he said, holding her gaze.

"How do I know that?"

"You know me well enough to be the judge. I'm not an undercover agent. I'm not a spy. I'm obviously not so good at that cloak-and-dagger stuff. You can believe me, I swear it."

A battle raged in her head. How much did he suspect about where she'd been? And how much of what he said could she believe? He was right, she did know him. They had been friends, and she'd even imagined they could be more.

She turned away from him and put her face in her hands. *Oh God, oh God, what to do?*

She felt him right behind her, first his breath on her neck, then his hands on her arms, gentle, cool. She wanted to shake them off in protest, but she couldn't conjure up the energy.

"Meg." He turned her to face him, his eyes searching hers. "Sit down and let me explain."

"You'll lie," she repeated dully.

"As I said, you can be the judge of that."

She let him lead her to the table and sit her down in a chair, then he sat down himself. He leaned to take one of her hands in his. She couldn't for the life of her understand why she didn't snatch her hand away.

"Okay, this is the way it went," he said. "Government funding for research does come with a heavy price tag. Understandably. National security guarantees, clearance for all employees, the works. Howie broke the rules. Now, maybe he didn't do it deliberately, but the fact remains, he did it. He put us all in danger, the whole world, theoretically. If Boris Lebedev uses Howie's research for biological warfare, the country he's working for could loose a deadly microbe on the world's population. Hold the world hostage. Meg, you know that, you worked in the field.''

She was frozen in her chair, his hands strong on hers, his deep blue eyes piercing her, pinioning her.

''For everyone's safety, for your safety and your baby's, Meg, you might want to tell me what your husband said in Vancouver.''

She recoiled, her hand sliding out of his grasp. Of course he knew. So she had been followed; Mark had carefully orchestrated the entire episode.

She took a quavering breath. How stupid she'd been. Then she looked up. ''Why didn't you arrest Howie?''

He regarded her for a long time and finally seemed to come to a decision. ''I told you I wouldn't lie to you again,'' he said. ''And I won't.''

''Go on.''

''Frankly, we don't have enough hard evidence to arrest and convict your husband.''

A moment passed. She tilted her head, trying to understand, her brow furrowed. Then abruptly everything fell into place. ''Oh, God,'' she whispered. ''You expect me to fill in the gaps. You think I'll confess what Howie said to me. All this time, all these weeks and weeks, you were just waiting for me to meet him and then come running back here to tell you everything.''

He nodded.

"You're despicable.''

"And your husband endangered the entire world.''

She bit her lower lip. ''I don't know anything. I don't know anything more than you already do. And even if I did, I couldn't…I wouldn't tell you. Yes, maybe Howie did something dreadful, something incredibly stupid, but you can't ask me to betray him, you can't…'' Her voice trailed away.

"I understand, Meg,'' he said. ''I'm just asking for you to think about it.''

There was nothing but caring in his voice, in his eyes. He'd never done anything to hurt her—ever. He'd cooked for her and taken her to the doctor. He'd done the dishes when her ankles were swollen; he'd been there for her constantly. He'd taken care of Brian, for God's sake.

What was the truth?

Attraction fought repulsion. Like the silly girl's game, holding a flower, plucking off a petal and saying, ''He loves me,'' plucking another, ''he loves me not.'' But changing the words: ''I love him, I love him not, I love him, I love him not, I…''

Her husband hadn't been there to see her belly grow. He'd never taken her to the doctor's office or indulged her irrational craving for pickles or chocolate or those special oil-cured Greek olives.

No, it had been Mark who'd done all that. Mark who'd acted more like a husband and father-to-be.

THEY PICKED BRIAN UP at eight-thirty sharp the next morning. Meg sat in the car while Mark went to the front door and rang the doorbell. She'd been afraid to say anything to Mark, but she didn't trust Brian to be ready on time, or if he was, she expected him to be dressed in dirty jeans and a death's head T-shirt, with his scraggly beard wandering across his face. She'd been so tempted to phone her brother that morning, to wake him if he'd slept in and to remind him to look decent.

But she knew that sort of behavior was typical of an enabler. Brian had to make the decision to be ready himself.

She needn't have worried. By some miracle, Mark emerged from Lucy's front door with a transformed Brian in tow. Shaved, his long hair slicked back, a pair of khaki slacks and a white shirt. His arm was in a sling, the cast on his wrist a brilliant white in the morning sun, and the bandage on his head stood out like a beacon. He looked like a very young soldier returned from battle.

He got into the back seat, and she put a smile on her lips. "Hi," she said, "you look great."

"Right," Brian said sarcastically.

Mark slid into the driver's seat and started the car. "You understand what this appearance is for, Brian?"

"I guess so."

"It's important to know what you're dealing with here."

"The judge looks at the police report and figures out what to do with me."

"That's close enough. But how you act this morning, your attitude, is very important. The judge holds your future in his hands."

"Yeah, so what?"

Mark pulled the car to the side of the suburban street, stopped it, killed the ignition, then turned around in the seat. "Look," he said quietly, "this is no joking matter. Your mother and your sister will be affected by what happens to you. They're innocent, but they'll be hurt, kid. You need to have some respect for them. They are your family. I know you think you're misunderstood, but that doesn't matter one little bit. You broke the law, you might have hurt someone or killed someone. You wrecked your mom's car. You take the goddamn responsibility for what you did, you hear me?"

Brian said nothing. Meg was afraid to look at him, but the vibes in the car made her heart race.

"You hear me?" Mark repeated in a low voice. The one he must've used on recruits, she thought.

"Yeah, okay, I hear you," Brian said reluctantly.

"I'll be watching you every second," Mark said. "Don't screw up. Because I can be a hell of a lot tougher than any city judge."

"Who're you...?" Brian began.

"Don't go there, kid. Just remember, I'll be in that courtroom and I'll be watching. You behave, you'll be rewarded, you mess up, you'll be punished. It's as simple as that. Got it?"

"All right, I got it." Grudging respect.

"Good, fine. I'm glad you understand. Now, let's go get this over with."

No one spoke on the drive into downtown Denver. Meg felt as if she were holding her breath the whole way.

Judge William Cortland was a middle-aged black man with hair so short the overhead lights gleamed on his skull. The clerk of the court called out name after name. Meg watched as people stepped up, one by one. The judge would ask a few questions, sometimes a lawyer representing a person spoke, then the judge dispensed his ruling and banged his gavel. "Next," he said each time.

Finally the clerk intoned, "Brian Deverall, 231 Laurel Street, Wheat Ridge, Colorado, student, arrested for DUI and reckless endangerment."

Brian stood and walked to the podium in front of the judge. Meg and Mark stepped up also. Brian's face was white, his lips pinched in a straight line.

"And who are these people with you, Mr. Deverall?" the judge asked.

Before Brian could speak, Mark said, "This is his sister, Meg Afferton, and I'm a family friend, Your Honor. My name is Mark Fielder. I'd like to vouch for Brian."

"I see." Judge Cortland looked from Meg to Mark, his eyes traveling over the mound of her belly, stopping there for a moment, eyebrows raised, and she flushed, knowing what the judge thought. "Mr. Fielder, are you…ah, in a relationship with…?"

"No, sir, just a friend," Mark hastened to say. "But I have a kind of special understanding with Brian. I'll take responsibility for him."

"Well, that's all good and fine, but Brian here

broke the law. He's going to have to pay a price."
He glared at Brian. "You realize the seriousness of
what you've done, young man? You could have killed
yourself or somebody else."

"Yes, sir, I mean, Your Honor," Brian said.

"I hope so. I don't believe in coddling you kids.
I'll set a date for a DUI hearing, and your license is
revoked as of this moment. You might want to see
about getting yourself a lawyer, son. Francis, a date
for a hearing, please?"

"November 21, Your Honor," the clerk said.

"Okay, November 21, see you right here, son,
9:00 a.m. sharp," the judge said to Brian, frowning,
"and you better not get into any more trouble."
Bang! went his gavel. *"Next!"*

They trooped out of the courtroom, down the wide,
echoing corridor, past many courtrooms. Meg felt
weak in the anticlimax of the arraignment. All she
could think was, *Thank God Mark was there.*

By the time they'd dropped Brian at home, and
Meg had made phone calls to the insurance company
about her mother's car, it was already late afternoon.
Her mother inquired about Howie, and Meg ducked
the questions as best she could. She knew that soon
she'd have to tell Lucy the whole story. Tell everyone, she supposed. But not until she was off the treadmill.

She and Mark drove back to her house in the dark.
They stopped for take-out, but she wasn't hungry, and
he didn't try to force the food on her.

"I'm going to bed," she said.

"You feel all right?"

"No. I really don't."

"You're not sick?"

"Not physically sick. Just exhausted."

"I know."

"Do you?" she said. "Oh, never mind. I can't believe that on top of everything, Brian would pull a stunt like this. Now he has to face the judge again."

"I have a few thoughts on that," Mark said.

"Thank you, and thank you for your help today. But it isn't your problem. And you may not even be here. The court date is weeks—"

"Let's worry about it later."

"Later," she said. But it seemed as if every facet of her life was on hold. When would it end?

She was in bed by eight, trying to find a comfortable spot, her belly in the way. She couldn't sleep on her stomach anymore, and the doctor had told her not to sleep on her back because the baby's weight would press on her lungs. So she moved from one side to the other, glad she had the whole bed in which to move about. Glad Howie wasn't there to complain about her tossing and turning.

Howie. What was he doing now? Getting ready to fly to Mexico, then onto South America?

He was too alone, too scared, too weak to start a new life all by himself in a strange country. And Howie was singularly bad at languages. A brilliant scientist, yes, but lousy at foreign languages. She couldn't imagine him living in a country where he had to speak Spanish.

She lay there and thought about Howie, then her musings turned to *Mark*. And, again, images assailed her: Mark in his bed just next door, lying there alone, his body sleek and muscular, his skin smooth except where it was roughened by hair. She could feel it under her fingers, she could smell his scent, she could taste his mouth.

But it was only her imagination, her love-starved yearnings. Mark was probably sleeping like a baby, as if she didn't even exist.

CHAPTER FIFTEEN

OCTOBER ENDED IN BRILLIANT days and chilly nights. To the west of Denver, hovering like sentinels, the mountains received their first significant snowfall, so that when the clouds cleared, the peaks stood out bright white against the sapphire sky.

Mark was called back to Washington the day before Halloween, and Janie arrived to replace him. Meg took the shift change in stride, or so it seemed to Mark. He wasn't sure how he felt about her apparent indifference. Relieved? Disappointed? But his feelings didn't matter. The important things were the tapes of Afferton's phone conversations with Joanna Riggs. The tapes, which were analyzed at DARPA headquarters, had been coming with greater frequency, and Mark's superiors wanted his input, especially his opinion on how the doctor's wife was going to react.

Mark said goodbye to Meg in the living room as Janie was carrying in her laptop and suitcase. "Look," he said, aware that Janie was listening, "I still plan on helping with Brian. The court date is a few weeks away, and I'll be here."

"I appreciate it" was all Meg said, her voice even. But did he imagine her hands were trembling where she held her sweater together? He wanted to believe that she gave a damn. He was astonished at how much he cared what Meg thought and felt. Astonished and worried. He was becoming too involved with her.

But how could he help caring about her? How could he help admiring her grace and courage in an impossible situation? Her occasional anger at him was richly deserved. She was beautiful and strong and soft all at the same time, and he had to fight the urge to take her in his arms every minute of every day. He wanted to protect her from the awful events in her life, he wanted to see her smile and laugh.

God, he was falling in love with her.

He arrived in Washington that same afternoon, checked his apartment and the junk mail that had stacked up. Both houseplants had withered and died. He threw them out with the dozens of catalogs, fired up his car that had been sitting idle for weeks in the parking garage and drove into DARPA headquarters.

A few catalogs, a couple of dead plants and a car. Was that the sum total of his home life? And yet he knew every nook and cranny of Meg's house, every tree and shrub and bulb in her garden, where the hammer and nails and screwdrivers were kept, which can of paint she used for her fences and which she used to cover the nicks on the interior walls. Her house had become *home* to him.

His boss stayed late at work that evening and filled Mark in on the reports from the agent who'd been monitoring Afferton's calls.

''We think the good doctor is ready to make a move,'' his boss told him. ''Meg Afferton is a big

question mark at this juncture. Our analyst believes
there's a chance she'll join her husband. We know
you think she'll remain in Denver. But spend some
time running through the tapes and see if you can pick
up anything we've missed. You can start in the morning, if you want.''

"I'd rather do it this evening," Mark said. Hell,
what else did he have to do? But the truth was he
needed to hear the conversations. He needed to know
if Meg was pulling the wool over his eyes. Was she
going to tell Howard Afferton that her life was in
Denver, hers and her baby's? He tried not to imagine
what that life would be, whom she would spend it
with.

Headquarters was quiet when he settled into the
analyst's office and closed the door. He examined the
tapes, their dates and times, then put on the head-
phones and popped the first tape into the player.

Most of the conversations between Afferton and
Joanna were short. Afferton had called Joanna right
at her home, unaware of the taps on the Riggses'
phones.

Mark listened to three conversations that had been
taped immediately after Meg's return from Canada.
There was nothing significant in them. But on the fifth
tape he began to notice the same level of heightened
tension in Afferton's voice that the analyst had picked
up on.

"But, Joanna, if you talked to Meg, why hasn't she
sent word to me? She was supposed to…make a decision. Have you even talked to her?''

By the sixth recorded conversation, Afferton was

losing it. "You're lying to me. I know my wife, she can't be silent on our...arrangement. I know her, god-dammit. What did she say?"

Then Joanna. "I'm not lying to you, Howie. I told Meg about every call. She hasn't sent a message back."

"I've got to talk to her myself. Is that man still at my house? *Is he?*"

"I believe so."

"Damn. What am I going to do? How am I going to talk to Meg..."

Then Joanna had arranged for Afferton to speak to Meg using Jerry's cell phone. Naturally Jerry had alerted DARPA, and everyone but Afferton knew the call was being monitored. Mark knew Afferton had to be at the breaking point or he never would have spoken directly to his wife. Hell, he was well aware she was under government protection.

Regardless, he phoned. And Mark sat in Washington now and listened to the entire recording.

"Howie, you sound...awful. Are you all right?"

"No, dammit, Meg, I am not all right. We had a deal, remember? You were going to meet me...."

"I never said that. I—"

"You sat right here in this goddamn hotel and promised you'd let me know! I have everything all arranged. Meg, what are you thinking? We have a plan!"

"*You* have a plan, Howie."

"You're my *wife*. What are you doing, screwing that agent?"

"Howie."

"What am I supposed to think?"

"Certainly not that." Her voice was very quiet.

Mark punched the pause button and sat back in the office chair. What the hell had Afferton said?

He reached out and hit rewind then played the segment again "...screwing that agent?"

He'd never felt embarrassment in his life, not like this. He was embarrassed for Meg, because she had been aware of how many ears were listening in. And he felt humiliation that his own co-workers—his *boss*—had heard this tape. What made him squirm even more was the fact that Afferton's comment wasn't too far from the truth. Mark had fantasized about making love to her.

It took a while for him to press play again and listen to the rest of the conversation. He was there to make a judgment call—would Meg run off with her husband or would her loyalty be to her country? But maybe his assessment was no longer objective.

Had his superiors known that? Was that why he'd been summoned back to Washington and Janie sent to take his place? Because he couldn't be trusted?

He finished listening to all the tapes but was unable to come to any conclusions. He heard the mounting tension in Afferton's voice. He heard mention of South America, but he had no clue what Meg might do.

The following morning he worked up a report. A useless report. And handed it to his boss. Swallowing every ounce of pride he possessed, he stood ramrod straight and said, "If you want to permanently replace me I understand completely."

But to his surprise, his boss replied, "Quite the contrary, we want you back in Denver."

It wasn't till later that night that he got it. They wanted him on the case for the very reason he was feeling uneasy about being on it—he'd grown far too close to Meg Afferton.

He spent a week in Washington, then boarded a plane back to Denver. At first he felt a swell of discomfort about plunging back into the Afferton situation, but as the plane banked and headed west, he shut that weakness off as if it were a faucet.

He guessed he'd done this particular job too damn well.

THEY BOTH HEARD THE CAB pull in at the same time, and Meg felt her breath catch. He was back.

Janie put down the book she was reading and stretched. "Ah, here he is now."

Meg didn't respond.

"I wonder," Janie said, "if you'd listen to some advice." She stood and walked to the front door where her suitcase and laptop were packed and waiting. "And what I'd like to say is strictly my opinion."

Advice, just what I need, Meg thought. *More advice.*

"Your husband is in serious trouble. But he could do himself a big favor by turning himself in before the attorney general issues a warrant for his arrest. With the right legal team, who knows, he might walk. He could plea bargain. Give the feds names and dates in exchange for a lighter sentence. The longer Dr.

Afferton hides, the worse it will go for him. And don't forget, Meg, we aren't the only ones interested in him.''

Meg could have denied any knowledge of what Janie Weathers was talking about, but she stayed silent. What was the point? They both knew that *she* knew exactly what was going on.

"Anyway, that's my advice. Maybe you could try to talk the doctor into doing the right thing, Meg. You're the only one who can.''

Mark was at the front door. "Why are you telling me this?'' Meg asked.

The door buzzer sounded. "I'm going to catch Mark's taxi to the airport,'' Janie said, in a hurry now. "But to answer you, I think you're an okay person. And you have a baby coming. You need to consider the stigma your child will carry around if his father is labeled a traitor.''

Janie opened the door and Mark walked in. She picked up her luggage, told him her reports were in the guest room, and then she turned to Meg. "Please think about what I've said.''

"Yes,'' Meg said.

"What did you say?'' Mark asked, but Janie was out the door. "What?'' he said again, putting his things down.

"Oh, nothing,'' Meg replied, attempting nonchalance. She hadn't realized how much she'd missed him.

She watched Mark disappear into the room recently vacated by Janie, and she wanted to run after him, touch his arm, see him turn and smile at her, say, "God, I'm glad to see you."

Then she hardened her resolve. That wasn't ever going to happen, so she had to be strong, take care of herself and her baby.

Somehow, someday, when all this was over, she'd get back on her feet. She'd managed before Howie; she'd manage again.

She heard Mark putting things away in the guest room; her house was a revolving door for government agents. He reappeared in the living room and gave her a half smile and a shrug. "So, how are you?"

"As well as can be expected." How could he stand this assignment? How could *she* bear it any longer?

"Your brother behaving himself?" he was asking.

"As well as can be expected," she repeated.

"Good, good. Look, I've got to read through Janie's reports, but then if you need to run errands or whatever—"

"Janie took me this afternoon."

"Good."

"How do you all tolerate this?" she asked abruptly.

"What?"

"This…waiting. And I can't…I can't really do a thing to help you, Mark, I just…"

"Waiting and monitoring is our job."

"But you carry weapons. Janie keeps hers around every minute. There must be times where everything just…happens at once."

He laughed mildly. "Oh, yeah, there are. But those

moments are few and far between. *This* is what we do most of the time.''

''Well, you can't wait forever.'' Oh, how she wished he could.

HE NEVER DIRECTLY DISCUSSED what was in Janie's reports with Meg or if she was still being shadowed by the Turghistanis. She really didn't want to know. He also made no mention of Howie's frequent calls to Joanna or of Joanna's subsequent calls to her. He certainly did not press her again about Howie. Time merely passed as if she had nothing more to do than get ready to have her baby. Was that Mark's plan—woo her into complacency until she eventually told all she knew about her husband's underhanded dealings? But she couldn't give Howie up. Something inside her wouldn't allow it. After all, he was the father of her child.

But she tried not to think about that, either. Life was easier when you could pretend.

There were unsettling moments that broke into her fantasy existence. The bill collectors had begun to hound her. There was no avoiding them. But there, too, Mark facilitated her existence by handling the calls.

''You know,'' he told her one freezing November morning, ''I could make the bills go away.''

She realized he was offering to pay them himself. Blood rushed to her face. ''I'll pay you back,'' she said vehemently, and he dropped the subject. He continued to run interference on the phone, though. And she let him, embarrassed and ashamed, feeling as if she were using him.

She thought she spotted a car on their tail several times, and she mentioned this to Mark. But all he said was "Don't worry about it. You've got enough on your mind."

Then a few days before Brian's hearing, they'd driven to her mother's, and Meg was certain she saw the same dark car parked down the block from Lucy's.

"I knew it," she said. "I knew they hadn't just magically disappeared. What the hell do they think I can do? Do they think I'll tell Howie to work with them? What a laugh. As if I have any control over my husband."

He shrugged. "Meg, this isn't going away, you know. You've got two countries with a lot at stake. What amazes me, frankly, is…" But then he hesitated. "Forget it."

"No, tell me what you were going to say."

"What the hell," he said, pulling away from the curb. "I was going to say it amazes me that they haven't found your husband yet."

Yes, she thought. *But they will.* The longer Howie stayed in Vancouver, the higher the risk the Turghistanis would find him. And she could change all that. She could tell Mark everything Howie had told her, and her husband would be arrested.

If only the baby would come, she mused, as if the child's birth was going to be a new beginning.

She was moving carefully now, not quite used to

her growing bulk. Even her hands swelled, her rings digging into her skin.

That night after they'd eaten, she muttered under her breath. "Damn rings."

"What?" Mark said.

"My rings are too tight. They hurt."

"Can you take them off?"

"My fingers are so puffy. I guess I could try soap."

She got up and went to the sink, poured some liquid detergent on her finger. Pulled at the rings with her other hand. "Dammit."

"Let me help." He rose and took her hand, studying her rings—a small diamond solitaire and a plain gold band. The skin under them was red and swollen. He tugged gently, then twisted the rings. "Does this hurt?"

It did. But she said, "Not too much." Heat rose to her cheeks. His hand was warm, strong, gentle. She wanted to pull away from him, but he'd wonder why, and the situation would be even more uncomfortable.

He worked at it, his head bent. She was acutely aware of his closeness, of his warm breath near her ear and the whiskers on his cheeks.

"Ouch," she said.

"Sorry."

"No, keep trying."

He held her hand under cold water. More detergent, a muffled sound escaped her, and the rings slid, caught on her knuckle, then came off. She looked at them in the palm of his hand, the gold and diamonds, the symbol of her marriage. And she was seized with a powerful sense of freedom.

Small things seemed to matter to him. Although he rarely referred directly to her condition, she knew he watched her, watched her belly grow.

Sometimes she caught the tender expression on his face—as if she and her baby were precious to him. And she rejoiced. Then she'd realize she was fantasizing. Mark probably practiced those looks in the mirror in hopes of making her dependent on him so she'd consider betraying Howie to please him.

One evening he took her out to dinner at Campo di Fiori, a new hot spot in Cherry Creek. It had taken some persuading on his part, her main excuse being her wardrobe.

"I have nothing to wear," she said. "I look like a whale, and every top I own has spots all over the stomach where I bump into things."

"It's not a dressy place."

"I have nothing *decent*."

"Nobody will care."

"I will."

"Nobody will notice."

"I'm kind of hard not to notice these days," she said wryly.

But she gave in finally, and took her time getting ready, appearing in a green top with a Mandarin collar, with a simple gold chain around her neck.

The restaurant was rustic Italian, with murals on the walls and small tables set close together, and chefs rattling in Italian in the exposed kitchen.

"I've never been here," she said, as they were seated with a continental flourish.

"I read about it in the newspaper."

He ordered cranberry juice for her and a glass of merlot for himself.

She found a smile. "This is nice. God, I haven't been out in ages."

"I know."

"Is this part of your job, too?" she asked, deliberately baiting him.

"Not exactly."

Their glasses appeared on the table. "Well," she said, lifting hers, "it's sweet of you."

"My pleasure."

She sipped, then regarded him keenly for a moment. "Tell me, Mark," she pressed, "is it a personal or a professional pleasure?"

He hesitated, obviously not caring to be drawn into dangerous waters. But he'd said he wouldn't lie to her.

"Can I take the Fifth?"

"I guess so." She picked up her glass again and drank, then set it down firmly, wishing it was wine to lend her courage. "Look, I'm going to be honest here. I have almost no money, no job, my mortgage is three months behind and I can't even sell the house because it's in Howie's name." She closed her eyes for a moment. "And here you are, Mr. Nice Guy, taking care of me. Offering to buy my *groceries*. I'm not sure how long I can go on like this." She leaned forward, the candle on the table flickering shadow and light on her hands. "I need to take charge of my life somehow."

The waiter came by and asked if they were ready to order.

"No, I'm sorry, not yet," Mark said. "Give us a few minutes."

"All right," she said when the waiter left. "Okay, that was my venting for tonight. Sorry, I'll behave."

"Meg..."

"Yes?"

"Look, I can't imagine what you're going through. I realize that. But, I swear, you won't have to worry about money."

"I need to take care of myself," she said bluntly.

"Don't worry about it tonight. Enjoy yourself."

"Okay, just call me Scarlett O'Hara. I'll worry about it tomorrow."

They ordered an antipasto platter and lobster risotto and veal scaloppine. People around them laughed and talked, clinking silverware, drinking wine, joking with the waiters.

She drank her juice, and when dinner came she had another. She pretended it was wine and imagined her cheeks turned pink.

"I never thought," she said over her risotto, "that this would last so long." She gestured with her glass. "I mean, you being around, Howie being...gone."

"It seems like a long time to you?"

"Doesn't it to you? Don't you want to get home? Maybe, I don't know, maybe to pat your dog or...or see a girlfriend, or, I don't know. Something."

"No dog."

She eyed him, waiting.

"No girlfriend, either."

"Why not? You're a—" she flushed for real "—you're a good-looking man."

"Thanks, but relationships take more than looks."

"Don't I know it," she said.

"My ex-wife could tell you more about my short-comings," he said dryly.

"What was she like?"

"A military brat like me. We had that in common, I guess—" he played with the stem of his glass "—but it wasn't enough."

"How long were you married?"

"Six short months of bliss," he said. "Can we change the subject?"

"To what?"

"To anything. Dogs, hey, why not? Do you like dogs?"

"I love them, but Howie wouldn't have one. Allergies." She made a face.

"I can't keep one where I live. But someday..."

"What about someday? What do you want to do with your life?"

"I haven't thought. Too damn busy."

She raised a forkful of rice to her mouth. "Sometimes staying busy is a defense."

"Oh, really. Against what?"

"Against knowing what you really want, against knowing yourself."

"Frankly, I thought I was just earning a living."

"Hmm," she said, chewing, her eyes on him.

It was cold outside when they walked down the street to where the car was parked. Without discussion she got into the passenger seat. He was beginning to know his way around Denver.

"It was nice of you to take me out," she said into the darkness as he drove. "You didn't have to."

"I know I didn't have to."

"I get bored, you know, and then I start thinking. I worry. I keep expecting something to happen, something awful. It's like waiting for the other shoe to drop."

"It won't drop."

"So you say. But I keep expecting it to. Crazy, isn't it?"

"There's a way you can end all this," he said carefully, and she tensed. "Meg, you know what I mean. Talk to me."

She heard the coolness in her voice. "Oh, I get it now, this was what dinner was about. Of course."

"Is that what you think?"

"Yes."

He was silent for a moment, and then he said, "You're wrong."

She opened her mouth to reply, then clamped it shut. The evening, a wonderful evening, was spoiled. Why make it worse?

CHAPTER SIXTEEN

MARK AND MEG PICKED Brian up the morning of his hearing. It was frosty out, their breath fogging in the cold air, the car's heater turned up high. The sky was clear, icy blue overhead, but to the west clouds rolled over the mountains, gray storm clouds that obscured the peaks completely.

Brian emerged from the house with the usual pout on his face. Lucy was at the door to say goodbye; she hugged him and said something, but her son shrugged her off and walked to the car.

"Hi, Brian," Meg said, obviously trying hard to be cheerful.

"Hi," Brian mumbled, ignoring Mark completely.

Mark rolled his eyes, shook his head and started the car. He wondered why he'd even considered helping this kid out. *Because he's Meg's little brother, is why.*

Ten minutes later, they walked down the corridor to the familiar courtroom. Lawyers waited on benches outside courtroom doors. People milled around—witnesses and family members, some cheerful, some pale and silent.

Mark followed Meg and Brian into the room, and they seated themselves behind several rows of petitioners. Brian fidgeted. Meg patted him on the arm, biting her lip, and it pained Mark to see her suffer. Damn that brother of hers.

The court clerk went through his litany, and the judge entered and sat behind his bench. "All rise for the Honorable Judge William Cortland," the clerk called, and Mark put a hand on Meg's arm to help her up. She seemed not to notice.

They waited while the judge dispensed his justice to cases prior to Brian's. "Fine of five hundred dollars, jail time already spent, drug testing." *Bang* went his gavel. "Ten days jail, community service." *Bang.* "Ah-ha, Mr. Nivens again? Two weeks, compulsory rehab, yes, you know where, Mr. Nivens." *Bang.*

"Brian Deverall, DUI, reckless endangerment," the clerk said.

Brian stood, Meg with him. But Mark said quietly, "Let me do it." She gave him a worried look but sat down again.

The judge peered over his reading glasses at Brian. "Is this your counsel, Mr. Deverall?"

"Uh, no, Your Honor. This is—"

Mark interrupted. "Mark Fielder, Your Honor. If you recall, I vouched for Brian."

"Okay," the judge said, shuffling his notes. "But didn't I recommend counsel in this case?"

"You did, Your Honor," Mark said, "but I think we can handle this without an attorney."

"Oh?"

"I agree that Brian needs to pay for what he did, but I have an idea I'd like to discuss with you. Would you consider a conference in chambers?"

"Are you a lawyer, Mr. Fielder?"

"No, sir."

"Well, you sound like one. I don't take kindly to wasting my time. Can't you tell us what you have in mind right now?"

"I'd prefer your chambers, Your Honor."

"Okay, okay," the judge said, irritated. "In my chambers at the lunch break." He banged his gavel. "Case continued. Next."

"What was that all about?" Brian asked, as the three of them left the courtroom.

"I want to talk to the judge about an idea I have."

"What idea?" Belligerently.

"Let's wait till I've talked to him" was Mark's final word.

At the lunch break, Mark left Meg and Brian sitting on the bench in the crowded, echoing corridor and found Judge Cortland at his desk eating a sandwich.

"Okay, Mr. Fielder, talk fast. I have a whole lot of justice to dispense this fine day."

"Judge, I really appreciate you hearing me out. Brian Deverall is a mixed-up kid. His father died when he was a little boy."

The judge made a disparaging noise around a mouthful of his sandwich.

"I know. I was in the military, and I trained a lot of sad sacks like Brian. I think some discipline would do him a whole lot more good than a fine or counseling or jail time."

"I'm listening."

"There's an eight-week boot camp for hard cases

like Brian at Fort Carson, the army base in Colorado Springs."

"I'm familiar with it."

"I'd like to take temporary custody of Brian and get him into boot camp."

The judge regarded him gravely, sandwich held in both hands.

"You can always throw the book at him if he doesn't hang in there," Mark pointed out.

"He'd have to complete the whole camp. And I'd want regular reports from whoever is in charge of him at Fort Carson. *And*—" the judge released a forefinger from the sandwich, directing it at Mark "—he loses his license for a year."

"Deal," Mark said.

Brian was the harder sell.

"You *what?*" he cried.

"One phone call and you start camp at Fort Carson next week. No phone call—" Mark hitched his shoulders "—the judge gives you whatever he feels like."

"Damn it all to hell," Brian burst out. "Boot camp? Like soldiers do? Crawling around in the mud and doing sit-ups? Who in hell do you think I am?"

Mark stepped up and pressed a finger into Brian's chest. "I think you're a spoiled brat with no goddamn direction in your sorry life. And I think, mister, that boot camp is a hell of a lot better than jail."

Meg said nothing. But she didn't look happy with Mark's suggestion.

"I'll just split," Brian said.

"You run now," Mark said, "you'll be running for the rest of your life."

There was silence. The last thing Mark heard was Brian mumbling, ''Boot camp,'' then swearing under his breath.

THEY DROVE BRIAN TO Fort Carson on a bright Sunday morning. He tossed his duffel bag into the trunk and sulked in the back seat, defiant and silent.

Meg was angry at her brother's childish behavior, especially after Mark had gone to so much trouble to help him out. Not that *Brian* considered it much help. She sat next to Mark, her hands clasped tightly in her lap, casting about for something to say, but nothing came to mind. And Mark and Brian, well, they seemed to be in some sort of a contest, the loser being the one who spoke first.

South on the interstate toward Colorado Springs, an hour away, the mountains glared silver under a strong sun. By the time they passed the burgeoning bedroom communities south of Denver, Meg was crawling with discomfort.

''Nice day, isn't it?'' she remarked.

Mark grunted. Brian said nothing.

''What time are you supposed to check in?'' she tried. Although she knew the answer.

No response.

''Ten, wasn't it?'' She tried again.

''Ten,'' Mark said.

Past the broad high prairies, past the Air Force Academy.

''Do I turn here or the next exit?'' Mark eventually asked.

She answered, ''Next one.''

There were nineteen other boys signing in at Fort Carson. Some were teenagers, some younger than Brian, some were obviously inner-city kids, some were longhaired suburban boys. All—including Brian—were a study in mutiny and resentment.

Army officers in starched fatigues handled the "recruits," their expressions giving nothing away. For a moment Meg was afraid of what Brian faced. What if he failed? What if he ran away?

As if reading her mind, Mark took her elbow. "He'll be fine," he said quietly.

"I hope…" She bit her lip. "I…oh, God, I hope…"

They left Brian there, her last glimpse of him breaking her heart, his thin face white and very hostile. And scared. He'd mumbled "Goodbye" to Meg; Mark he'd pointedly ignored.

She drew in a deep, quavering breath as they drove away.

"It'll be the best thing that ever happened to him," Mark assured her.

"He can't even call out or get calls."

"Not for the first two weeks."

"What if he gets sick or…or something like that?"

"There's a base hospital."

"But…"

"Forget about Brian for now. He's on his own, Meg, probably for the first time in his life. Whatever he does he gets immediate reward or punishment for. Training."

"Like a *dog*," she protested.

"A dog without training can turn out dangerous,"

he said without rancor. "He's going to come out of this just fine," he assured her, and somehow his words gave her comfort.

He drove through Colorado Springs, a pleasant, sprawling city tucked between plain and mountain.

"Hey," he said eventually, "you hungry?"

"A little."

"I heard about this old hotel that has Sunday brunch."

"The Broadmoor."

"That's it. Supposed to be pretty good."

"It's expensive."

"My treat."

"I don't know…"

"Come on, live a little."

"I'll feel so guilty, with Brian at that awful place, and—"

"Meg."

"All right. Fine. Whatever you want."

"What do you want?"

"Oh, I don't know. I'm acting like a jerk, aren't I?"

"Uh-huh."

"Let's do the Broadmoor, then."

The Broadmoor Hotel was a bastion of European grandeur dating back to the early 1900s. It rested serenely amid emerald-green golf courses, the mountains lifting directly behind its golden stucco and red-tile roofs.

It seemed trivial, but Meg wished she'd worn something nicer than black maternity slacks and a blousy red top. A dress, maybe, or a skirt. She pulled down the visor and combed her hair, applied fresh lipstick. She'd never been to the Broadmoor.

Sunday brunch was crowded, most of the tables were occupied by families and hotel guests. In one corner was a team of young ice hockey players wearing their jerseys, being watched carefully by coaches and parents.

"Nice," Mark said, looking around.

They sat down at a table near a window, and a waitress poured them coffee. "The buffet is right over there," the waitress said. "You can go back as often as you like."

There were sweet rolls, muffins, croissants, pepper-crusted bacon, sausage, French toast, smoked salmon and bagels, pancakes and waffles, eggs and omelets cooked to order, fresh fruit. All in crystal and silver—a cornucopia of delicacies.

"I can't possibly—" she said.

"Try."

Plates heaped, they sat down to eat. Meg knew she couldn't finish the food. With her growing belly it seemed as if there was less room in her stomach. But Mark had no such problem.

"Now, this is more like it," he said.

"It's ridiculous."

"When I was a kid, I loved buffets. Growing boys, you know. Whenever I visited my grandparents, my grandfather would take me out to his favorite buffet, and we'd have a contest to see who could go back the most times."

She watched him smile. "Who won?" she asked.

"When I was a little kid he did, but then I got

bigger and he got older and... Boy, I remember the first time I beat him. I was sick all day from eating too much, but I won.''

"That's a man's sort of contest,'' she said.

"Yeah.''

It occurred to her that all the diners in the restaurant probably assumed that she and Mark were a young married couple expecting a baby. She and Mark. Oh, how she wished. She studied him as he buttered a muffin, ate scrambled eggs. She'd grown to love the way he looked, the way he moved, the timbre of his voice. It resonated deep inside her, as if there were a tuning fork in there, vibrating to perfect musical notes.

She ducked her head and picked at a bowl of fruit salad. Oh, God, how dumb she was, crazy about him when she was married to another man. Worse, she was carrying that man's baby.

"Hey, take a look,'' she heard him say, and she felt him lay a hand on her arm.

He was pointing out the window. "That's an eagle, I swear it is.''

A dark bird soared on outstretched wings, far, far above the golfers.

"Beautiful,'' he said.

But she was only aware of his touch, and it sent shivers along her spine. She withdrew her arm, sat erect and trembling in her chair.

"Did you see it?'' he asked.

"Yes,'' she replied. Lying.

"Hey.'' His eyes rested on her. "Are you still worried about Brian?''

"No, not really."

"You okay?"

"I'm fine."

"I'm going back for more. Want me to get you something?"

"Ah, no thanks."

By the time he returned, her mind was made up. She'd been toying with the idea for some time, and now she was going to do it. Perhaps it was her realization that the longer he stayed with her, the worse her predicament would become. Until she simply couldn't bear it.

"Mark," she said, leaning toward him.

"Uh-huh?"

"Mark."

He looked at her then, put his fork down.

"I need to get something off my chest. I haven't told a soul this... That morning—the day Howie disappeared—he..." She couldn't confess *that*. Instead, she said, "I tried to tell him that I needed a break from our marriage. I guess I didn't get my point across. Anyway, when he didn't come home, I thought he was mad and punishing me. Of course, I realized later that was absurd, still... The thing is, my marriage was over before all this happened. I knew it. I didn't know how to go about leaving him."

She realized she'd been staring at her hands and looked up. "True confessions," she said, attempting a smile. "I just needed to say that to someone."

His eyes were on her.

"Well, say something."

"I'm glad you told me."

"Are you? Really?"

"Yes, Meg. I am."

She took a breath. "Okay. Good. Now I want to tell you about Howie." She felt her heart begin to pound.

He waited with perfect stillness. He was very good at waiting.

"In Vancouver, he...he told me what happened." She spoke in a low voice, and he leaned close to hear, his eyes never leaving hers. "He told me he'd been sending his research to this man, the one who rented the car."

"Lebedev. Boris Lebedev."

"Yes. He'd been sending stuff to him for a couple of years."

"In what form?" An utterly professional tone of voice.

"Disks, computer disks. Lebedev said he wanted the information to treat an Ebola-like disease in his country."

"Turghistan."

"But eventually Howie realized there was no such disease in Turghistan, so he stopped sending disks. And...that's when they threatened him, and Lebedev came to Aspen..." Her voice broke. The story was almost too ridiculous to repeat.

"I see."

"He didn't mean to do any harm. That man lied to him. He thought..."

"He took money. Sold the information. Your husband's not that naive."

"I know," she whispered.

He removed his glasses and massaged the place where they'd rested, thinking.

"Mark?"

"All right, you're doing great, Meg." Glasses on, back to the interrogator. "How long ago did he start sending disks? How did he send them? Did Riggs know?"

She answered as best she could. Her voice shaking, near tears.

He leaned close to her. "Do you think his research could provide Turghistan with an infectious biological warfare agent?"

She shook her head. "I don't know."

"Would Riggs know?"

"I don't know. I'm sorry, I don't work there anymore. Howie didn't talk…much about his work. I—"

"Okay, Meg, you're doing fine." He hesitated then asked, "Did he give you any details? Names, places, amounts of money?"

"Not much. He did tell me he had an account on Grand Cayman at the…" She thought back. "I think it was the First British Limited Bank. He gets money wired to him in Vancouver from there."

"Okay," he said as if to himself. "What about the men he dealt with?"

"You know about Boris Lebedev. He didn't mention any other names."

"Anything else? Take your time."

She shook her head. Then she drew in a deep breath and forged ahead. "Listen, Mark, what if I could convince Howie to turn himself in? And then you could ask him everything you want to know."

His eyes were like lasers, burning into her. "Do you think he'd do that?"

"I'm not sure. But he's, oh God, Mark, he's a mess. He's desperate. Really frightened—of you and of the others." She took another deep breath. "If I could get him to come home and…and talk to you, could you promise to be lenient? Could you, Mark?"

He sat back in his chair and studied her for a long time. Around them people conversed and laughed, and there was the clink of silver and crystal.

He finally spoke. "I could work something out."

"But can you promise leniency? Or immunity, you know, whatever you call it."

"I can't promise immunity. It's up to the attorney general. But I can take Howie into custody myself, I'll promise you that."

"If he tells you everything, though, will they go easier on him?"

He picked up a fork and tapped it against the table, his countenance unreadable. What was going on in his head? What contingency was he analyzing?

"Mark, please say something."

"What do you want me to say?"

"That you'll…surely you could influence your superiors. Couldn't you do that? I mean, if he turned himself in, and you got the credit…"

An expression chased itself across his face, a split-second shift of his features into—she tried to decipher it—distaste, no, more a grimace of disgust. At her suggestion? At Howie?

She shivered inadvertently. She shouldn't have brought up this idea; it was insane. She'd made a terrible mistake. She pressed her lips together and fought panic.

Mark laid the fork down with exaggerated care, his attention turned inward. Then he straightened and ran a hand over his face.

"Mark?"

"I'll arrange it, Meg, but only with the understanding that he cooperates fully."

Relief swept through her. Howie would listen to her; there was no other way out for him. "I only want to keep him from going to jail," she said. "He isn't a criminal. He made a mistake."

"A whopper."

"I'll be grateful, Mark, you know that. I'll do anything I can." Her lips were stiff. She'd presented her plan as if she were sure she could get Howie to surrender to Mark. What if she couldn't?

He gazed at her intently, and she could see the sunlight refracted in shards in his glasses. "Look, Meg, even if this works, and Howie serves no time in jail…you and your baby deserve better than Howie Afferton. You're doing the right thing."

She shifted uncomfortably in her chair, her belly heavy, the baby moving inside, her heartbeat loud in her ears.

"Meg." His tone had softened.

"Um?"

"Look at me."

She glanced up. The interrogator was gone. Mark—the man she knew—was back. Her heart melted.

"I'm sorry," he said, "you've been put in this position."

She tried to smile. "Maybe in the long run this will turn out to be for the best."

"Let's hope so."

She looked around the elegant dining room. "Can we go? I...I don't think I can sit here any longer."

He rose, reached out a hand to help her up. "The last thing on earth I want to do is hurt you, Meg."

She closed her eyes. If only the past didn't exist. If only she could have Mark and the baby, if he could feel for her the way she felt about him.

Oh, how ridiculous she was being. The same old naive idiot, believing, hoping Mark could love a stupid, married, *pregnant* woman.

She stood and took her shoulder bag from the back of the chair, tugged at her red blouse so that it didn't ride up on her stomach and made her way out of the dining room of the Broadmoor Hotel.

The drive back to Denver was accomplished in taut silence. There was nothing more to say, she supposed.

Once, as they passed the picturesque outcropping that gave its name to Castle Rock, he asked, "Are you all right?"

"I'm okay, thanks."

She went to bed that night, weary, her ankles throbbing and swollen, her mind racing. What would happen next? Would Mark give her an ultimatum of some sort, or would he let her initiate her plan on her own? What should she do? How would she manage to convince Howie? Would he even listen to her?

And then—the same refrain that had tortured her

for months—she wondered how she was going to support herself and the baby. Mark would leave when this horror show was resolved one way or the other. He'd go back to Washington, glad to be rid of her. Then what?

Maybe she could talk Jerry Riggs into giving her back her old job as a lab technician. The money was excellent. And when she needed childcare, there was a marvelous state-of-the-art facility right next door to the lab. She would make it work.

There was one problem—R and A Biotech would only survive if Howie came forward and told the entire truth, clearing Jerry of any involvement in the dealings with Turghistan. A big *if*.

Okay, she thought, suppose R and A Biotech did not survive Howie's treachery. There were other labs all over the metropolitan area. Surely she could get a job at one of them. And she could move out of the cold ugly monster of a house, let the bank take it back. Sell the condo if she could. Probably the government would attach Howie's assets, anyway. Well they were welcome to all of it.

She'd make it work. She could. She'd managed before Howie; she'd manage again. She and the baby.

But first, before all that, she had to see her husband one last time.

CHAPTER SEVENTEEN

SHE GOT OUT OF THE CAR and gave Mark a shaky smile. "I hope this works," she said.

"You'll do fine" was his reply. That was all—no advice, no last-minute suggestions. She was glad *he* thought she could pull this off, because she wasn't at all sure.

She walked up the path to Jerry and Joanna's home. It was a simple, older suburban Denver house; a beige clapboard split level in a neighborhood in Parker, fifteen miles southeast of Denver.

She'd always admired the area. The trees and shrubs that had been planted twenty years ago were mature, and she'd never been here when there weren't children and dogs on the streets.

The Riggs kids were nowhere to be seen when Jerry answered the door. She figured he and Joanna had sent them off to friends, not wanting to chance their children overhearing the conversation Meg would soon have with Howie. She couldn't blame the Riggses. The family had suffered enough.

Joanna appeared from the kitchen. She was drying her hands on a dish towel. "Hello, Meg," she said. "You've got a little time. Would you like coffee or a hot tea?"

Meg declined the offer and sat with Jerry and his wife in their living room, Jerry's cell phone resting on the end table next to her elbow. She checked her wristwatch. Five minutes till Howie was supposed to call.

"You look great, Meg," Jerry said, sitting across from her.

"Thank you," she replied. "But I feel big and fat and ready to burst."

"I remember those days," Joanna said, and she gave Meg the first genuine smile she'd given her since Howie's disappearance. "When is your due date again?"

"Mid-January. But my doctor told me not to count on an exact date. He said, 'Think winter, and you'll be on time.'"

They all laughed, but the moment was edged with tension. Meg folded her hands in her lap and tried not to glance at the cell phone. Her palms were damp.

She knew Jerry and Joanna had to be terribly upset about the situation. Sure, they'd both been cooperating with the federal government for months, and thus far the grant money for R and A Biotech had continued to flow in. Still, it would be so much better for everyone concerned if Howie gave himself up. And this prearranged conversation was Meg's last hope of convincing her husband to do just that. If she failed, Mark was ready to have Howie picked up and held by the Canadians till his extradition could be arranged. And then a sharp lawyer would advise her husband to stay silent, and without Howie's confession, Jerry's integrity would remain in doubt. But if

Howie came forward and told the truth, Jerry would be cleared.

The question remained, could she convince her husband to do the right thing? He was so crazy now. Even worse than ever this past week, calling the Riggses at all hours, demanding that Joanna talk to Meg and convince her to join him in South America. Meg hadn't heard the conversations, but Joanna had told her everything. Then, yesterday, Meg had gotten up her courage and asked Joanna to set a time for her to speak to Howie herself.

She glanced at her watch. *It's all or nothing now,* she thought, and despite the chill November day outside, sweat broke out on her neck.

"I wish he'd call," she mused aloud. "I wish this was over."

Jerry cleared his throat. "You know," he began, "Joanna and I were talking this morning and, well, we believe we both owe you an apology. None of this was your fault. We know that. And we've been less than...understanding with you."

"That's all right," Meg said.

But Joanna interrupted. "Better just let us speak honestly, Meg, before we chicken out. Jerry is right. We've been rude to you when you needed friends the most. It's unforgivable."

"Well, I forgive you," Meg hastened to say, her eyes straying to the phone again. "I would have felt the same way if I had been in your shoes."

Jerry nodded. "But will you be okay, Meg? I mean, you'll always have a job waiting for you at the lab, you know that, and you'll always have us—"

"Jerry," his wife cut in, "are you blind? She *has* someone."

"Huh?"

"He's sitting outside in the car," Joanna said, and she shook her head at her husband's naiveté.

But Meg had no time to respond or even to be embarrassed or confused, because just then Jerry's phone rang. She jumped at the sound, then picked up the cell phone.

It rang again in her hand, shrill and demanding.

"Should we leave?" Jerry asked in a whisper, as if Howie could already hear.

"Thank you," Meg said. "I guess it would be easier for me," and then she clicked the talk button.

She was taking a breath, was ready to say hello, but Howie's voice slashed across the distance. "Meg? Meg, is it you?"

"Yes, Howie, it's me, I'm here."

"And you're using the cell phone? They can monitor us, you know. Don't put anything past them, Meg."

Obviously Howie wasn't thinking. He'd called her on the cell phone, so of course she was using it. But, more important, he didn't seem to realize the government could listen in to any device it wanted, especially a cell phone, where their words could be snatched right out of the airwaves bouncing off a satellite.

"Did you hear me, Meg?"

"Yes, yes, I did. I'm on the cell phone, Howie. It's okay."

"Good, good," he rasped. "When are you coming? It's been weeks. I was thinking, Meg, maybe it would be better if you just join me in South America. Leave everything. I don't give a damn. I've got money. I told you. Or did I? In the Caymans?''

"Yes, you did. But there's something you should consider, Howie. Will you listen for a minute?''

"What is it?'' he said impatiently.

"Well, what if you could get out of this awful mess and come home to the States?''

"Ha."

"No, listen, if you could strike a deal with the government, tell them everything in exchange for leniency, then maybe—''

"No, no, no!'' he cried.

"But, Howie…''

"Goddammit, no!''

She had to drop the subject. Her heart squeezed painfully.

"What about South America?'' he asked. "I think you should fly there and meet me. Next weekend. That gives you all week.''

"I need to see you in person first,'' she said, desperately casting about for a way to get him back to the States now.

"No, no, I have to leave here. It's a miracle Boris hasn't tracked me down by now. I've got to get out of Canada.''

"Then come to Denver.''

"No! Are you nuts! With that *man* there, that agent!''

"But, Howie, I can't fly to South America, I—''

"You mean you *won't*.''

"No, it's...it's the baby, Howie. The doctor said—"

"Baby?"

Dear God. "Our baby. You remember."

"Oh, God, of course, what was I thinking? Are you all right, is something...?"

"Howie..." She thought fast. "Look, I can't discuss this on a phone. I need to see you. In person."

"Not Denver. No."

"Aspen, then. What about Aspen?"

There was a pause, then he said, "I guess I could...I guess I could get across the border. But not at the condo. They'll be watching the condo, Meg. Not there."

"Okay, not the condo. How about the institute? You could..."

"The bridge," he interrupted. "You remember the footbridge? Below the music tent?"

"Yes, on the Rio Grande Trail, right?"

"That's the one. I'll meet you there. You can walk, can't you?"

"Yes, I can walk. When, Howie? When can you be there?"

"Give me three days. I can get there in three days."

"Wednesday?"

"Yes, I guess that would be Wednesday. Hell, Meg, I'm not even sure what month it is, much less what day." He laughed then. A sick, throaty laugh. "You should see me. I'm as thin as a reed. You always fed me so well. You remember how I forget to eat?"

"Yes, I remember."

He went on about his appearance until she finally said, "What time? What time on Wednesday?"

"Oh, that's right. Let's make it five in the afternoon. And for God's sake, Meg, ditch that man. Don't let yourself be followed."

"All right, Howie. Then it's this Wednesday at five at the bridge. Right?"

"I'll be there. I can't stay, though. No. I'll keep going till I get to the Mexican border. I'll just about be in South America by next weekend. Then you can—"

"We'll talk on Wednesday."

"Okay. And Meg, I'll make all this up to you. Whatever you want. We're rich. You'll see."

"Yes, Howie," she said.

She left the Riggses' house after thanking them and promising she'd let them know what happened in Aspen as soon as she could.

"They'll arrest him, you know," Jerry said at the door. "If you don't convince Howie to turn himself in voluntarily, they'll take him into custody so fast your head will spin."

"Yes, I know."

"It's for the best," Jerry said, and he hugged her and kissed her cheek. "You take care of that baby, you hear?"

"I will," she said.

The Audi was running when she got in. She'd been sweating inside the house, now she was chilled to the bone.

"Cold?" Mark asked, reaching for the temperature lever on the dashboard.

How odd, she thought. Anyone else would have jumped all over her with questions about her phone call. Then she remembered Joanna's statement: "She *has* someone."

They were out of the subdivision before she finally said, "Aren't you going to ask me what Howie's going to do?"

"You'll tell me when you're ready," Mark said, his eyes on the road.

"Well, it's done."

"He's turning himself in?"

"Not exactly," she began.

DUSK FELL EARLY IN NOVEMBER. By four-thirty the sky was a uniform gray, clouds settling on the mountaintops around Aspen, a faint glow in the west where the sun was setting.

Why hadn't she thought to make the meeting earlier? But she'd been so intent on getting Howie to meet her at all, she hadn't considered the time of day.

It didn't matter. Nothing mattered but persuading him to talk to Mark.

She stood at the doors to the back deck of the condo and felt shaky. Scared. Knowing how much was at stake. Knowing it was all up to her.

Mark had informed her that DARPA agents had followed Howie to Aspen. But she didn't know what condition Howie was in. Was he lonely, afraid? Or was he only thinking about starting a new life in South America with her and all his riches?

She could hear Mark in the background talking on his cell phone. He had men stationed all over the place here. Earlier he'd told her the agents from Vancouver who had tailed Howie across the border were certain no one else was on her husband's trail, but she nevertheless worried. What if the Turghistanis had spotted Howie? Probably not in Canada. But here? What if they'd been waiting for him to show up in Aspen all this time?

She heard Mark fold the cell phone. "All set?" he asked from across the room.

Her heart fluttered. "I hope so," she said, trying to smile.

He opened his jacket then, to check his pistol, pulling it out, checking the clip, sliding it back into his shoulder holster.

"You're not going to need that, are you?" she asked, horrified.

"It's just part of the job," he replied dispassionately.

"You're sure? Howie will freak if he sees it."

"Howie will never see it."

She sighed. Mark knew what he was doing. She only wished she was as certain as he was. "What if Howie still won't listen to me? What then?"

"Meg, you know we have to pick him up. We've been over this a dozen times."

"I know, I know. I just can't help worrying. I feel as if it's all up to me. Maybe I'll say the wrong things. Maybe... Oh, God, I don't know."

He came around to face her, reached out to grasp

her arms in both hands. "I have complete faith in you. I know you can do it. It'll be over soon."

She pressed her lips together and nodded. She resisted the temptation to fall against him, sob on his chest, beg him to take her away, take care of her. Love her. There was no time for any of that; she had a job to do.

She was dressed warmly in a camel's hair coat that barely buttoned over her stomach, boots, gloves, a green scarf and a black beret.

Mark was going to drive her down to the entrance of the Rio Grande Trail, park and let her out to walk the half mile to the bridge where she was to meet Howie. He would follow behind her. The two-man team following Howie was supposedly already in place on the riverbank above the bridge. Everything had been planned with absolute precision.

As soon as Howie agreed to give himself up, Meg would walk him back to the car, where Mark would meet them.

Piece of cake.

She got into the car, and Mark drove down to the Rio Grande. Silence engulfed them; they'd talked and talked about how this would go down, and there was nothing left to say.

When they got out of the car, she felt as if she was about to say goodbye to her old life, as if she was closing the door behind her and opening one in front of her.

"Hey, break a leg," Mark said.

"You only say that to someone going on stage."

"Close enough." Then he approached, holding her

eyes with his. "We can call it off, you know. Right now. I'll tell the men to pick him up. You don't have to go, Meg."

"Of course I have to go. I can't let that happen to Howie. Lure him here and then..." She shook her head. "No."

"All right. Just remember, you'll be covered every second. I'll be nearby, and the other team is already in place."

She shivered. "They must be freezing."

"They'll live."

The first few flakes of snow drifted out of the leaden sky as she began her trek. The trail was paved and used constantly by runners and walkers and bicyclists. A scenic route, it wound along the Roaring Fork River, among fields of wildflowers in late summer, stands of aspen trees, tall cottonwoods and spruce trees. People walked their dogs there, and mothers pushed baby carriages.

But no one was out on this gray, blustery Wednesday at five in the afternoon. Maybe that's why Howie had chosen it for their rendezvous.

She walked quickly, arms swinging, trying not to think of what lay behind or ahead. Funny that she'd volunteered to influence Howie when he'd been the one to control her life so completely.

He was there on the narrow, arched footbridge, resting his arms on the railing, peering down at the black river that slid by below him.

She halted for a moment, watching him, struck by his gaunt appearance. She'd slept with this man for six years. She carried his child. Yet she didn't know him. She had never really known him.

Seeming to sense her presence, he straightened and turned toward her, the wind tugging at his raincoat that might have served him well in Vancouver but looked out of place here.

She'd been preparing herself for three days, going over her greeting, all her lines.

"Hi," she began.

But he cut her off. "You're late. God, Meg, you're always late."

"Sorry," she managed to say. The old timid Meg. But she let her apology stand. She'd never been able to deal with him.

"No one's with you?" He looked around.

"No one's with me."

"Not that...that *man*?"

"No."

"You didn't tell anyone?"

"No," she lied.

No hugs or kisses or questions about her health, she thought sadly.

His eyes traveled over her face, down to where her coat buttons strained over her stomach, and his expression mutated. "God, you're...big."

"I'm pregnant," she said patiently.

Then his expression altered again. "I know, I know. It's done. We'll deal with it. We'll get you a girl, a nanny or whatever. Help will be cheap where we're going. Hey, it'll work out."

The wind died and snowflakes calmly floated out of the sky. She blinked and forced herself to remem-

ber her speech. It was so hard, though, *looking* at him.
He'd been handsome. Always clean shaven, his
clothes neat and perfectly tailored, every hair on his
head in place. And now he was…haggard. She felt as
if she was talking to a stranger.

"Look…" She took a breath. "Howie, look, we
have to discuss the future."

"The future? Haven't you heard a word I've
said?"

"I don't think you've considered everything. The
running, the hiding—"

"Of course I have."

"There's a better way."

"What the hell do *you* know?"

"I know, Howie."

Abruptly the old Howard Afferton was back. He
eyed her as if she were a moron. "You don't know
anything, Meg. You never did."

She almost turned on her heel. But she'd expected
this. Tried to prepare herself. She looked past him and
took another breath. Her exhalation came out in ragged plumes in the cold air. "I can help you," she
said. "If you come with me right now and talk to a
friend of mine. It's not too late."

He swore then and stalked away from her to the
end of the footbridge, then back. She could see he
was angry and she had no idea what was to come.

"You've betrayed me, haven't you?" Something
in his eyes seemed to buzz.

"No. No, I'd never betray you. But you need
help."

He kept staring at her and then he exploded. "I

should have known. I should have known!'' His voice rose. ''My *wife*. Oh boy, oh boy, you are a stupid woman. But you're still my *wife* and you're going to Argentina with me. You bet you are!''

''Howie, for God's sake, listen to me.''

''No, no, no. I'm through listening. It's time to go.'' He reached out and snatched her arm, and when she tried to draw away, he clutched her and began to drag her along, off the bridge.

''No, Howie, no,'' she cried, wishing Mark could hear her. She was scared. She'd thought she could deal with Howie on her own, but she couldn't. She needed Mark's strength.

''You're coming with me, you little bitch.'' He was panting with the effort, and dragging her, and she felt dizzy suddenly, the baby kicking, her weight unwieldy, her breath short.

At first she didn't realize what had happened. There was a noise, a loud crack that echoed between the banks of the river. She felt Howie pause, as if hesitating, and then the pressure on her arm slackened.

There was no time to be afraid. She merely turned, thinking, *what?* But he was sagging, his hand slipping off the arm of her coat. Her confusion increased, and she thought again, *what?* His fingers grasped the cuff above her gloves then released her, and he was on the ground, one leg twisted under him, his arms outflung.

She stood frozen to the spot, staring at him, trying to make her brain work. The snow drifted down ever so lightly, and she could see individual flakes settle on his face and on his open eyes. That's what she'd always remember, the way the snow touched and melted on his eyes.

"No," she whispered, then louder, "Please God, no!"

She dropped to her knees beside him. "Howie, Howie!" She touched his cheek, took his hand—a limp, heavy hand—and shook him, crying his name over and over.

She was dimly aware of subsequent cracks in the air, but they seemed very far away. She kneeled over her husband. Sobs tore out of her as she tried to keep the snow from falling onto his face.

Time halted. As she knelt next to her slain husband on the riverbank that cold November day, the clock stopped ticking for an eternity before reality set in.

She heard a voice. "Meg."

Then again. "Meg."

She still couldn't move; she was frozen there, sheltering Howie's body, her mind unable to cope with more than that.

"Meg, do you hear me?" A hand on her shoulder, then a body crouching down beside her. "Meg?"

She sensed him close to her, an arm around her shoulders. "He's gone, Meg, I'm sorry." Then there was a passage of time, a vacuum of nothingness, and she felt his arm tighten around her. "Come on. Come on now, let me help you up."

She finally levered herself up with his help, then her knees buckled, and he caught her and held her, her face buried in his chest.

"Oh, Meg." His voice caressed her, cutting through the fog and the dawning horror.

"He's...he's..." she began.

"Yes, he's gone. He was shot, Meg. By one of Lebedev's men." His hands were strong on her back, supporting her.

"Lebedev's men?"

"Yes." His voice was kind and patient...and familiar. She clung to him. Slowly he let go of her and placed a hand under her chin, tilting her face so that her eyes met his. "Can you hang on for just a minute? I have to... I have a few things to do. Okay, Meg?"

She nodded, unable to speak, trembling.

He took his coat off and draped it over Howie. Two men were there—she hadn't seen or heard them coming. Another two ran across the bridge and down the bank of the dark swirling river to a man who lay half in and half out of the frigid water.

She was aware that Mark was on his cell phone giving orders. She watched the men drag the Russian up the bank, where he hung between them, wet and half dead, his clothes sodden and bloody. She noticed that one of the agents carried a long rifle that dripped water. She was aware of everything, but it was as if there were a veil between her and what was happening.

A few minutes later the scene changed from slow motion into fast forward—a policeman arrived, running, out of breath. Then another. Urgent voices, sharp exchanges. Mark, totally in control, talking to several policemen.

Meg just stood there, shaking, waiting... After a time, Mark left the growing crowd and came to her.

He took her hand, gently. "I'm getting you out of here," he said.

"Shouldn't I...?"

"There's nothing you can do here."

"But... Howie..."

"He'll be taken care of."

She let him lead her away. She managed to walk, slowly, his arm around her, until he helped her into the car and drove her back to the condo.

Stripping her coat and scarf and hat off, he pressed her down onto the couch. He fetched her a glass of brandy and put it between her cold hands.

"Drink," he said.

"I shouldn't."

"One lousy sip."

She raised the glass to her lips and sipped. Fire hit the back of her throat and she coughed.

He took the glass, then sat beside her on the couch. "Meg," he said, "I'm so sorry it had to happen like that."

She looked down.

"We should have seen it coming. I should have. The Turghistanis must have had someone in Aspen this whole time," he said.

"But how...?"

"We were followed down to the trail. Either that, or Howie was spotted earlier today in town. He wasn't exactly thinking straight. He got here this morning and didn't do a whole lot to stay invisible. I'm sorry, Meg. I blame myself."

But she was shaking her head. "No. It was Howie's

fault. He did…this to himself. It's almost as if…as if he *knew* there was no way out and he—''

"Don't torture yourself. Lebedev's responsible. We'll get him. I'm not at liberty to say precisely how, but he'll be in custody soon. He'll pay.''

"I know you're right. And in the end it really doesn't matter, does it? Maybe nothing matters.''

"You matter, Meg.''

She shook her head.

"You and your baby.''

She looked at him. There was a curious expression on his face, a softening of his features. He took his glasses off and met her eyes with his. Naked deep-blue eyes filled with…

"Meg?'' He put a hand on her cheek, and she pressed into it. "Look, this is a hell of a time, but…I have to say it. I'm here for you if you want me. I'll be here for you and your child. Always.''

It took her forever to digest his words. She turned her face up to his, tears wetting her cheeks. "Mark,'' she breathed, "you don't have to… I'll be all right. And I have the baby, I'll…''

"Shh,'' he said. "I love you, Meg. I think I have since the first time I saw you.''

"But…but, what about the baby?''

"What about the baby?''

"I mean…''

"I've been with you since the beginning, haven't I?''

"Yes.''

"Then let me just love you. The two of you.''

She stared at him, astonished. When everything

was black and hopeless, a door had just opened and beyond it she could see light, beautiful light. She stepped through the door.

She took his hands in hers and rested her head against his shoulder. "I love you so much," she whispered.

EPILOGUE

EMILY MAE FIELDER TURNED one year old on a cold, blustery January day, and her parents planned a party with balloons and a cake and presents and invited guests to mark the milestone.

"Not that she'll understand what's going on," Meg told her husband.

"But we will." He grinned.

The occasion was celebrated that afternoon in the Fielder's cozy three-bedroom house in Colorado Springs, where Mark had transferred to work for the Defense Department in its Cheyenne Mountain facility.

Emily's grandmother Lucy drove the hour and a half from her home in Denver with her uncle Brian. Joanna and Jerry Riggs arrived with their children, and several of the Fielders' new neighbors were there, too.

Emily was just beginning to toddle; a bright, cheerful child with fat cheeks and her mother's dark red curly hair. She loved being the center of attention, giggling, clutching at the frosting on her birthday cake with a chubby fist, smearing her face, the tray of the high chair, her new bib with colorful flowers embroidered on it. Meg tried to wipe away the worst of the mess, but gave up when Emily threatened tears. Her grandmother, however, told the little girl a funny story and was able to clean her sticky fingers with no trouble.

Jerry Riggs and Mark had become quite good friends over the last year, with Mark acting as a kind of facilitator between R and A Biotech and Merrick Pharmaceuticals. The firm was now secure, with a new biotech specialist handling the research for Jerry.

"No technical talk," Joanna warned her husband.

"It's okay," Meg said, handing out cake and ice cream to the adults. "It might be nice for Mark for a change. All he gets around here is baby talk."

Emily was banging on her tray with a silver spoon she'd been given as a present. When Meg reached over to take it away, she cried and banged harder.

"Choose your battles carefully," her next-door neighbor Connie advised, and Meg stored the words away. After all, Connie had three kids under the age of eight and was surviving nicely.

"How are your classes?" Meg asked her brother, always a little anxious about his reaction. But he'd finished his boot camp and gone back to school at CU and seemed to be doing all right.

"The semester starts next week," Brian said, "and I got into the psych class I wanted."

"You figure out what you want to major in?" Mark asked.

"Not yet. At the rate I'm going it'll take me a million years to finish. But I really like the science courses."

"Runs in the family, I guess," Mark replied.

"Well, my grades in English and history suck...
oops, sorry, they're, uh, bad."

Emily was still banging away, bits of frosting flung
off her spoon, her plastic bunny cup on its side, sticky
with frosting. Meg sighed—she'd have to scrub the
walls at this rate.

The party was a success, even though the guest of
honor fell asleep in her mother's arms, her fine curl-
ing hair stuck to her cheek with butter frosting, her
party dress spotted with food, her tights bunched below her diaper, one patent leather Mary Jane still on
and one missing.

Lucy gave her sleeping granddaughter a kiss.
"Good night, darling girl."

Joanna hugged Meg. "You look so happy," she
said. "I'm glad for you."

"I am happy," Meg replied, holding her baby.

The guests took their leave, donning coats and
gloves and scarves against the cold, bustling children
out to cars. Phrases drifted back on the cold air:
"Bye, see you soon... Call me... Talk to you next
week."

Then Meg and Mark closed their front door to the
winter night and looked at each other and smiled.

"It was a good party," he said.

"It was, wasn't it?" She hitched Emily up on her
shoulder. "I've got to get her to bed. She's all
sticky."

"I can't believe she's a year old," he said.

"And what a year." Meg went down the hall to
the baby's room and flicked the light on, Mark following. The walls were pastel plaid wallpaper, the

furniture painted white, stuffed animals on shelves. And lots of children's books from her librarian grandmother.

Together they washed Emily's hands and face, changed her into her sleeper and laid her in the crib, which had an animal mobile hanging over it.

"She's so beautiful," Meg mused aloud, studying her sleeping child—the pale, veined eyelids and dark lashes, the curly hair and pink cheeks and clenched fists.

"She looks like you," Mark said.

"Oh, she's much prettier than I ever was."

"Not true."

He put his arm around her, and they stood over Emily, watching her sleep.

"When do you think we should start thinking about giving her a brother or sister?" he ventured after a while.

"Um," she said, "well, we might want to start thinking about it in, oh, say, seven months."

He looked at her in surprise. "You mean, you're..."

"Uh-huh," she said.

*These New York Times bestselling authors
have created stories to capture the hearts and minds
of women everywhere.
Here are three classic tales about the power of love—
and the wonder of discovering the place
where you belong....*

FINDING HOME

DUNCAN'S BRIDE
by
LINDA HOWARD

CHAIN LIGHTNING
by
ELIZABETH LOWELL

POPCORN AND KISSES
by
KASEY MICHAELS

*Available only from Silhouette
at your favorite retail outlet.*

Silhouette®
Where love comes alive™

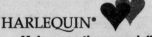
HINTLTW

EMERGENCY!

The Family Doctor
by Bobby Hutchinson

The next Superromance novel in this dramatic series—set in and around St. Joseph's Hospital in Vancouver, British Colombia.

Chief of staff Antony O'Connor has family problems. His mother is furious at his father for leaving her many years ago, and now he's coming to visit—with the woman he loves. Tony's family is taking sides. Patient care advocate Kate Lewis is an expert at defusing anger, so she might be able to help him out. With this problem, at least. Sorting out her feelings for Tony— and his feelings for her—is about to get trickier!

Heartwarming stories with a sense of humor, genuine charm and emotion and lots of family!

On sale starting April 2002

Available wherever Harlequin books are sold.

HARLEQUIN®
Makes any time special ®

Visit us at www.eHarlequin.com

HSRE